THE FALL OF MAN

Printed in Australia
First published November 2025

Cover design by It's Made By Brooke
Internal design by Jessica Chaplin

Paperback ISBN 978-1-7637529-8-6
eBook ISBN 978-1-7637529-9-3

More great titles can be found by visiting www.matthewcirsonauthor.com.au

A catalogue record for this work is available from the National Library of Australia

THE FALL OF MAN

Matthew Cirson

Also by Matthew Cirson

The Depths Within: Part One
The Depths Within: Part Two

Leviathan

CONTENT ADVISORY

This novel is a work of fiction set in an alternate version of World War II.

It contains themes and depictions relating to the Holocaust, war crimes, and human suffering. While the events and supernatural elements are fictional, the historical atrocities of the Holocaust were real, and their memory deserves solemn respect.

Reader discretion is advised. This story is intended to explore the nature of evil through speculative fiction, not to diminish or reinterpret the historical suffering endured by millions.

Throughout history, mankind has proclaimed many gods. They have worshipped them, sacrificed to them and then, as civilizations died out, or became conquered, they forgot them. No matter where you look, there is always a god, or more. If you look back to Ancient Egypt, you will find the Sun God – Ra, amongst others. Come forward a few thousand years and you will find Zeus perched on Mt Olympus. In today's age, we have the two great deities, in the Christian Lord and the Muslim Allah. Of course there are more, there always is. One thing that can never be questioned, is the relationship between gods and war.

As if two edges of the same sword, religion and the ghastliest acts that mankind can commit, come almost hand in hand. The same can be said about soldiers on the ground and their beliefs that the crimes they commit are nothing more than God's work. There is evidence of this, as far back as man dates. Think of those that were sacrificed in the name of Ra as the pyramids were constructed. Think of the prayers that would have been thrown at the feet of Ares, the Greek god of war, as the Spartans massacred their way across the Peloponnese. Of course, all of this is overshadowed by Nazi Germany and their "Final Solution", along with the words that I could never forget: "Judenfrei" or "Jewish Free". But even in these acts, we find the question, as was asked by many US troops in that gruesome campaign: "If God be for us, then who be against us?"

No matter what religion you look to, if a god exists, then there must be, for all intents and purposes, its antithesis. Would the Greek Hoplites have ever prayed to Zeus or Ares, if they were not concerned about what waited for them in Hades? The same question could be asked about the Norse and their ferocity in battle, if they didn't believe that they must die in combat to find Valhalla. But is it the gods, or the chaos that is man, that drives us in war? I want to believe it is the latter; I want to believe that with all my heart and soul. When I think of my time in the European theatre and beyond, I cannot bear to think that any god has anything to do with what I saw, what I felt and what I still fear to this day. As to admit that there is a god, no matter the name, you must admit that there exists an anti-god. That this battle between the light and the dark does exist, and if that is so, then it means that all these horrors, all these terrible things, are real. If that is so, then the good has already lost, and we come closer every day to the fall of man, and the world of darkness, horror and hunger that awaits.

PREFACE

My dear friend,

Before you begin to work your way through the contents of these pages, there is something that I must explain. If this elephant in the room is not addressed right now, then I have no doubt that you will merely believe this to be a work of fiction. The scrawling of an old, tired, and obviously insane man. Although I cannot explain everything to you in this preface, you must have it as an understanding before you move on. I implore you, if our friendship has meant anything over these years, then please, let it be that you accept the words that come next.

The history that you have grown up with, is false. At least, it is to me. It is difficult to explain every minor detail that I claim to be false, as before the events I am about to recount, I was just another young man, with no concern about the world outside my own vision. It wasn't until I woke up, detached, displaced, and confused, that I put my soul into the research that led me to meet you. You know that I served in the invasions in Europe, you know that from what I have told you. But there were many things that I omitted. Part of the reason was so that no one thought I was insane, but there was a large part of me that hoped that I was. If the history contained in the pages that I read along with you was true, then perhaps there would be some hope. As time went on,

I became confident that this was not the case.

June 6th, 1944 is a day that I am sure you will know off the top of your head: D-Day, The Allied invasion of France. I told you that I was there that day, and part of that is true. The lie was that the allied invasion I took part in did not occur on the 6th of June, but the 23rd of December, 1944. At that stage, France was still under occupation and no hope of liberation was on the horizon. But this is not where the story starts.

Knowing you, I can already imagine your eyebrows raised as the above-mentioned date clashes with what you know to be true. I know this doesn't match what you think happened, but I've studied the commonly taught version of history, trying to map out the differences so that I could explain them to someone, someday. It's worth remembering that I can't compare the worlds history to my own, all I have is my memories of how the war began. You have libraries, I on the other hand, merely have fragments. A lot of that is lost to me, and as I sat down and attempted to write my argument to you from the position of a historian, I realised there was little point. So, I will do the best I can to explain the world situation, as it was for me: a boy, nothing more.

As far as I know, the key difference must be with the mindset of Adolf Hitler. On the 11th of December 1941, after the attack on Pearl Harbor and the US declaration of war against the Japanese Empire, Nazi Germany *did not* declare war on the United States of America, of that I am certain. The US was dragged into the war after Pearl Harbor, but only into one theatre. I did not serve in the Pacific and therefore my knowledge of the fighting that took place is non-existent. The atomic bombs were set off, as far as I am aware, on the same day across both histories; the differences do not lie here and hence I will move on, leaving the Japanese altogether.

Countless books, articles and stories have explored the age-old question: "What if Hitler had won the war?" There is a general consensus that there was no chance of this happening once the Eastern front was opened. I agree with this wholeheartedly. The distracted, underpowered and under-resourced Wehrmacht of Western Front in your history, is the greatest example of this.

The excellent book, *The Wages of Destruction* by Adam Tooze, details the economic war of Nazi Germany in your time; numbers that do not lie are told within these pages. It speaks of the giant economic effort that Nazi Germany undertook to mobilise every ounce of its resources to sustain the fight as long as it did. The only thing I can say to you is, imagine the Third Reich with unlimited resources.

This would entail a power beyond belief in those times. Although the Wehrmacht and Waffen SS forces that we faced did not have unlimited resources to draw from, they were certainly more substantial. But the question I want you to ask is, at what cost did they achieve this?

With the far superior strength of the Wehrmacht on the Western Front, it was only natural that Lebensraum (living space) would be sought in that area as well. Czechoslovakia, Poland, France, Belgium all fell and quickly, as in your history. But France was not where they stopped. With the failure to gain a surrender from the United Kingdom despite the constant battering from the Luftwaffe, Operation Sealion took place on the 2nd of June 1943, after considerable resources were poured into the Kreigsmarine. Even in this realm, this took considerable time and resource allocation. The development of the Panzer divisions and the mass manufacturing of armaments continued, but not to the extent that would have been required to launch a mass land invasion, as was seen with Operation Barbarossa.

An assault force of sixty thousand men crossed the English Channel, while ten thousand Fallschirmjäger (paratroopers) secured the ports and the forward area of their landing sites. The British fought bravely but withered under the blitz. London fell within three weeks; the royal family was astonishingly captured at Buckingham Palace in a widely publicised raid led by infamous SS man, Otto Skorzeny. Still, the British Empire endured.

Those that survived the invasion held their land as long as they could, but there was little anyone could do. Eventually, England and Scotland fell to the Reich and as a last-ditch effort to prolong the war effort, fifty thousand soldiers and two hundred thousand civilians were evacuated to British controlled territory in Northern Ireland. Plagued by harassing fire from the Luftwaffe, some ships never made it across the Irish Sea, but many did. There, they resisted, beset by the constant ariel bombings, and land skirmishes with the revolting Irish, until a glimmer of hope that was shrouded in the darkest clouds came their way in January of 1944.

Frustrated with the refusal of the dwindling British to surrender, the entire royal family was publicly hanged in Piccadilly Circus. The crimes they were charged with included supporting the propaganda machine against the greater German Reich and a list of completely fabricated treasonous acts, which included those apparently committed by thirteen-year-old Princess Margaret. All of this was televised. The sight of the two squirming children's bodies as the rope drew the life from them, sent the Western world into an outrage. I remember standing on a Chicago street, screaming along with the other workmen who had stopped what they were doing to witness the execution.

King George VI, Queen Elizabeth, and Princesses Elizabeth and Margaret, all perished under the wrath of the German Reich on the 9th of January 1944.

The United States of America declared war on the Third Reich two days later. The act that was meant to crush the last spirits of the trapped British armies had, in fact, stiffened their resolve. Propaganda flyers that showed a United States soldier running across the ocean toward Ireland and a black mass that depicted the Third Reich, were scattered everywhere. The posters were plastered on shop windows in the US and were even distributed throughout the last remaining sovereign soil in Northern Ireland. They carried a message for the British soldiers:

"Hold on, Tommy!"

"We are coming!"

It was there, in Northern Ireland, where my story begins. Amongst the broken down, the starving, the dead. My first taste of violence, thrown into the blitz of the German war machine.

PART ONE

Millisle – Northern Ireland

September 1st 1944

1

The rain seemed to echo inside my head, as each heavy droplet panged against the steel of my helmet. The sound of it was almost enough to drown out the crashing waves only a hundred feet away. There seemed to be no escape from the rain when it started. The days of sitting in wait while the pangs of hunger slowly and surely ebbed away at my strength, meant that morale was low. I would've liked to have laughed at the situation, but instead I huddled myself closer to the wall of the trench that I lay in, in some hope that the sandy walls may offer some cover.

If the gods would permit, I might even be able to get some sleep while the endless autumn day of manning the line ticked away. As if inspired by the thought, I checked my wristwatch. The old Gruen Tank that my father had given me before I shipped out, still ticked away as well as the day it was made. Although there was barely enough daylight to make out the numbers that surrounded its face, I could make out the position of the arms well enough. *Five a.m., definitely time to try and catch some shut eye*, I thought as I closed my eyes and rested my helmet against the sandy trench wall.

'Cody,' the sound of my name startled me and I jumped, accidentally kicking the man that had woken me. 'Now Private,' the man said in a poor representation of an offended English officer. 'Sleeping on watch, are we? That sort of mischief would have you straight off to see the leftenant.'

'Keep working on that accent, Jackson,' I said in a sour tone. 'One day it might be passible.'

Jackson looked down at me from under the rim of his helmet. Water ran down the smooth surface of steel and dripped down on my arm. Jackson was in his mid-twenties. The carefree ways of his youth had remained after our time in basic training, despite the efforts of our drill sergeant, who insisted it would be the death of him. The young man's M1 Garand was slung over his shoulder, with the muzzle down in an attempt to keep rain out of his barrel. Both of his hands were wrapped around a pair of binoculars, which he held low at his waist.

'Seen anything this morning?' I gestured at the binoculars.

'Nothing,' he said through his smile. 'It's still too dark. I can barely see the waves break.' Always eager, Jackson seemed to spend every spare second he had perched behind those binoculars, looking for the signs of German approach. Almost as if he wished for them to come. 'Here,' he said as he held them out. 'You give it a try while I take a load off.'

I yawned as I took the binoculars from him and stretched as I got to my feet. Sand and silt fell from my damp clothes as I stood, and a cold shiver ran up my spine. It was amazing how the water soaked into a man when he laid still. The way it soaked through his clothes and almost into skin. Each drop bringing a cold change that sucked from his strength, staunching the fire within drop by drop. Jackson groaned as he leant his M1 against the trench wall and lowered himself to sit down next to it. More sand fell from the walls and showered over his coat as he too yawned and pulled his legs up to his chest.

As I stood up, my head cleared the trench and I saw the first hint of the daylight through the rain. Although the sun was nowhere to be seen, the rolling movement of the waves of the Irish Sea were visible before me. White foam capped the breaks of the waves as they came crashing down. Gulls cawed as they flapped away up the coast toward

Bangor; I raised my head to the sky as I watched them disappear. All the days spent watching, either for signs of the Luftwaffe, or the barges that we had expected to see break the horizon. But no, days were spent sitting in the sand waiting, growing weak and restless.

I raised the eye cups to my face and peered through the binoculars out past the beach. When we joined, we were in a blood rush. We wanted to come here and fight, to avenge the acts of crime that the Nazis had committed. We felt strong, confident, and invincible. But when the fleet arrived at Castlerock, we weren't met with cheers. The Englishmen barely even looked at us. Their eyes were to the sky. Men hurried around anti-aircraft emplacements while Spitfires droned overhead. Men were unloaded, as was the food and the few tanks. Then it seemed that for every man that set foot on the last remaining land of the United Kingdom, five stepped off. Women, children, the elderly; all of them refugees of some sort. They all departed, while those that remained were left behind with even less than what they had before.

Soldiers stepped off, carrying with them arms, munitions, and food, and what they found was an army that had little of any. Any excess was spread out, leaving less for everyone. We stepped off the boat, ready to fight, ready to push back, but we were in no shape to invade England. So instead, we stood, sat, and waited for more. Every day, we waited for the Germans to land the killing blow and cross the Irish Sea.

Through the binoculars, I watched wave after wave rise and break like a cycle of life. The surge of the sea was almost like a heartbeat. Constant and soothing. It was difficult to see much; as Jackson had said, there wasn't enough light to make out much, just the white breaks that stood out from the darkness and gloom of the sea, which was almost as black as the German's reach over Europe. I scanned from right to left, blinking sporadically as the rain pattered down and speckled the lenses. Then, there was something. I almost had it, then it was gone again, vanishing like our hope, behind a swell. Too small to be a boat. Too small to be anything at that distance.

I blinked and pulled the binoculars away from my face. Tugging the sleeve of my coat over my thumb, I rubbed at the ocular lenses to remove the accumulated water and salt. Noting the location where I thought I had seen something, I threw the binoculars to my face again. It took me some time, but eventually I saw it.

'Anything?' Jackson asked as I heard him light a cigarette.

I strained my eyes as, with each second, more and more light gave me a better chance to make out what had pricked my interest. I watched a wave break, and there it was, something small and black that rode the waves like a piece of junk that had been washed out to sea. I watched it, as it rose again with a swell, and then a wave broke in front of it and it was lost again.

'Well?' Jackson prompted again as I turned to look down at him.

'Nothing,' I muttered as I handed him back the binoculars. 'Just a piece of trash. Got any spares?' I nodded at the cigarette.

Jackson exhaled as he looked up at me. The smile on his face was gone as he squinted through the rain that splattered off his helmet and into his eyes. The expression on his face was as if he was contemplating how much he actually liked me, whether it was more or less than the few cigarettes that he had on his person. After a while, he held out the soft paper packet to me, and I looked down through the tear in its top.

One left. 'You sure?' I asked, although my hand was already reaching for it.

'Sure,' he laughed. 'There'll be more where they come from when we cross the sea.'

Maybe he was right, I thought as I lit the last cigarette and tasted the stale tobacco as it rolled around my mouth. I could understand his eagerness, every American felt it. We had not faced the Jerrys. We had not been beaten back from our homes. We had come over to fight. Instead, we stood and watched as our supplies ran low. The worst part was that the low morale of the English was catching. Almost like a cold, that festered in your body. Idle hands were the devil's work, my mother used to say. Our hands were plenty idle where we sat now.

Maybe Jerry would come soon? Maybe whatever happened when they did, was for the best?

Everything good must come to an end, the age-old proverb. As if ringing true, the final cigarettes that were in our possession were finally snuffed out by the rain, taking with them even more of our morale. It seemed like an age that we sat there, our backs to the sea wall and the never-ending stalemate. My stomach growled in protest as the weeks of rations that barely sustained my weight took their toll. Like the ocean gripped in a viscous storm, my stomach rolled deep within me. Lashing out at the body that held it within, just as the oceans broke themselves against the beaches to my back. Finally, I stood and felt my body ripple as my muscles worked against the dampness of my clothes.

'Keep watch,' I said to Jackson as he peered up at me through the rain that had now turned to sleet. 'I'll try and rustle up some rations.'

I barely received a nod in reply as I slung my own Garand rifle over my shoulder and set off up the trench. Men huddled together in the trenches as I made my way through the lines. Gaps in the line left sporadic holes as weeks of sitting idle had left men complacent. Like I could talk; in the past two hours I had spent no more than three minutes watching the waves or the sky. It was as if every man was relying on the next, to let them know when the war was here. The boards that lined the bottom of the trench clunked and groaned as they took my weight. The lack of attention that our front line deserved generally eased my progress, until I hit the sporadic clumps of men that sat around each other, either laughing or sleeping in the rain. I had to take care not to step on them. I finally reached a cut out in the trench where an M4 Sherman had been driven down a built ramp to sit behind a wall of sand, silt, and sandbags as a forward line defence. The matte green of the tank seemed to shimmer as the water ran down its silent hull. The seventy-six-millimetre cannon faced forward, while the barrel of the M2 fifty calibre that was mounted to its turret hung up in salute to the rain that no doubt signalled another eventless day.

The life of the camp seemed to exist outside of the trench. As I walked up the ramp that had been built for the Sherman, a deuce and a half truck trundled by with its load of soldiers and civilians, all of whom looked glum as they peered out at the world from the safety of the canvas canopy. A howitzer trundled on its axle, behind the truck.

I frowned at the cannon as I watched it jostle and bounce on the rough terrain. Most of the heavy weaponry had been positioned behind the Strangford Loch, which, if we ever faced the ocean, lay at our rear. Allied command had flooded the loch, in case of a German spearhead making ground through our defences. With the loch flooded, the lines of advance would become bogged down in the marshy swamp that had once been lush farmland. The only issue that I could see with that, was that if the Germans secured a beach head against us, how the hell were we supposed to escape?

The truck's engine bellowed as it made its way down to Bally Walter, no doubt to reinforce that part of the line. As each day came and went, the geniuses that flooded the loch received new information. The German assault would come at Coleraine, and they would attack from Port Ellen. Men and resources were moved from point A to point B. Then the attack would come at Bangor and not Coleraine, and the resources and men were all moved back again.

Part of me thought that command had no idea, the other part of me wondered when the next load of men, tanks and planes would come. Would it be before the hammer fell? God could only hope.

As I walked my way inland, my rifle jostled at my side. Other groups of soldiers scattered the marsh. I saw the first-aid station, where the docs and nurses scanned the locals and the refugee English for signs of malnutrition. Luckily there were no Americans in that state, yet. A little further on, another deuce and half was jacked up over a swathe of timber boards. Its rear driver's side wheels were all removed as the mechanic, who was packing the bearings, wiped rain away from his brow with a grease-covered hand.

I was forced off the drier centre of the road by a platoon of Shermans that clattered past; it was good to see Sherman tanks. Although how they would fare against the seemingly unstoppable Panzer divisions, I was not sure. Nevertheless, I was happier to see them than not.

Most of the armour that landed along with Patton's first army was sent inland and south. A war of two fronts – another reason why the fleet had to risk landing at Castlerock, a port that was all too close to the coast of the occupied UK. With the Third Reich only a stone's throw away, the Irish had revolted against the Crown. Patton feared that the Nazis would land armour south of the border, in the seemingly less-than-neutral Ireland port of Dublin. In all honesty, many Americans thought that their first fight would be against the revolting Irish, rather than the Germans that they had sailed all this way to depose. But as soon as the Americans set foot on North Irish soil, not a single shot was fired, in any direction.

Finally, the mess came into view and my shoulders slumped so low at the sight that my rifle almost slipped from its perch. The line for any food seemed to stretch for a mile. Civilians eager for anything clotted the line, their empty looks of despair only matched by the vacant bowls that they clutched to their chests. Speckled in the ranks were the drab green of the Americans and the khaki brown of the refugee English forces that remained.

I joined the end of the line behind an RAF lieutenant and was occupied by my own thoughts until a hand slapped down on my shoulder, waking me from my daydream.

'Cody, fancy running into you here.'

I jerked my head at the disruption and smiled.

'Thanks for holding our spot in line,' Private Jacob Little boomed loud enough for the mass of people that had gathered behind me to hear. 'Always happens to us, we join the line up and the captain wants us for something special,' the large man said with a grin as he unslung his Browning Automatic Rifle (BAR) and allowed the butt to rest on the ground. Although a large man, he seemed to find the weight of the automatic rifle cumbersome.

'The louder you say it, the more truth there is in it, is that right?' I smiled back at him.

'Something like that,' Corporal Joe Skinner smirked as he pushed his way in front. Skinner was the platoon's 2IC, behind Sergeant Carrera. Skinner was shorter than most, standing at almost half of Little's height, with slicked back hair and a pointed nose. It always made me laugh that Skinner and Little had developed a brother-like relationship almost instantly. 'Where's Jackson?'

'Back in position. You seen anyone else? Seemed like I fell asleep and when I woke up everyone was gone.'

Little laughed. 'Maybe the Germans had come and taken us all out, only missed you because you were sleeping. Is that what you thought?'

'No,' I said flatly. 'More like a truck of food and women came through and you assholes ran off without waking me.' The other two laughed.

'Carrera is off talking to the captain. He sent Walker and O'Reily off to command, to see if they could replace Baker.'

'And Laffey and Clark went to collect the mail,' Little finished.

Private Matt Walker was the squad's support gunner, a role that meant that he was supposed to shadow Little everywhere he went. Most of his pack consisted of carrying ammunition for the BAR, as the automatic rifle chewed through more than what Little could carry. This meant that he only carried an M1 Carbine for himself, a rifle smaller in calibre and size than the standard issue M1 Garand. Privates Jacob O'Rielly, Mark Laffey and Tim Clark were all rifleman in this underpowered squad.

At full strength the fourth squad of first platoon consisted of twelve men. At current standing, the squad stood three men short. Not due to losses sustained in battle, but by a tactic of spreading the men thin to cover more ground. Bill Carrera, the squad's leader, insisted that this was a short-term measure to cover the ground that the English couldn't fill. Whether it was true or not was yet to be seen. I suppose at that time, we didn't need a full-strength squad to sit around and wait.

'Any news on when the reinforcements are due?' I asked Skinner.

'No idea,' he dismissed. 'You didn't see Jerry before you left?'

I laughed at the stupid question. 'Oh yeah, I saw him. But I figured he was still far enough away for me to grab Jackson and myself some grub before he got here.'

Skinner laughed. 'And to think you weren't going to get me any.'

Conversation continued as the line progressed toward the mess. It went quicker having another two men from my squad to talk to. In many ways we were brothers, all of us. Although some had closer friends, like Little and Skinner, and in many ways myself and Jackson; all of us loved each other.

Finally, we made it to the front of the queue. I readied my mess kit as I neared the front, then put it away as I saw what was on offer. There was no hot food. The first man was handed a can of bully beef, the second was handed two biscuits that looked as though they had been made in the First World War and were only now called upon from surplus. Little looked down at his hand, and the two biscuits that barely made up the enormity of his palm.

'Share with the soldier who has the can of beef,' were the words of the fat man behind the counter.

'Hey, I'm getting food for my pal back in the tren–' I tried.

'You and everyone else, buck. Move along.' The fat bastard cut me off.

I stood there for a second, thinking what to do with this lousy piece of garbage, when something happened. A sound seemed to cut through the chatting of the people and clanking of the cans. A sound that I should have instantly recognised but for the lack of action, it didn't register. I held the can of beef in my hand and looked at Skinner. The colour had washed out of his face. I instantly reached for my rifle, to make sure it was still there. As I turned back to the road within the tents that I had just recently walked past, soldiers were running everywhere. Civilians, caught up in the mix, started to scream. The can of beef fell from my hand; I felt it hit the toe of my boot and I looked down and watched as it rolled off into the crowd of people that were now in full panic.

Skinner grabbed my arm, and I turned blankly to look at him. 'Cody, come on. We need to get back to the line. Jerry's here.'

I blinked and finally the sound that had started the whole

commotion registered in my head. As if to signify my understanding, AA guns that scattered the line began to fire, as the air raid siren warbled its horrible tune.

'Jerry's here.'

2

As the anti-aircraft guns hammered in the distance, my heart skipped a beat. There was nowhere to hide, nowhere to go but the trench that I had lain in only moments before. While the air raid siren howled, the scene before me turned to chaos. Men ran into each other as they rushed to their positions. I watched one man fall, only to be trampled by the men that followed him in their panic. I never saw what happened to him and never knew if he even made it to the line. All I remember is his hand as he reached out for help, that for as far as I knew, would never come.

Finally, my body sprang into action, and I became one of those that barrelled through the masses to reach the safety of the trench. While I ran and slipped on the mud-caked road, my eyes darted here and there in search of the planes that would no doubt spell our doom. Through the noise of the men that surrounded me, and the cracking rapidity of the Bofors cannons, I thought I could hear the faint rumble of aeroengines in the distance. Beneath it all my heart hammered in my throat and my head was filled by the gushing of each breath that I sucked into my lungs.

Already, I had lost Little and Skinner in the chaos. I paused for a second and looked back for them, just as someone slammed into me, knocking me to the ground. I felt the mud splash into my eyes, blinding me for a second as my M1 skittered away from me. I spat mud and silt out of my mouth as I pushed myself from the ground, when another GI's legs slammed into my ribs, sprawling me once more. The private that had tripped over me went sliding into the chaos, taking a few other men down on his way. *What the hell is happening?* I thought, as again I tried to right myself while the drone of the aeroengines seemed to swell in the air. Finally, I regained my feet and had just started the search for my M1 when I was hit with such a force from behind that I thought I had been hit by a deuce and a half. There couldn't be anything else on the island that could've hit me that hard. The world went quiet, all the air seeming to be sucked out of it, as my legs were lifted from the ground. Nothing could penetrate the silence that replaced the chaos of everything that came before. I travelled fifteen feet through the air; it felt like two hundred. Around me, other men had been thrown asunder as well, and nothing could penetrate my mind for the blankness that had come over me.

When I hit the ground, I didn't even feel it. I had no idea if I was in pain, if I was bleeding, or worse yet, if I was alive. All I recall seeing was my arm out in front of my face, and a grey vision of the world in front of me as I looked directly at the truck that the mechanic had been working on just moments before the German bomb had come down on the mess. The mechanic was still under the truck. For all I could tell, he was looking right at me. His expression was blank, and his eyes didn't even blink as the shower of silt and dirt, men and shrapnel showered down from the air in the aftermath of the explosion. I always remembered that man, even to this day. It must have been the bomb that had dislodged the jack; it had to have been. Either way, the bare hubs had crushed the man's chest as the full weight of the axle came down on him. I wonder how long he remained alive with that weight pressing down.

In all that time, I had not taken a breath. I couldn't. I opened my mouth and tried to draw the air into me, but nothing would come. Over to my right, I felt the shock as another bomb went off, then more to my left. One after another, they came and fell.

Dirt and mud filled the air, as did the blood and limbs of men that had once scurried for their lives, like rats from a hawk. As if a switch was flicked inside of my head, my airways opened and my head swam with the onrush of oxygen. At the same time, my hearing came back. Slow at first, then all the way, and to be honest, I wish it never had. How my life would be so much different…

Explosions filled my head, but even they weren't enough to drown out the screams of those around me. I groaned as I sat up and looked around. Men and civilians were littered all over the road. The mess was gone, there wasn't even a suggestion that it had existed. A truck lay burning on my right; I didn't even feel it land, nor did I feel the heat as its canvas backing was licked by fire that danced in the light rain. My mouth fell open as I watched a hand reach up from the fiery mess of canvas; it trembled, as if in fear, its fingers splayed wide for a second before the flame consumed it and then there was nothing. Nothing but the explosions, horror and screams around me. How could we ever win against this?

Two hands tore me from my paralysis and dragged me to my feet.

'On your feet, soldier!' The man who had hold of me growled over the sound of the chaos. 'On your feet!' he screamed in my face.

Although now aware that I was alive, I was still unable to answer him. He held me before him, I remember seeing his eyes below the rim of his helmet. The drab of his uniform seemed grey to me as more silt showered down on us and he shook me while screaming something that I couldn't hear over the latest explosion.

I placed my hands on his and shook my head, and I saw the frustration blink in his eyes. He shook me again and tilted his head forward so that our helmets clanged together.

'I said, get back to the line!' he screamed in my face.

I had no idea who this man was, or what rank he held, but I assumed he was higher ranking than I. 'I have no rifle, sir!' I shouted back, finally finding my voice.

He released me suddenly, as new screams from my right drew his attention. We both looked over and saw a GI dragging himself out from the fire of the truck. His legs were gone, and flames licked at his blackened body while his hands sloshed through the mud, blood, and shit.

The supposed officer stepped away from me and took one final glance back toward me. 'Look around, son, there are plenty to choose from.' He turned and rushed to the mortally wounded, burning soldier.

I turned as another explosion came from behind the motor pool. The heavy truck rocked on its suspension, which triggered the nerve endings of the dead mechanic. I shielded my eyes as more dirt showered down on me before I took the officer's advice. I looked around.

M1s were everywhere. Scattered on the ground amongst the dead, wounded and those that were trying to hold everything together. I saw a Browning Automatic Rifle and stepped past it, to retrieve an M1 that was in the hands of a dead GI. From the looks of it, he had died holding his rifle to his chest, while his blood had drained from multiple shrapnel wounds in his guts. I pried the weapon from his dead hands and checked the chamber. It was time to return to the line.

As the first bombing wave moved on, a squadron of Spitfires hurtled out to the ocean above my head. Their superchargers howled as those majestic planes headed off to what could only be their end. I shouted in praise as I ran back to the trench, while the Bofors continued to hammer and hammer, peppering the skies thousands of feet above my head. Carnage was everywhere. I passed a burning Sherman on my way back to the line. The body of the driver lay silent over the frontal slope of the armour that couldn't stand up to the German armament. Finally, I was back at the slope that led down to the static Sherman that was built into our trench defence.

Men were clambering over the armour, passing tins of thirty calibre inside, while others were passing in more seventy-six. *The invasion must be happening now,* I thought. *It must be now.* I ran through the trenches as I looked to the sky again to see if the clouds had cleared, but no luck. In fact, they seemed to sit even lower than before. The rain sleeted the sea as it rolled and churned, unaffected by the carnage on the shore. The trench seemed so crowded compared to before, slowing my progress.

Faces of men that I had seen before but did not know. Faces that showed fear, faces of boys not yet men. But I supposed few were, back then.

I was almost back in position when the screams of the men around me made me stop. 'What the hell is that?' one man called.

'The sky is on fire!' another shrieked.

I turned to the ocean and looked to the sky. A portion of the grey cloud had turned yellow, as if all the power of the sun had been focused on that point. My progress slowed, until I finally stopped. Like all the other men, we stood there and watched as the yellow spot grew and grew and finally turned red.

'Oh my God,' I said as the other men screamed and ducked their heads.

'Get down!' another soldier called. And like a good soldier, I did.

The German Junkers bomber was more fireball than plane. It burst through the clouds like a comet from the stars. One of its engines screamed, as if in its death throes, as fire engulfed it. The other was silent, its prop standing out from the flames like the cross of Christ as its body hurtled toward us. I threw myself down, atop of the other men that crowded the bottom of the trench. As the heat washed over us, the sound of the dying aeroengine consumed the world.

As fast it came, the heat disappeared, and we were left there on the bottom for no more than two seconds before the bomber crashed behind our lines.

I raised myself to my feet, bringing my rifle with me. Fire shot up in the air behind our lines. A fireball that rolled and illuminated the world that had become even darker since dawn. 'Christ,' I said to myself as I began to head back to my position. As I started off, another soldier called after me.

'Christ can't help us now, kid. He shipped out with the women and children.'

When I finally made it back, Jackson's eyes were wide. He stood at the trench line, his M1 resting on the lip of the sandy edge.

'Jesus, Cody, I didn't think we'd see you again.' He touched my shoulder as I fell in beside him, as if to make sure that I was real.

'No shit,' I said as I tried to regain my breath. 'Next time it's your turn to go the mess, I ain't leaving this trench for no one.'

'Say that again when the Germans are in it.' Another familiar voice barked further down the line. I looked beyond Jackson's wide eyes and saw Walker and Clark. 'Any idea where Little is?'

I was happy to see that at least some of the men had made it back. I was just opening my mouth to reply when another voice cut over me.

'Sorry ladies,' Skinner said in his usual Boston twang. 'Would've been here sooner but some lousy Kraut decided to park his bomber almost on top of us.'

Both Little and Skinner joined the trench from the rear. Little grunted as his full weight slammed into the forward face of the shallow trench. We fell into silence as Little set up the Browning on its ungainly bipod, while Walker moved in beside his position. We were all certain the time would come now; the only question was when.

With half of our strength still missing somewhere in the chaos, we waited as the rain fell on us, our rifles poised at the ocean that continued to swirl and break on the beach. As I stood there, looking over the hooked sights of my M1, I thought that I'd never really noticed before how little we could see. Beyond the first break of the waves, the ocean was lost to us in a swirl of sea spray and sleeting rain.

Our breaths broke up the monotony of the rumbling aeroengines and the second wave of explosions that came mostly to our back. One bomb did land roughly on the trench line and sand and spray was thrown high into the air, but this was well right of our position. More planes came down, fighters too, but in the distance and not in our line of sight. The only key difference between the bombs and falling bombers was the sound they made when they hit the ground. No matter what it meant, I now have no doubt that lives were lost with every impact, whether they were German, English or American. To me, looking back on this day, it made no difference.

I cannot tell you how long we stood there waiting for the inevitable. It felt like hours. But no doubt, barely a second had passed before something in the swirling waves caught my eye again. In fairness, only minutes had passed since the first bomb had landed.

'Jackson,' I said without tearing my eyes away from the front. 'Pass me those binoculars.' I held out a hand while I laid my M1 on the sandy edge of the trench. I heard Jackson rustle through his gear as I squinted my eyes again, straining through the grey to make out what I had seen. Finally, the binoculars were placed into my open palm and once more I scanned the ocean, looking for what had piqued my interest.

It took some time before I found it and when I did, a line creased my brow. I remember thinking how surreal it was to focus on something so small in the water, when so much was happening around me. It was the same piece of garbage I had seen before. The same piece of black scrap that rose and fell with the waves, but for some reason, it was in the same place as before. I lowered the binoculars as concern washed over me. More bombs exploded to my rear as I raised the binoculars a final time, only then had I noticed that the air raid siren had finally ceased its warbling.

Thank God for small mercies, I remember thinking, as I found the piece of garbage once more. I redoubled my grip on the casing in my hand as I frowned. The black circle came down the face of wave, and as it did, I saw the water break around something that seemed to be standing up from it. A vertical line, directly from its centre. Not only that, it didn't seem to get pushed from side to side – even if one of the waves broke crooked, the circle stayed true.

'What the hell is that?' I spoke aloud as I squinted.

'Where?' Jackson asked as he leant forward, following the direction of my gaze. He squinted into the sleet, reclaiming the binoculars.

'Just there, say one o'clock,' I pointed in its direction. 'I saw it before; I thought it was garbage but it couldn't still be there.'

It didn't take Jackson long to find the item in question. 'It's not stationary,' he said as he adjusted the focus.

'I know that, it's moving with the waves.'

'No, I mean it's coming ashore, but slowly.'

'Give me that,' I said disdainfully, not believing his words. Jackson handed me the binoculars again and it didn't take me long to see that he was right. It was no more than a hundred feet out from the shore when I first saw it. Now it seemed it was closer to sixty. As I watched it rise on a wave again, I saw it jerk, as something that was connected to it pulled it against the roll of the wave. 'Jesus,' I said as I lowered the optics from my face.

'What?' Jackson asked, but I didn't have to explain.

Thirty feet from the edge of the beach, something was coming out. A commotion started down the line while men to my left shouted out at the same time. As I looked from right to left, more and more of these things started to become visible. The waves broke around them, like they were rocks that had been washed ashore by the churning sea. But they didn't stay still. Closer and closer they came, until the rise of the sand bar exposed their hulls to us.

'Oh God,' I heard Walker say beneath his breath. Up and down the line, the men shuffled in the trench, trying to get an idea of what it was. Some rifles cracked, the first shots of the war for us, and they did nothing.

Higher and higher the bulking shapes came, exposing the rubber tube that came out from their top and drooped over their backs. Higher and higher still they came, the tip of their cannons breaching the water now, only partially and then completely.

The squared front of the MKIV Panzers rose from the sea like a Leviathan of mythic fables. It wasn't long before the sound of their engines and the clattering of their tracks were audible over the crashing of the waves and the howl of the battle above us.

Not knowing what else to do, I raised my M1, centred the sights on the closest Panzer, and began to fire.

3

Those first shots of the war seemed redundant. I will never forget the first time I held an M1, back in Fort Worth – the weight of it. The sense that we, as men of the US 1st, would be armed with the most powerful weapon of war ever conceived. Even more powerful than anything that the Third Reich, the technological superpower, could devise. I felt invincible, as I am sure almost every other man in my company did. Yet, the butt recoiled against my shoulder, and I viewed the steel beast through my sights. Round after round, bark after bark, did nothing. Finally, the eighth round hammered through me and the receiver ejected the clip into the air with a telltale twang, to be lost in the sand with I don't know how many lives. That feeling of invincibility was gone. I was afraid for my life.

I reached into my bandolier to reload the M1, as I watched the progress of the Panzer. Up and down the line, men were firing. I heard the short rapid bursts of the BARs and the slow methodical cranking of the thirty calibres, but nothing big. No fifties spoke up to silence the rest, no fire from the embedded Sherman to my far left. No artillery ruptured the beaches, not even the AA continued its rattle anymore.

As I rammed home a clip and the bolt of my M1 slammed forward, an explosion occurred on the frontal armour of the closest Panzer.

'We scored a hit!' I remember screaming. I don't know why I thought this, maybe it was hope lying somewhere down deep in my stomach; maybe I was just a fool.

Men cheered as the heavy iron continued to roll up the beach, but not even a hint of a smile reached my face as the turret of the MKIV traversed first left then right, as if freeing its joints from its submersion. On the frontal glacier, the machine gun in its ball socket waggled about furiously as the rolling armour came to a stop.

I didn't raise my rifle again. I was lost for words. The tank that now sat free from the reach of the ocean detached its snorkel from its cupola. There seemed to be a second of silence from the American line, almost a breath of contemplation, before all the Panzers on the beach began to fire into us. The Panzer closest to us fired a round from its long-barrelled seventy-five-millimetre cannon, straight into the ground almost an inch before the line of our trench. Sand flew into the air in a furious torrent of debris and flesh. Men started to scream as the engines revved and the tanks began to crawl forward again.

I ducked my head as the bow gunner raked his machine gun fire across our line. He fired so fast, I could not differentiate one shot from another. More sand flew into the air and sifted down over me like coarse rain, while another seventy-five slammed into the beach further down the line. Another bellowed in some other place, while the German machine gun fire now drowned out the sound of the American rifles.

I looked up and down the line. To the left, men fired into the tanks with no effect, while others stayed low, reloading their weapons. Thirty feet down to my right, our trench had collapsed against the first seventy-five-millimetre shells. Amongst the sand and broken timbers, I saw the lifeless shape of a man's arm, the only part of his body left uncovered by the collapsing cover.

I sucked a breath into my lungs; the air tasted of death and fear. Lifting myself above cover, I began to fire again into the tank. Two rounds, quick and fast, before the bow gunner's MG tracked back over my position and I was forced down again. Before I had a chance to raise into a firing position again, I was grabbed from behind and spun around. My first thought was that the Germans had already made it into our trench, that I was about to be skewered by the bayonet of some sturmtruppen. But above me was Bill Carrera, back from HQ.

'Don't fire at the tanks!' he screamed in my face as the German machine gun fire raked over our position again. 'Little!' he screamed at the squad gunner who had just rammed another magazine into his BAR.

The big man looked up from his weapon to our sergeant, with a blank expression. The world was awash with gunfire, cannon fire and the rolling sound of engines and war that echoed above us. 'Paratroopers have landed behind the lagoon!' Bill turned his own attention to his Thompson sub-machine gun, as he readied it, 'we have more infantry inbound from the–' he cut himself short as the rolling sound of aeroengines changed almost instantly.

Throughout the steady drone of the engines and gunfire, something had started to scream. A horrible sound cut through the world of chaos and disaster, running down my spine. It fixed my feet to the crumbling ground beneath me. Higher and higher and higher in pitch it screamed, and I could do nothing but follow Bill's gaze into the air. With the relentless fog, smoke and shit that filled the sky, I could see nothing, but the scream that filled the air filled my heart with dread.

'Cover!' Bill screamed as he drove his shoulder into me and threw me into the ground.

Men had started to shriek in panic as the wail of the falling death filled the air. I felt the cold of the ground beneath me and the heat of Bill on top of me. His breath was on my ear and sweat lined his flesh, as he raised his head to be heard over the Jericho sirens. 'Stuka! Cover!'

The rest of that moment was lost to the frightened shrieks of the men that surrounded me. The siren howled on and on and on. It grew louder with each second that marked its course toward us. The sound of its cannon fire was almost a godsend, as it marked the ending of the Stuka dive bombers' run. The cannon fire seemed like it was from another world, far away.

Then came the impacts that shot up the beach like a ripcord of death. Men wailed in fear and fired blindly into the air as some of the fire ripped up the centre of the trench. I felt the thud as the shells drove into the sand. If there was a distinction between the sound that sand or flesh made, I didn't hear it. That thought was lost almost instantly as the machine cannon's fire washed over us and was replaced by the deafening explosion of the Stuka's payload.

The explosion slammed through Bill and myself, as if a Panzer had run over us. The air was pushed out of my lungs, and as the sound of the aeroengine washed away into the distance and the shriek of the Jericho trumpets dissipated, I was left in another battle to draw air. With my mouth open, gaping for life, sand and silt fell into my open maw as the fallout from the bomb came crashing down. I managed a small breath before something heavy slammed into Bill's back, driving the small respite out of me. Bill grunted as he shifted to the side and tried to gain his feet. As the pressure from my chest lifted, I sucked in more air and choked as I dragged sand into my lungs.

Machine gun fire swept over us again as I spluttered and choked, starbursts forming in my vision. Aware of the screams around me and fighting still for breath, two hands dragged me to a sitting position and finally air poured into me again.

Bill's face was an inch from mine. He slammed something into my chest as he screamed into my face, 'Infantry ashore, get up there and stop them!'

With that, Bill was gone, and American rifle and machine gun fire filled the air. I clambered to my feet and wiped sand from my eyes. I lifted myself to the top of the trench line and was then forced down again as the Panzer's machine gun raced in my direction. Again, sand flew and I tempted fate by rushing up again the instant I felt the fire pass. I threw my M1 to my shoulder, determined for retribution, and my sights fell on a landing craft that had seemed to appear from nowhere.

Grey men, almost invisible in the salt spray and the falling sand, were running ashore. Some fell as they were cut down, and I fired into them, fast and rapid, not even aiming but just wanting them to die. I saw men fall, having no idea if it was me or the other GIs that had hit them. They fell to the beach, and as I fired into the places where they had stood, they fired back at us from their prone positions on the beach. Sand kicked up in my face and blinded me partially, so I ducked down to clear my eyes.

In my blurred vision I thought I saw someone at my feet and I tried to make out who it was, but nothing was coming through. I swore as I kneaded at my eyes and felt the grit of the sand against the globes. I gritted my teeth and through the tears that had formed I saw a dead soldier at my feet. It was Tim Clark; the colour had washed from his face as he lay there on the ground, looking right into my eyes. I paused. I remember the way his helmet sat almost beneath his head, which lifted his chin towards me. Sand fell from the air in a tirade from another torrent of German fire, and I saw it land on his eyes and his lips. He didn't blink, didn't even wipe away at the particles that sat on the edge of his lips. Even as the vibrations of the advancing Panzers forced them one by one, over and into his gape.

Something broke in me and I forced myself to the side of the trench as I shouldered my M1. I pulled the trigger hard, again and again and again, trying my best to aim. It wasn't until the tenth time I had pulled that trigger that I noticed the gun wasn't recoiling. It had jammed before I had even noticed Tim. That sobered me. If anything in the war was going to kill me, it would be not being in the right mindset. I needed to get my shit together and it needed to be now.

I cleared the jam and dumped the rest of my clip on the sand. With a new clip in place, the bolt of the M1 slammed home and I brought it to my shoulder and fired.

As waves of men had now landed on the beach there was no

shortage of targets. The smartest of the Wehrmacht raced to the Panzers and sheltered behind them, while others ran as far up the beach as possible before they were either killed or driven to the ground to try and find cover. Each man fought their own war, each man gambled with his life to gain an inch or die. I cut down possibly my first German in that moment, as he ran across the beach in front of me to make it to the safety of the rear of a Panzer. I led him almost instinctually and cut him down as he ran. I remember the way his Mauser flew out of his hands as I took his life from him. It was almost as if the action was like a surrender. Like he didn't even want to be holding it. It made no difference; it never did in the end.

Another man drew my attention as he lay behind the bodies of his fallen comrades and fired up at us. I fired five times into his position, unsure whether I was killing the man or just driving my leaden fire into the back of the dead Kraut. The twang of the clip's ejection drove me back under cover to reload. Four more clips I emptied into the mass of men on the beach as I did my best to dodge the machine gun and rifle fire that peppered at me after a few rounds. I had just finished loading another clip into my M1 when again Bill grabbed me.

'Panzers advancing!' he screamed into my face and pushed me down the trench to my left. 'Take Jackson and get to that Sherman and get us some goddamned fire support!'

He returned to the trench line and dumped half of his magazine forward of the line before he was driven back below by intense German fire. Bill had not had his head below the trench for more than a second before he burst back above the line of cover and dumped the rest of his magazine downrange. As he worked to reload his Thompson, he noticed that I had not moved and he regarded me for a second with a look of bewilderment. 'Now, Private!' he shrieked before he racked the sub-machine gun and returned to the defence of the line.

Finally, I dragged myself to my feet. Unaware of my surroundings, I looked around and saw Jackson to my left, engrossed in his own battle to stay alive. He was engaged, like everyone else, in the defence of the trench line. As I hunched over and moved toward his position, I watched him try to raise himself above cover to lay fire down. Almost instantly, he was driven back down by bursting fire at his position. I couldn't help but think, as I laid a hand on him to gain his attention, that Bill had saved his life by dragging him away from the trench line. Some Kraut down on the beach had singled him out and at some point, Jackson's luck would have run out.

'Jackson!' I raised my voice as I shoved him. He raised his head to consider me and not even a look of recognition was visible through the fear that was in his eyes. 'On me, down the line.'

He nodded through his distress and I didn't even check if he had fallen in behind me as I worked through the chaos to head down our line of defence back toward the Sherman.

Our journey back down the trench, through lines of crossing fire, death, blood, and sand, was horrific. I remember seeing one soldier raise himself above cover to fire on the Germans, only to have his helmet blown off his head almost instantly. His M1 fell from his hands as his arms shot outwards from the shock. I remember the butt of the rifle sticking out above the open air of the trench as the soldier fell to his knees. As he came down, I saw the top of his head had been replaced by a mess of blood and wrinkled matter. The surprised look on the soldier's face remained until he crumpled at the base of the trench, twitching. We moved over him and beyond.

More soldiers screamed, while others moaned as they held their hands to the wounds that leaked their lifeblood out over the sand and rotting timbers of the trench floor. Those that had strength called out for medics who were no doubt overwhelmed by the carnage that had ensued in the past twenty minutes. Unable to assist their friends, soldiers stole glances back to those that suffered in the safety of the trench. They reloaded their M1s before throwing themselves back into the line of fire to hold off the German advance.

It was hard to move past those men that needed our help, to brush away the desperate grasps of those that were dying, that only wanted someone to tell them they were going to be alright before they passed. But we couldn't spare a second; even as we progressed down the line, the sounds of the Panzers' engines revved and the clatter of their tracks signalled the doom that was to come.

By the time we reached the Sherman I had no idea if it was too late or not. There was chaos everywhere. Fire had spread behind our trench line and the open area that sat behind the Sherman was lost to me in a cloud of darkness, where the fire from the overturned deuce and a half had spread almost beyond control. The men that I had once seen loading thirty calibre into the steel beast, now lay around the tank in a mess of blood, gore and limbs that left them indistinguishable from one another. The way they had been chewed up beyond recognition left me no doubt that the Sherman had been the main target of the diver bombers' attack run.

The tank sat silent in the chaos; I had no idea what to do. We had left our positions to find fire support, but the closest embedded tank had already been taken out of the fight by the loss of its crew. I would like to say it was me that had leapt into action, but I was not that brave, not then, and I doubt I ever was.

As I stood and looked down at what remained of the crew, my M1 limp at my side, Jackson leapt onto the tank. He ditched his M1 on the back deck as he raised himself into the view of the enemy and was about to disappear into the turret when a man with black smears of grease appeared in the opening.

'No!' he screamed at Jackson as my friend was preparing himself to enter. 'You man the fifty, keep those Krauts off us.' He looked around and his eyes fell on me. 'You there!' he screamed with a look of desperation mixed with anger. 'Standing there holding your goddamned pecker! Get your ass up here and man the gun. Let's cook us some Germans, boys!' he screamed as he disappeared into the turret, his voice resonating out of the open cupola. I couldn't believe what I had just seen, nor what I had heard. But the next thing I knew, I was following him.

*

The Sherman was cold beneath me. Its engine was dormant, not even running to power its traverse. The back deck was slick with blood and empty shell casings from the fifty, which had come into action before the operator was chewed to shreds by the Stuka fire. I slipped, lost my footing, but remained on the tank as German small arms fire began to patter off the armour. I swore, but did not panic as I raised myself even higher and then fell into the safety of the turret as the ear-splitting roar of the fifty began to thunder into the morning.

The sound inside was surreal, almost special, as the roar of the fifty washed over the heavy steel plate. The sound that managed to sneak inside the turret echoed and bounced like thunder rolling in the clouds. The gunner had moved to the left side of the turret and was levering the breech open manually when I came inside. He looked up at me with wide eyes as he strained with the weight of the breech. 'Right side, forward,' he spat. 'See that hand crank?' Everything was white inside the Sherman's turret, except for the breech to my left. I fell heavily into the gunner's seat and looked around. I saw instantly what he was referring to – a small vertical lever that sat to my right just in front of me.

'Got it!' I proclaimed as I latched my hand over it.

'Use that to traverse. Look in front of you, see the eye piece? Look through there as you turn, I'll load the gun.'

I leant forward and looked through the periscope before me. If I thought the world inside was surreal, then the view through that periscope was otherworldly. Germans lay on the beach, dying, while sand and shit was thrown up over them. Their comrades ran for cover over the dead and dying. I spun the traverse handle one way and stopped as I corrected my rotation to turn toward the right. While leaning forward, the motion of the turret was eerie. Smooth and silent below the dulled fighting outside. As I came about, I saw more carnage on the beach, even the way the blood ran down the sand and mixed with the ocean, only to be swept up to stain the beach over and over in its relentless motion. Then finally, I saw one.

The MKIV had progressed most of the way up the beach, and almost reached the grassy plains before the trenches. Behind it, a line of soldiers advanced with the monster, safely behind its armour. Those that were on the outside and further back were picked off by Americans who had vantage points on their flank. I moved my head to the right and saw another periscope, but this time with a reticle. I traversed and went too far.

'Shit,' I groaned as I tried to stop the traverse. The Panzer was almost in sight. 'Ok,' I said as I started to come back. 'Almost there.'

'There's a foot pedal to your left!' Jackson shouted. 'You shoot when you're ready. It's the right pedal.' I heard a slam of steel, and he shouted just afterward. 'Up. Gun ready!'

I didn't even question him. I felt it with my foot, and he directed me a little, but I could tell he was wary of the recoil of the cannon. I saw the Panzer come into view, and I pushed down hard with my foot. When the co-axial machine gun fired, my heart sunk. Tracers flew and hammered into the side of the Panzer; the tank didn't even slow.

'Your other right, genius!' The gunner roared.

I looked away from the periscope and down at the pedals. I saw my error, lifted my foot, and jammed it down hard on the pedal I had missed. The seventy-six-millimetre cannon to my left erupted in a furious motion of power and burnt cordite. It slid backwards on it rails and the breech flew open, expelling the case and gun smoke into the turret. The force of the cannon fire shocked me and rung through my ears. My eyes bulged at the pain in my head from the concussion and all I could do was look over at the gunner as he slammed another shell into the open, waiting breech.

'Up!' he screamed as the breech slammed home and he backed away from the cannon. Slowly, I turned my head back to the periscope and looked through. The Panzer had stopped. I had no idea where the first shell had gone, but I saw that the tank had stopped further forward of where the reticle lay.

My heart hammered like a machine gun against my ribcage as I traversed the turret. The fine lines of the reticle tracked their way over the dark steel of the Panzer to rest on the line of the turret. A chill ran up my spine and my chest seemed to clench against the staccato of my heart as the Panzer shifted in the gloomy view of the periscope, its own turret turning towards me before stopping.

As I looked right down the barrel of the Panzer's long gun, I stamped hard on the pedal again and the Sherman rocked under the power. The force of the concussion rocked me away from the periscope and again I had no idea if I had hit it. As the gunner moved to my left, I drove myself forward to see what was happening, and was confronted by the sight of the Panzer's barrel once more. I tensed as I waited for it to fire, with my foot poised above the pedal, waiting for him to say the word once more. My head thumped as the fumes from the gunpowder filled my senses, and part of me thought that was what I saw in the periscope – the fumes of the cordite dancing before my eyes. But it wasn't until I saw the sparks of fire through the dark hole I had made in the side of the tank, and the man trying to make his way out through the cupola, that I knew we had killed it.

'Hit!' I screamed as I watched in awe as the Panzer crew tried to escape the burning wreck of its hull. I watched one man make it out of the wreck, only to be gunned down by the Americans only twenty feet before him.

'Move on! Find another target!' The gunner screamed at me. 'Gun ready! Armour piercing!' He shouted as he slammed another shell home.

I blinked as I saw another crewman fall on the burning wreck of his tank and I traversed right again. Forcing myself to ignore the scenes of chaos, I was in search for the MKIV that was threatening my squad. While I squinted to see through the smoke that was billowing out of the first Panzer, the turret began to pang as if hard hail was falling on an iron roof. I pulled away from the periscope and looked to the gunner in concern.

'Small arms fire. Keep hunting!' He waved me on. I didn't realise it then, but he looked more frightened than I was. He didn't want to be there, and as bullets panged off the steel all around us, I didn't blame him.

As I strained my eyes while scanning the beach for the next Panzer, a clump of sand was thrown up in front of the tank, completely blocking my view. 'Panzers targeting us!' he screamed. 'Get a line on them!'

I blinked and moved back to the wide-view periscope but couldn't see a damned thing. It was now my turn to do something stupid. I raised myself up and lifted my head through the open cupola above me. It was the most terrifying thing I had ever done.

Tracer rounds rushed toward me, panging off the hard steel of the Sherman and ricocheting off into the distance. I saw the dead and dying, and Germans raise their rifles against me, but most importantly of all, I saw beyond the smoke, the Panzer that was advancing up the beach from my squad. It had stopped and its turret was facing us; we didn't have long.

As I ducked back down into cover, the intensity of the small arms fire increased tenfold. I forced it to the back of my mind and rushed to traverse the turret. I scanned through the wide-vision port as a screech of steel and the shudder of the turret made me turn to look at the gunner again.

'Glanced! Hurry up, goddamn it!'

I returned to the periscope and felt as though I was in the right spot, but waves of smoke made me unsure. 'Where's the elevation?' I screamed, as through the whisp of the smoke I saw the hint of tracks in the uppermost portion of the periscope.

'There! Left!'

I saw where he pointed and should have known. My left hand naturally fell in place as soon as I saw it. With the panic now engrained into both of us, I returned to the periscope and swung the barrel up into the air.

'Almost,' I said to myself as more small arms fire hammered into steel. 'Almost.' I poised my foot over the fire pedal, and through the periscope the smoke washed away again, caught by some heavenly breeze. Once more, I saw the Panzer and slammed my foot down.

4

The body of the Sherman jostled under the recoil of the seventy-six. Smoke filled the turret as the empty casing was ejected from the cannons breech and fell into the basket below. I trained my eyes as I struggled to see through the periscope again, but the smoke of the first destroyed Panzer had been buffeted down by the rolling sea breeze to obscure my view.

'Armour piercing!' the gunner screamed as he rammed another shell into the breech. As it slammed shut, I couldn't help but feel invigorated by the gunner's confidence. So much so, I slammed my foot down again without even being sure of my target; there could be no way that the Panzer could have moved beyond my line of sight in the short time that it took the gunner to reload. Again, the hull of the Sherman rocked behind the walls of sand that protected it and more smoke filled the turret as it spewed out the empty casing. The world outside seemed to mean nothing at this stage, nor the pangs of small arms fire that ricocheted off the armour of the Detroit rolling iron. Not the sounds of explosions, as grenades exploded along the front or the machine gunfire. None of it seemed real beyond the armour.

It didn't even seem real when the German shell hit us. The rupturing of the armour and the tearing of steel dissipated almost as soon as it cut through my day dream. As something hard hit me on my left and I was thrown against the outer ring of armour, stars appeared before my eyes. I still remember the shock of the moment and the taste of blood, as my vision reeled. Slumping down further in the turret, the chair that I was perched on seemed to disintegrate. I struggled to draw a breath, but the thickness of the powder smoke was even more abhorrent than before. My lungs rejected the poisoned air, and I was shaken by a cough that rattled my head. Almost as a safety mechanism, I scoured the floor with my feet, desperately in search of a firing mechanism to step on. No matter how hard I searched, I had lost my orientation in the moment of the impact.

'Jack—' I tried before another cough racked my body. 'Jackson!' I managed, before I finally pushed myself up from the turret basket. 'Jack—' I tried again as a stabbing pain in my side cut my voice off way down within me. 'Ahh…. Shit.' I groaned as my strength left me for a second and I slumped back down into the basket once more. My hand brushed a jagged chunk of steel that protruded out of my flank. I gasped as I inspected the damage before I was forced to close my eyes as my vision reeled again. My helmet clunked against the turret ring and the steel echoed through my concussion.

I am not sure how close I came to losing consciousness; I don't think I knew it back then and I sure as hell don't remember now. Yet, as I pulled each inch of steel out of my flank, my whole body shuddered. Each inch that felt as though a mile of pain had stretched out of the wound to my side, each shuddered breath that kept it all inside of me. Finally, as I pulled the shattered hunk of armour free from my flesh, a shudder of relief fell from my body. As the piece of steel clattered amongst the rails of the basket, I finally saw what had become of the Sherman. The cannon mantlet had shattered under the power of the German shell. The sheer force of the impact had driven the breech of the cannon a foot over in my direction.

'Gunny!' I tried this time, resigning myself to the fact that if the Sherman was hit so hard and if so much damage could have occurred inside of the armour, then anything outside must surely be dead. The only source of help I could find, must be the gunner. 'Gunny!' I screamed again as I struggled to rise. My hands slipped on the cracked breech as my aching body finally found its feet. 'Answer me goddamn it!' I spat as I pulled myself over the breech of the cannon. 'You can't be…' I started again as my eyes finally fell upon him.

The German shell had impacted the turret casing to his back. The shell, even after it had punched through the weaker side armour, had still had enough force to tear the man in half. His upper torso lay in the basket alongside the empty seventy-six casings. One of his lungs had been torn from within and lay out beside him like a sack of wasted flesh thrown aside. The smoke that filled the turret was not from the unburnt powder of the Sherman's breech, but from the man's clothes that had caught after the intense heat of the melting armour had sprayed up his rear.

'Cody!' I heard Jackson scream but I didn't answer him. It couldn't be true. Surely the voice was his memory in my mind. I was lost to the horror of the tank crewman that lay below me. The horror of seeing the fragility of man so clearly in that moment, and how the only thing that kept me alive was the breech of the seventy-six that sat between us.

'Armour piercing,' I mumbled to myself, as above me the sound of my name rolled over deaf ears again. I became increasingly aware of heavy machine gun fire. The racket of the fifty calibre Browning's that were mounted to the back of most US Vehicles was commandeering. I finally turned from the mess below me and struggled to raise my head through the open cupola. If the sound of the fifty was intense within the turret ring, the concussion of the monster increased tenfold when there wasn't half an inch of steel to dull its thunder.

I breathed air that was filled with the salt of the Irish Sea, and I had never felt anything so beautiful compared to the strangling sensation that the powder fumes had within that tank. Jackson was standing on the rear deck of the knocked-out Sherman. The barrel of the fifty calibre was depressed enough to be used in an anti-personnel capability. The barrel hammered back in the frame of its large square frame with each shot.

Large, artillery-like casings fell beneath the blackened steel with each cyclic action of the weapon. Spilling all over the back deck which was interlaced between brass and steel links.

'Cody!' Jackson screamed, as he raked the fifty back over another section of the beach head. I remember seeing his face as he did so. He looked as though he had aged a decade as the fire spitting from the muzzle of the cannon in his hands cast shadows over his face. "Infantry, Infantry!' His mouth shaped the words as they were lost over the thunder of the machine gun.

As my vision swayed for the final time in my concussion, then snapped back to reality, I turned my head away from Jackson to the beach head. The sight was surreal. A few Panzers littered the beach, black smoke trailed up in the air as sparks of fire flickered up the inside of their hulls and open cupolas as the munitions inside cooked off.

Dead Krauts littered the shore around the steel monsters. Blood stained the sand, as water lapped at their heels. The barrels of their Mauser's buried by the footfalls of the men that had rushed over the top of them only to fall against the withering American fire. Yet, for each Panzer that sat burning in the sand, three rolled up the shore. For ever Wehrmacht man that lay dying or dead on the last British frontier, twenty screamed for 'volk und Führer' as they fought their way to the trench line.

As my eyes panned the carnage of the beach front, three black specs tracing the air caught my eyes. Three aircraft, flying in a tight formation toward the beach front, banked and swept down low, increasing their speed as they washed off elevation in their attack run. Again, the screams of the Jericho trumpets forewarned the incoming of the Stuka. If I thought the sound of one of them was bad, the combined howl of three dive bombers hurtling towards a man as each second counted down to either the spray of cannon fire or the explosion of a five-hundred-pound bomb, was earth ending. As if I was a man on death row, a man that knew the date and time of his own death. Each moment beforehand became a profound torture.

I was horrified as they came down on us. Frozen in fear as the wailing pitch drove itself into my soul and rippled in my ears. As I screamed and held my hands over my ears, Jackson swung the fifty calibre and hammered a stream of continuous fire at the screaming eagles. The barrel jostled and the casings tumbled over the rear slope of the turret, as Jackson reigned fire into the sky. I don't know when the fear broke, I don't know if it ever did. One of the Stuka's dipped its nose while its trumpets warbled its horrible siren. Without a jerk, the Stuka sailed straight into the beach amongst other German soldier's and vehicles. Its fuselage shattered as its prop drove into the ground and the tail jerked upward as its spine broke. There was fire, but nothing as impressive as anyone would expect. The horrible howl of the siren was lessened the instant it hit the ground.

Still, the two remaining Stuka's continued their assault. Perhaps it was then that I felt myself moving. My foot clambered atop of the shattered cannon breech and my bleeding flank pushed clear of the cupola. All the while, the fifty-calibre continued to hammer its monotonous thud. As I pulled myself free of the cupola, my feet slipped on the smooth surface of the armour. As I leapt, my feet slid on the steel, lessening my momentum but still, I had enough force to slam myself into Jackson's side and drive him from the rear deck of the Sherman.

As we crashed into the sodden earth, the ground trembled in fear as the Stuka's cannon fire tore up all that fell beneath. The steel of the Sherman twanged under the impact and the wail of the sirens lifted as the Stuka's lifted themselves back into the air.

I hoisted myself from the thrashing man beneath me, and the mud and the wet sand clung to me. Jackson was writhing on the ground, shrieking as he tried to push himself away from me. Visually, I inspected him, but nothing stood out. I ran my hands over him; I didn't even think of my own wound that I had suffered, my only thoughts were for him. As my hands touched him again, he struck me in the jaw. I tumbled into the muck and in an instant, he was on me.

Dazed by the blow, I couldn't understand what was happening.

My helmet had tumbled from my head in the instant that I had fallen, I felt his fingers work through the strands of my hair and clench, he held my head up for a second and bellowed into my ear, 'Fuck you, Kraut!'

My face was driven into the mud and wet sand below. He screamed as he did so, I remember that much. I opened my mouth to try and talk him down, but mud and grit washed into my mouth and splashed against the back of my throat. I coughed and spluttered, all the while the force doubled on the back of my head. I pushed my hands into the grit to lift myself, but I couldn't gain a purchase. Still, he screamed. The sound of gunfire, explosions and engines washed around me.

Suddenly, it stopped. The pressure, the screaming, and the incessant struggle for life. To look back on this moment now, I didn't know if I had perished, or if Jackson had worn a stray bullet. But as I lifted my head and spat the debris from my mouth, I heard him there sobbing. I turned and saw him, still perched atop of me, looking at his hands in bewilderment.

'I... I...' He stammered. 'But I... you...'

I heaved him off me, scrambled to my feet in desperation as the war continued around us. I clenched one fist around the cuff of his shirt and with the other hand I brought it, open palmed across his face in a swift movement. His eyes widened at the blow, and he finally looked at me again.

'We don't have time for this!' I shouted over the din. Jackson didn't say a word. 'We need to regroup with Carrera. Are you with me?'

His eyes still wide, his mouth opening and closing as if trying to grasp to something solid. Almost non-existent, the faintest of nods reassured me that he was at least somewhat in control. I dragged him to his feet, turned back to the crippled Sherman and retrieved our M1's. I thrust one into his hands and instinctually, his hands closed around it.

'Stay on me. Don't fall behind.' I checked the chamber of my rifle and moved back into the trench line.

Chaos and panic were all that remained in the line of defence. The Wehrmacht troops and the remaining Panzers had advanced within twenty feet of the trench line. They were close enough now that their shouts of desperation and barks of command intertwined with the Americans. Almost as if they battled to be heard over one another. We ran through the trenches, heads down to avoid any fire from our enemy that was so close now that I thought I could even smell the water that soaked their clothes. The smell of their rations on their breath. The rot in the dying flesh.

I had never realised until this point, but one stretch of trench was dug shallower than the rest, and as we moved, we were forced into a crouch to remain in cover. The boards clacked under our feet as machine gun fire sent showers of sand and muck into our faces. The faces of the men we passed were grey. Fear had sunk into them; although they had killed their fair share of attackers, the fight had still come closer. The shrieks of the dying, the howl of the Stuka's and the roar of the Panzers all dug at the foundations of each man's sanity. As men stood to fire at the enemy, the odds of them ducking back to safety became slimmer and slimmer. Any consecutive attempt of repeating that action in the same position, meant almost certain death.

The bottom of the trench was littered with the dead and dying. In some places it was impossible to step around them. At first, I hesitated, but it became a reality that we needed to step on our own, to move on. I saw many men die, their faces torn into unrecognisable lumps of flesh, bone, and sinew as they rose to slow the German advance. Others, in such fear for their own lives completed the action with such pace, that their shots could almost certainly have counted for nothing.

My uniform was soaked from the rain and mud. I could feel the crust of the sand and the stickiness of my blood. Still, we progressed through the chaos, not stopping to fire our own weapons, not daring to take the chance. We were finally back into a sufficiently dug out portion of trench that allowed us to stand and our pace had increased once more, when above the trench line I heard the Germans barking orders and almost instantly the roar of an engine. I paused as the clatter of tank tracks rumbled through my body. I looked to the walls of the trenches and saw grains of sand and silt trickle through the cracks in the boards. Behind me, Jackson pressed into my back. I turned and regarded him. Fear hung in his eyes like the body of man that swung from a rafter. No doubt I had my own hanging man in my eyes as well. I'm sure we all did.

As the world was lost in the vibration of the advancing Panzer, I heard the charging cry of the Germans that remained on the beach. A breath shuddered in my chest, hesitant to take hold by the incessant rumbling as ten feet in front of me, the lip of the trench crumbled beneath the weight of the MKIV.

I watched awestruck, as first the main cannon of the long barrelled seventy-five millimetre reached out into the open air and the world seemed to darken as its bulk broke the supporting timber braces of the trench. The men below the monster screamed as they pushed against those at their sides to escape the rolling death that appeared above them. Its nose dipped at first as more and more of its weight was left unsuspended. I remember seeing the bogeys droop as the leaf springs relaxed. The nose drove hard into the opposite wall and amazingly pushed through. Sand and rubble, broken timber and shit poured into the trench, burying the men below—alive or dead—in a premature grave.

One man was only partially buried; the top half of his body remained free. Having discarded his weapon, his hands worked to free his legs while above him the Panzer cleared the trench and stopped. I had just started to move, to help the trapped soldier, when Jackson stopped me. I heard him say something but any sense of it was lost in the moments that came next. The trapped soldiers snapped his head up to the trench line, as something drew his attention.

'No, no, no, no!' he screamed as he raised his hands out before him in surrender.

A single rifle shot, one in thousands that had fired that morning, rings out in my memory. The bullet passed through one of the desperate man's hands and onward through his face. The life left him instantly and his body collapsed. He slumped over, still stuck in his partial tomb as the Germans flooded into the trench around him.

What happened next is only a blur to me now, all these years later. It all happened in such a small amount of time. The Wehrmacht flooded the trench. Men dressed in drab grey greatcoats and their bucket helmets stormed the collapsed section of trench before me. As I raised my M1 to fire on them, others breached the trench mouth directly in front of me. I fired on one man who was armed with a Schmeisser sub-machine gun, and who had barely recovered from the fall when my bullet drove into his side. He fell without making a sound as I moved my M1 onto the next man.

Again, I fired into the chest of a Wehrmacht man who was turning his Mauser on me. Then I fired into another and another and another. Behind me, Jackson was in his own fight for his life as he fired in the opposite direction at other invaders. I do not recall how many rounds I fired into the advancing Germans, but I can only imagine it was eight, as once my M1 ejected the empty clip and the sound twanged through the air I charged the remaining men. Running over those I had already shot, not caring where my feet fell. I drove the butt of my rifle into the body of one man and didn't slow my pace in the action. I raised my rifle over my head and again brought the butt crashing down in an overhead swing into the back of another man's head who had just leapt down before me.

Someone crashed into me, and I felt myself lose my grip on the M1. I felt something hard press into my chest and my vision was covered by the grunting, sopping wet man above me. As I tried to writhe beneath him and work my hands under what I could only imagine was his rifle, he lifted himself as he screamed something in German.

I remember his face. Like all the other men I had seen that day, his face was lacking colour, his eyes were determined and lacked emotion. As he spat words at me, he drove his helmeted head forward to cave my face in. Somehow, I managed to evade the brunt of the blow, but my right ear rang in protest as the steel grazed the side of my face.

Likewise, I swore at him. Cussed and cursed as I kicked my legs and finally got my hands under the Mauser still pressed into my chest, just as he raised it. He drove it once into my side, sending a wave of pain through my body. As I writhed in pain as he raised it up high to crush my face. I burst upwards from the ground in a fit of rage and desperation.

Around us, I was vaguely aware of others fighting and screaming. The sound of gunfire had evaporated. The world was in a struggle of one-on-one conflict where there was no room for rifles.

I drove my hands into the man's face and managed to topple him sideways. His rifle became lost in the chaos, as had mine, and we were left to pummel our hands and legs into each other as we rolled back and forth on the trench floor. The German grunted in my ear as I drove my fist into his gut. I screamed in his face as I offered another flurry of blows that seemed to have little effect on the man. Then, he was atop again and from somewhere I saw a glint of steel in his hands. I instantly lunged for the knife or bayonet, I never saw what it was, but I felt its edge slice through the flesh on my arm in the struggle. As blood coated my hands, my grip started to waver. I redoubled my grasp again and again, and I saw the look in the German's eye as he fought against me: he knew that it wouldn't be long before he could move on.

That was the last expression that ever crossed that man's face. It was destroyed in the next instant when a rifle shot erupted nearby. His weight collapsed on me, and I gasped for air as I struggled to move away from him. My eyes darted here and there as I tried to take in my surroundings and my next target. The US soldier that had saved my life had moved on to lay fire onto other Wehrmacht men that were bridging the collapsed section of the trench to support the Panzer. As I clambered to my feet, I watched his course of fire, until another shot rang out behind me and the soldier collapsed face forward in the mess to become another one of the dead. I spun around to see who had fired and saw Jackson engaged in a similar struggle against another grey soldier.

As I moved towards him, I removed my bayonet and swiftly dug it into the side of the man as he drove Jackson into the trench wall. He grunted at the pain but wouldn't relent. Again and again, I drove my bayonet into the side of the German, who never once turned to look at me. Slowly, his strength began to wane, and he fell to the ground as

Jackson swore and continued to fight him as he fell.

'Come on!' I shouted as I dragged Jackson away. 'He's done. We need to regroup.'

I pulled Jackson away with me, toward the collapsed section of trench, ignoring the chaos that was happening around us. We turned to the collapsed section of trench as we both picked up M1s that lay on the ground.

The Panzer had started to move forward again, no doubt in assault of the scattered structures that lay behind our line of defence. Its main cannon roared a breath of fire just before its tracks sprang into motion once more. A line of Wehrmacht had assembled behind the armour, while others remained in the trenches, engrossed in their own struggle with surviving GI.s. I raised my M1 and fired point blank in the side of the head of one such Wehrmacht man who sat astride a dying GI. I didn't pause to watch him fall; I moved on and fired into the back of another man. I saw Jackson intervene in a fight where a US man was on top, he placed the muzzle of his rifle on the man's face and fired. We needed every man who was able, to be on their feet. There was no time for fair fighting.

As my M1 ejected an empty clip, I discarded it for a German Schmeisser that lay on the ground. I raised the pressed steel machine to my shoulder as another wave of Wehrmacht men ran across the collapsed section of trench. The Schmeisser rattled steadily, as I directed my field of fire into the mass of the men and let those that were behind run into the fire. Men fell and rolled down the sides of the new embankment, over the corpse of the partially entombed GI., while others ignored me all together and continued to find cover behind the advancing Panzer.

When the Schmeisser ran empty, I let it fall to the ground and retrieved another M1. Jackson was there with me as I began to move toward the collapsed embankment. 'Jackson,' I panted as I moved over more dead men. 'Move up.' I continued to encourage, more for myself than for him. 'Move. Come on.' Out of breath and only running on adrenaline, my body kept moving despite the exhaustion and loss of blood.

We mounted the collapsed section of trench and threw ourselves into the hole on the other side. The scene on this side of the embankment was just as abhorrent. A GI. screamed and writhed as a German drove his bayonet into his back. Another greatcoated soldier pulled a Luger from his side and fired it three times into the GI's throat. He collapsed in a bloody heap, his fight done. Amongst all the other fighting, a single potato masher grenade fell into the trench amongst the Germans and the US alike. I spun and drove my shoulder once more into Jackson and pushed him hard into the embankment as a dull roar erupted behind me.

I spun, raising my M1 once more as the screams from Germans and US alike ripped through the air. Men were crawling on the ground, trailing disfigured legs behind them, while others suffered in silence, too shocked to complain as their life drained out of them. We moved on through the wreckage, not expending a single round of ammunition to silence the wounded and maimed.

We came across a section of trench where a standoff was occurring. US troops had cleared a section of trench where a series of corners had been installed to prevent sweeping actions. Jackson and I expelled the Wehrmacht men that were fixed in assaulting the trench beyond the cut outs. The five Germans, were too focused on their forward assault and had left none to cover their rear flank. All fell within seconds. As we approached the section, Jackson went to move forward, breaching the point of cover the Germans had occupied seconds before. I grabbed a hold of his coat and dragged him back as a volley of heavy BAR fire lashed out at him.

'Thunder!' I screamed down the trench line, as Jackson skated backwards on his ass. 'Friendly's moving up. Thunder!' I repeated the call sign again.

'Flash!' Was the single syllable answer that allowed nothing else below the intensity of the gun renewed gunfire.

I motioned Jackson on as I covered our rear. Not wanting to make the same mistake as the Germans before us. We moved down the line and the wave of emotion that ran through me when I saw Little's face behind the BAR that was covering us, was inexplicable. Our squad was pinned within a small outcrop that was meant for a thirty calibre Browning machine gun. Little urged us on, as he leant out of cover and didn't speak a word to us as we passed. Bill Carrera's attention was on the assaulting Germans on the far side. Sporadically, his eyes would dart to the top of the trench line and scour the edges before his attention would return to their front.

'Jackson, Cody, back sir,' I said as I fell in behind him.

Carrera looked at me. Blinked, then returned his eyes to Laffey who had leant out of cover to fire twice down the trench line. Laffey swore as he dove back into cover and the wall adjacent to him was hammered with machine gun fire. 'They've set up an MG, sir.'

'We're at risk of being overrun,' Walker said behind us.

Carrera turned on him with a flash of anger. 'In case you can't tell private, our position, like every other goddamned position, is overrun.' He turned and spat to the trench floor.

As he spat, a German potato masher grenade skittered into the trench intersection before Laffey. Instinctually, he moved out of cover to kick it back down the trench.

'Laff…' Was all Carrera got out before the MG 42 ripped into Laffey's side. He fell silently, atop of the grenade. Carrera turned in an instant and threw himself a top of us. The explosion was dulled by Laffey's weight, but my eyes were open when it detonated. I saw his body raise into the air as if to stand, then his momentum threw him on his back in dead weight.

'Fuck.' The word was all I could find. 'Fuck.'

Carrera was up again; he grabbed me by the shirt again and pulled me to my feet. 'Move up, take point,' he growled, then shoved me to the trench intersection where Laffey lay. I drove my shoulder into the crumbling trench wall and waited. Being careful not to allow any part of my body to slip into the intersection.

'Who's got smoke?' Carrera shouted, and I heard the men of my squad rustle amongst their belongings. While they searched, I was left to look at the remains of Laffey. The entire front of him was a mess. What the MG 42 had not destroyed, the grenade had completely obliterated. Most of him was gone, an unrecognisable mess that apart from his boots could not be distinguished as US or German.

'Here,' I heard Skinner say as a metal cylinder was passed forward.

Little's BAR opened up at that point, in a short thudding burst as more German's assaulted our rear.

'Skinner, O'Rielly, swap out with Little I need the BAR over here.'

'Sir!' was returned as men shuffled position and shortly the rattle of the BAR was replaced by the snaps of M1 fire.

In a few moments there was heavy shuffling and Little spoke up, 'Little, here sir.'

'Cody,'—I felt a hand on my back— 'move aside. Little, wait for smoke, then we need base of fire on that machine gun position. Jackson, you move up. Twenty feet, no more. There is another nest to your right. There is a radio, you need to call artillery support on this position.'

'What about—' Jackson started.

'What about nothing.' Carrera finished the sentence for him. 'We need to wipe out what's left of the Panzers before they get too far beyond the trench.'

'Sir,' I asked, 'you said German paratroopers had landed amongst the guns. How do we know that they haven't been overrun.'

'We don't.' He pulled the pin on the smoke grenade and threw it.

5

My life seemed to flash beyond my eyes in the moment that I watched the cannister disappear over the trench wall. My mouth fell open in disbelief of my orders, as Carrera directed me back to the intersection, stacked up behind Little. The other men did not contest this order, despite the serious threat to their own lives that an artillery barrage would bring. Perhaps they all understood this was the only way. My mouth had gone dry, but I wasn't sure if it was the weight of the orders that rested on my shoulders, or Hitler's buzz-saw that waited for me beyond the intersection that unsettled my nerves.

Below the crackle of gunfire, the roar of Panzer engines and the howls of men, a faint pop was heard beyond the trench intersection, and I attempted a dry swallow as I checked my M1 again and released a shuddering exhale in preparation.

Calls from the Krauts down the end of the trench line came in panic as the MG 42 opened up blindly. Little lowered his head as the adjacent wall erupted in a shower of fire. The MG 42 was lightning quick in comparison to the old Brownings we used. Even as I watched the trench wall ripple under the withering fire, I could not ascertain one shot from another. The sound was a wail of death and metal. The stream continued, on and on and on. The wrenching scream of Hitlers buzz-saw worked away at my resolve until finally the barrage ended.

Little took no time in moving into action. As soon as the stream of fire lifted, he shifted his position and started firing on them in short bursts to maintain his magazine.

I felt a hard shove in my back as Carrera moved with me.

'Go! Go! Go!'

I shot up and ran, my heart in my chest and my eyes pinned open in a wide, horrified glaze. I leapt passed Little and darted to the far wall so as not to run in front of his fire. As I faced the gauntlet before me, I gasped and almost hesitated. It was like something out of a horror novel: a killer mist that rolled down the main streets of a city, so thick that bullets seemingly couldn't even penetrate it. These are all the thoughts that ran through a bewildered young man's head as I watched the wall of white and grey roll toward me. It weaved and tumbled over itself, as thick as it was. I took one hurried step towards it, as I sucked as much air into my lungs as possible and plunged into the abyss.

The world within the smoke cloud was surreal. I instantly lost all sense of orientation and as the thudding of Little's BAR behind me continued to rattle off bursts of fire, I expected to wear a volley in the back. I hesitated for half a heartbeat as I continued to run blindly. My right shoulder brushed something.

Yes, I thought as I swapped my M1 into my left hand, feeling its butt rub against the trench wall in my movement. As I picked up my pace once more, I held my right hand out and felt the wet, rotting boards of the trench under my fingertips. I exhaled at that point, my heart hammering in my chest as my feet pounded the boards beneath them. Another volley of fire from the BAR behind me and I felt the wind lift in the wake of the bullets, kissing the sweat on my neck. Before me, the Germans were shouting, and I could hear the metallic clatter of them trying to bring the MG 42 back into a firing state.

Just another step, I thought, *just another one and then you'll find cover.*

Yet with each step I took, my fingers continued to brush the wet timber of the trench wall.

Just another step. Just one more.

As I heard the slick movement of the machine gun in front of me and the heavy slam as its top cover was closed, the wall beneath my finger-tips disappeared. I let myself fall to the right as the ripping fire filled the air before me. Through the smoke, the world turned orange. Fire from its muzzle blasted and even the smoke itself seemed to shudder at the furious disruption of the air. I howled in relief as I fell to the ground and pushed myself deeper into the smoke-filled alcove, watching the orange-tinged smoke that flickered before me like a dying light.

The air felt stale now, poisoned by the smoke that had kept me alive, while I felt like a layer of chalk was building up on my tongue. I shuffled forward on my hands and knees, no longer confident of where I was going. My hand brushed something that was softer than timber and it moved slightly under my touch. I shifted back and clenched my grip around my M1 once more. But nothing moved, and nothing made a sound.

As Little relented under the MG fire to my rear, I regained my feet. Finally, the wisp of smoke had started to clear. I remembered thinking at that stage, as my vision started to come back, that this was what it must be like to go blind. Suggestions of items began to reveal themselves to me as the smoke rolled on and upward, thinning as it spread.

Becoming surer of my surroundings, I began to move into the alcove. The higher things were, the easier they became to see. As if the smoke had some sort of weight to it, it remained thick as morning fog a foot off the ground.

The torn tarp roof lining flapped in the sea breeze. Tables and chairs were arranged around the perimeter of the square alcove, with the only opening behind me. I scoured the littered tables, looking for the bulky radio. Maps and other notes stirred on the tables as I tripped around the room, stumbling on things that lay below the line of heavy smoke. I heard the shout of Germans in the trench behind me, a stiff reminder that I needed to hurry.

Just then, I saw the stem of a radio microphone, standing upright on one of the desks. I shuffled towards it and knocked it over as soon as I reached it. I swore as I righted the microphone and looked blankly at the panel before me. The gauges and bandwidth indicators were all blacked out.

I swore again as I flipped switches here and there, always switching them back when I failed to see an immediate response. Finally, I flipped something and a faint light appeared behind a single gauge, where a small needle was lifting and falling sporadically.

'Yes,' I reassured myself as more German cries came from the trench line, shortly followed by a stream of MG fire. I flinched at the sound, but did not take my attention away from the radio. Someone was talking but I couldn't hear them.

On the crowded table I searched, brushing pages atop of which was a map of the trench line with grid references. I held onto that sheet and finally found the headset. If I thought my situation was bad, the commotion on the radio was horrific. Soldiers requested support up and down the trench line, some calling for air support, some called for ammunition, others reported the moving of the German infantry, but no one seemed to answer. No one seemed to offer any sort of help.

I looked blankly down at the sheet with the grid references and saw scrawled hastily at the top, "NM C." 'Nutmeg,' I muttered as a grenade exploded in the trench.

I looked across to the opening of the alcove and just as I was about to try to raise the artillery, two German soldiers appeared at the alcove mouth. My mouth fell open as I saw them swing their Schmeisers around, my M1 lying uselessly on the table next to me. Just as I thought my war was finished, their flesh erupted in a crippling barrage of fire, and in the short distance I heard the heavy mechanical thudding of Little's BAR. I was out of time – this needed to happen now.

I returned my attention to the radio set and depressed what I thought to be the transmission button. 'Urgent. Nutmeg Charlie Red Alpha. Fire mission.' I paused as I consulted the map. I released the transmission button almost hesitantly as I consulted the reference.

'Charlie's gone, soldier. This is Nutmeg Easy, what are the coordinates?'

Gone? The Germans did find success against the artillery units after all. 'Nutmeg Easy,' I answered him instantly. 'Sector blue, Sierra One through Sierra niner, German armour, acknowledge.'

I let the grid reference sheet fall from the table as I retrieved my M1. I heard Nutmeg Easy call back on the radio. His voice was faint, but his acknowledgement and the offerings of a flight time fell on deaf ears as more Wehrmacht spilled into the alcove. The M1 clattered against my shoulder, one round after another as men fell as they rushed through the alcove opening.

Again, my M1 ejected the empty clip from its breech and as I reloaded the weapon, a whistling sound rang out above the din of the battle. I lowered my head as I waited for the impact. I took a breath then let half of it back out as I cowered in front of the radio. Somewhere, a shell hit. Then another closer this time, then another further away. Three shells. None of which seemed to land on the trench line at all.

I raised the earpiece to my head once more as somewhere I heard someone yelling my name. I placed the headset down again and listened over the din of the battle.

'Cody! Down one hundred!' It was Carrera down at the trench intersection. 'Tell them, down one hundred! Fire for effect!'

I leapt for the microphone switch again, flipped it and spoke rapidly. 'Down one hundred… Nutmeg Easy. Down one hundred, fire for effect!'

'Roger that–' was all I heard before the radio exploded before me. I fell back away from it, dazed by the sparks and the shock of the impact. I thought at first that the explosion had come from the artillery support, but to my left I heard the working of a bolt-action rifle. I looked over and saw a Kraut advancing on me as he hurriedly reloaded his rifle. As I regained my feet, he fired again and missed. We came together in a clash of helmeted steel, swearing and spitting as the fire from hell fell around us.

We fell together as the earth shook beneath our feet. The screams of the shells as they raced in from above were almost as horrific as the explosions that followed. Worse than the bombing, worse than the Stukas – the rapidity of the explosions was unfathomable. The roll of the hammering, the constant shower of debris, and over it all the screaming and whining of the shells as they raced to the ground.

I don't know if I lost consciousness throughout the barrage, or how long it went on for. All I know is that I was on the ground; the fight between myself and Kraut ended almost as soon as the first shell detonated. But when the last shell fell, and the screaming stopped, as did the rain of dirt, sand, and horror, I lifted my helmet so that I could see, and I noticed for the first time how my hands trembled. I sat there, almost wonderstruck by their shudder as a scream of rage echoed next to me and again, I was dragged back into the fight.

Having also surviving the artillery strike, the Wehrmacht man resumed the fight. He threw himself on top of me, punching and clawing at my face. His first blow hit well and stunned me. Luckily enough, most of his blows fell in a flurry that had little effect. Yet still I offered no fight to the man. I was stunned, helpless to defend myself, as blow after blow came down on me. Finally, a gunshot echoed, and the life vanished from the man in the very instant before he toppled off me.

I continued to lay there, shaken to the bone by the events of the past hour, if it had even been that long since the first bomb fell. To this day, I never knew, as the watch my father had given me stopped working somewhere throughout this first fight. As my vision settled and the sounds of the war started rolling back in on me, I found another man standing over the top of me. Bill Carrera was looking down at me, a grave expression on his face. He knelt by my side and ran his hands over me.

'Cody, are you alright?' he said as his hand touched my side where the jagged remnant of Sherman had pierced me. I winced away from his touch. Bill drew his hand away and we both saw the red of my blood that lined his hand. The colour seemed to drain from him as he considered the blood.

'I'm alright, Sarge,' I said as I tried to sit up, but my body seemed to be drained of all energy. 'It was from before.'

'Medic!' Carrera bellowed as he pushed me back against my struggle to sit up. 'It's alright Cody, we will get you patched up. You did well son, now you need to rest…' He had barely finished this last word before he turned his face back to the opening of the alcove and howled impatiently for a medic once more.

Then Jackson was there, Little and Skinner. All of them looked grave, except for Jackson. He knelt by my side, opposite Carrera, and smiled at me. 'Hey, Cody,' he said softly as he took my hand. 'You gave them a pounding.'

'It worked?' I said, truly amazed.

'You bet your ass,' Skinner said, his positivity doing a poor job of shining through the worried look on his face.

'You took out a few Panzers with that barrage.' Carrera frowned again. 'Forward observers will use artillery to mop them up.'

'Good, good,' I said as I tried to sit up again.

'Hey, hey,' Jackson said as he pushed me back to the ground again. 'You rest up. Wait for the medic.'

I looked down at myself, now wondering what had happened to make them all so concerned. 'Where am I hit?' I asked as panic started to run through me.

'Don't worry about it,' Carrera added as he tried to calm me, but it was too late.

Panic had set in now, as I pawed all over my body to find no pain apart from the standard aches that came from the events of the last hour.

'Here,' Jackson said as he took my left hand and pressed it to my side. 'Bayonet wound,' he said glumly.

I looked at him with disbelief. A part of me believed him, until I pressed down and felt the pain in the same place as it had been since the Sherman. I had to laugh. The confused look that was exchanged between the four men that stood above me, made me laugh even harder.

'I told you it was from before. I ain't dead yet,' I said as I finally sat up and looked before me. The laughter died in my throat as I finally saw the alcove smoke free for the first time.

Officers, enlisted men and non-coms alike, lay twisted where they fell in front of their work stations. Being able to see clearly now, the alcove held a forward observation post that was manned by radio operators and logistics personnel. When the Germans had entered the trench line, each one of the men had been cut down trying to get out of the trap their shelter had become. Blood covered paperwork and maps; men had died, falling over the tops of those that had fallen before them. None of them had a chance.

'It's alright, son,' Carrera said as he finally dismissed the thought that I was going to be KIA, and helped me to my feet. 'If you're not dying, then you can rejoin the fight and we can thank Jerry personally, for everything he has done here today.' Before we headed out of the alcove, we all stood there for a moment longer and looked at our fallen. All of us were eager to get our own back – an eye for an eye, no matter who went blind. We wanted revenge.

6

After-action reports of the following days were bittersweet. The Nazi invasion of Northern Ireland had failed to take a foothold, and those that hadn't been pushed back into the sea were taken prisoner. But there was no argument that they had bloodied our nose.

There was little respect shown to the prisoners. Hundreds upon hundreds of grey-clad Wehrmacht men mixed in with the brown camouflage of the Fallschirmjäger, the German paratroopers that had mostly decimated the artillery behind the lagoon. If the remnants of the British 47th – or 2nd London as they preferred – hadn't been scheduled to swap out some GIs on the front, the whole situation could have been different. No one likes to count strokes of luck in an after-action report, but with Nutmeg Bravo and Charlie companies decimated, the Fallschirmjäger had turned the US artillery on its own armour, with surprising accuracy. Of the four platoons of M4 Sherman's from the 2nd Armoured that were in operation around Millisle, less than a third remained.

It was blatantly obvious that the Fallschirmjäger had intended to take no prisoners. Of the two companies of rear line men that were assaulted in the drop of elite German soldiers, only those that ran for their lives remained to tell their stories. Executed GIs numbered in the hundreds. With no time to line them up, they were shot where they stood or knelt as they tried to surrender. Although with their own distaste for the Germans at having been expelled from their own country, it was left to the British to guard the German prisoners; the brass felt they could not trust their own men with the safety of their prisoners of war.

These were all stories that spread naturally throughout the camp. Those, amongst others, who were still on the hunt to capture survivors of the Luftwaffe action who had bailed out. Corpses of men continued to wash up on the shore every day. Bloated and only recognisable by the remains of their uniforms. The difference of numbers between RAF, US, and Luftwaffe pilots I do not know, especially as amongst those recognised as Germans were not distinguished between Fallschirmjäger, Luftwaffe, or Wehrmacht, all of which suffered losses to the Irish Sea.

It was not long after we left the trenches that the P-38 Lightnings and P-51 Mustangs descended from the sky to assist with aerial reconnaissance. With the artillery raining down on the remaining Panzer corps, they fell into panic. A platoon further down the coast from our position became lost in the flooded marsh behind the line. The troops that abandoned their bogged down Panzer IVs were promptly surrounded and after short exchanges of fire, were taken prisoner. All that we were left with, as survivors, was the mopping up of the remaining Wehrmacht troops that had made it either into the trench line or beyond. Men who had hidden themselves beneath corpses and lashed out with pistol fire or grenades as unsuspecting GIs went about the work of cleaning up, did not help their cause.

The casualties that occurred after the failed invasion were small, but held a lasting impact. Ammunition was cheap, and lives weren't. It soon became common practise to shoot any German soldier, whether they were dead or alive, to protect one's own skin.

I am not proud of the actions I took to preserve my own life, and I don't believe any of the men I served with would feel any different, but that didn't matter back then. The men we fought were desperate, put into a position by their peers. It is said in 'your time' that the SS were the main contributors to the war crimes that Nazi Germany committed, and my experiences led me to see nothing different. Yet, when they were facing a new foe that did not distinguish between the multi-faceted tiers of the Third Reich, I feel they were forced to do anything but be captured and risk universal persecution.

I wonder how this thought, as if spoken from beyond the grave, would have felt as I stood above the ruined trenches and looked over the beach front. Seeing the thousands of men lying ruined on the shores of the final refuge of the British Empire. I turned back and saw the bodies crumpled in the trenches, men lying half buried either by sand or by those that fell atop them. Men that died in protection of the crumbling Empire, lying alongside those that came to kill it. None of it seemed to matter anymore – we were all just meat destined for the grinder. Cattle being led up the gangway to enter the killing floor.

We remained on high alert for the following week until further reinforcements arrived to bolster our troops. More men, more tanks, more planes. This time, very little refugees left, only the German POWs were extricated for their own protection. With this second reinforcement, supplies seemed to come thick in hand. It seemed like more men arrived every week; it didn't take us long to feel strong once more. Perhaps not invincible – that smitten mask had been stolen from us forever when our nose was bloodied. But with strength, the US gaze lifted beyond the protection of Northern Ireland. The die was cast and soon it would be our turn to attack, our chance to invade.

PART TWO

South of Liverpool – Occupied Wales

December 23rd 1944

1

Months had passed since the failed German invasion of Northern Ireland. The blood of the fallen Wehrmacht and Fallschirmjäger had barely been washed away from the sand and soil of the last vestige of European freedom. The loss of friends clawed deep at our minds, with nothing left to do but mop up the dead and welcome the reinforcements. Idle hands are the devil's work; that statement could not be any truer when it came to dealing with the things that we saw. Action pushed death to the rear of the mind, orders gave a man something to carry out. Even in Northern Ireland, in these early days of the war, idleness led to dwelling. Dwelling led to depression, and depression led to drink.

When a man could lay his hands on the bottle it was like a blessing from Christ. It was as if there was a cancer inside of the gut of each man. Something that ate away at him, from the inside out. A man could only put up with that knowing sensation for so long before he needed to give in, needed to put the fire in his belly out. Like a wave of morphine, or the first wave breaking over the sun-baked rocks that had been cooking since the fall of the tide, the first wash of liquor was a godsend. After the first it didn't matter; it never did and never would.

As I sat in the WACO glider, I looked down at my hands. A tremble had worked its way into them. Idle hands were the devil's work, and now I had nothing to fill them with. I couldn't get up and go for a stroll, I couldn't even have a drink. We were somewhere over the Irish Sea, heading to glory. Three hundred planes, towing three hundred gliders. Some contained Jeeps, others artillery. Ours contained our rifle squad.

Bill Carrera sat toward the front, looking over the pilot's shoulder at the world beyond. Little and Skinner sat across from him; neither of them spoke. Walker and O'Rielly sat directly across from me, then there was Jackson by my side, as always.

Stuart Leach, one of the replacements for our losses, was not a large man, but apart from Little, I suppose none of us really were. His slender face looked gaunt beneath the rim of his helmet. Hazel eyes that may as well have been grey for the little amount of light that there was in the glider. His mouth was moving, and I noticed that his eyes were fixed on a point somewhere in between myself and Jackson. The way in which he drove his gaze into that spot told me that his focus must have been five thousand miles beyond the balsa wood wall of this flying coffin.

I clenched my fists to cease the trembling. As I did, I turned my right hand over and looked at my old Gruen watch: 6:18, the same time it had been for the last three months. The time that seemed to have stopped somewhere on the beaches of Millisle. Although the watch had stopped, I couldn't stop myself from checking it. As if at some point the gears might re-mesh and the mechanism respring, suddenly bringing my father's gift back to life. I laughed to myself as the glider rocked in the air, disturbed by some invisible force as the C-47 Skytrain dragged us through the sky. To my right, the second new addition to our squad lit a cigarette and the glow of the cherry in the dark drew my eye.

'Flash,' I muttered and the smoking soldier raised the rim of his helmet to consider me. Jeff Gordon, nicknamed Flash for the similarity of his name to the new comic strip, *Flash Gordon,* was a tall, slender man with a hooked nose and a face that always seemed freshly shaven. Apparently, in his physical assessment back in the US, as Flash lined up with all the other recruits, he was rejected from the air force and fighter training, and was pushed toward becoming a Sherman driver. His height and reach were perfect for the selector shift of the tank. As if to spite everyone, he joined the front line infantry. To be honest, I am not sure there are any right decisions when it comes to selecting what branch of the armed forces one is going to serve. What matters is that the decision was made in the first place.

I held my hand out to Jeff and kissed the air. Jeff blinked, then without a word he reached into his pocket and withdrew a soft-shelled packet of cigarettes. Down it came, one by one, we all took one. Idle hands were the devil's work, so it was best to fill them.

As my hand that held the smouldering cigarette rested on my knee, I watched the jitter of the glowing cherry in the dark. Each drag passed a few seconds. Little by little, the stem of fire worked its way closer to my hand. What would I do when it ran out? What would I do when we landed?

I think that sums it up, the way we all felt as we sat there waiting for the war to begin anew. If we were walking, we were in control. If we were on a boat, we could jump and swim if need be. But here, now, we couldn't do a damned thing. Sit and smoke and allow the devil's work to seep into our heads and writhe within our minds.

Hell, if something went wrong after we detached, we couldn't even swing around to go for another pass. The WACO gliders had no engine. Once we detached, twenty seconds was all that was left between us and the Almighty. The only engine sounds were that of the Skytrain that laboured before us. A dull throb that echoed in the back of my mind as the light frame of the WACO jostled in its slipstream.

The wind that coursed its way across the fabric that was stretched taut over the timber and alloy frame was the loudest contender. It was enough to drown out the sounds of idleness, the shuffling of the men who sat deep in thought. The lighting of cigarettes and the chatter of the pilots. Some men laughed that the ones who 'piloted' these flying death traps were the Clayton's pilots of the US expeditionary force. A pilot when you didn't have a pilot. But as I alluded to before, it took men with guts to sit in the powerless fabric-lined boxes. Men that knew they only had one shot to land themselves and their cargo, or else all was lost.

Bill Carrera shuffled in his seat as he leant closer to the pilot before him to see clearer out of the cockpit. Somewhere before us, something like a streak of lightning illuminated the sky and a short snap of brilliant light swept through the cabin, casting surreal shadows across the backdrop. Like the spirits of all the men leaving their bodies, the likeness was there one second and then gone the next.

'Ok,' Carrera said loud enough for us all to hear. 'Here we go.'

The rest of the squad stirred in their positions and most leant forward to see past the men and out into the dark abyss. All except Leach. His eyes had now closed, yet his mouth continued to move in his silent mantra. Perhaps he was the smart one, as what I saw was fear striking the hearts of every man inside that cabin.

The light that had coursed through the cabin was created by the detonation of the engine of one of the many Skytrains that littered the air. It only lasted a second as the wing let go from the aircraft and with it, the fire and light disappeared below, gone forever.

'Brace!' Carrera shouted as he wrapped one of his hands around the alloy struts. The Skytrain that had lost its wing was gone. It had disappeared below and off to our left an instant after its wings had been clipped. The glider crew that had seen the demise of their lifeboat had detached themselves, leaving them adrift in the powered column. Whether they had lost control or had been forced to alter their course, I will never know, but they didn't drift along with us – they banked across in front of us. I saw its bulk rush towards us, its airspeed washed away faster than the Skytrain vanished. I closed my eyes and prepared for death, a death that I was powerless to avoid, but it never came. Not yet.

'Fuck, that was close,' one of the men said and I exhaled as I opened my eyes. Suddenly the world around us became louder. Distinct explosions, one after another. Left to us, then right, then behind and in front. My brow furrowed and I wrapped both of my hands around my M1.

The glider's frame jostled again and was almost thrown twenty feet down and to the side in the change of the air. I opened my eyes, and wished that I had left them closed. FLAK had zeroed in on our column. Large puffs of peppered fire exploded at our precise altitude.

To our right, a glider broke apart, torn to shreds by shrapnel that was thrown into its carcass by a nearby FLAK shell. There was no explosion from the collapse of the airframe, it just disintegrated. Men fell from its crumbling façade, and tumbled through the air, parachute-less, to their death. The C-47 that had lost its cargo continued, oblivious. All that remained of the WACO was its nose cap, which trailed dangerously behind, swinging around in the wind.

The men gasped, and short words were exchanged between a few but none that I heard. Another C-47 exploded nearby, and seemed to stop dead in the air by the force of the shell that had hit it. The trailing glider closed the gap instantly, and was torn apart by the fragments of the plane that had towed it. Again, light was sent through the cabin and I remember seeing all the men's faces at that point. Eyes wide in terror, their mouths set, others open in fear.

Leach remained quiet, only his mouth moved and his eyes remained fixed on that spot. Meanwhile, the destroyed C-47 and WACO, descended as one, consumed in flame.

It wouldn't be long now until we were released, we all knew that. If we were being hammered by FLAK, then we must be over land. Seconds were passing as minutes and soon the tow line would be cut and it would be what felt like hours in freefall. Sure enough, as that thought ran through my mind and my fingers pressed hard into the timber stock of my M1, Carrera turned to face us.

'Brace yourselves, twenty seconds!'

As he said it, I watched the pilot on the left reach up and drag a lever down. Suddenly the glider lurched in the air and the Skytrain before us lifted away. Almost instantly, the whole attitude of the glider changed. My stomach lurched deep within me and the wind that coursed over the taut fabric seemed to increase in its ferocity.

We were plunged into silence as the WACO fell below the FLAK fire. Jackson groaned beside me, and I can only imagine it was from the fear and the anticipation of our freefall. I could not blame him. I closed my eyes again and rested my helmet against the muzzle of the M1. With the vibrations and jostling of the airframe, the metal clanged against each other and the sound of it was enough to drive me insane. The thought even crossed my mind that one pull of that trigger, while my head was over the muzzle, would end it all. Just one pull.

'Field ahead,' one of the pilots called out. 'Fifteen seconds.'

It was now that the words that Leach was repeating became audible to me. 'He is my refuge and my fortress, my God in whom I trust.' His eyes were closed, and the words came rapidly from his mouth as he held his M1 before him, its butt resting on the floor of the airframe. 'You will not fear the terror of night, nor the arrow that flies by day.'

'Tracers!' A pilot screamed over the top. 'Machine gun fire!'

As the steel of my helmet rattled against the muzzle of my M1, the fabric of the airframe was torn around us, as the German MG fire raked through the frame. Perspex cracked as many rounds passed through the windscreen and Walker began to scream.

'Nor the pestilence that stalks in the darkness, nor the plague that destroys at midday.'

There was a horrible crack and a dull thud as one of the pilots was struck in the face by MG fire. The airframe shook at the loss of strength on the controls and lurched to the left.

'Oh shit!' the remaining pilot screamed. 'Obstructions in the field! Ten seconds!'

'A thousand shall fall at thy side, ten thousand at thy right hand. But it shall not come nigh thee.'

I opened my eyes as the wind became even louder, and I saw that a large slit had been created in the fabric liner before me, to Leach's rear. Walker continued to moan as O'Reilly was pulling at his coat.

'The trim is shot! I have no control,' the pilot called out again. 'Oh God. Oh God.'

I turned my head and looked out through the blood-caked Perspex of the cockpit. The glider was headed for a field; the angle of the descent was too sharp. The ground was littered with poles that stretched straight up into the air, like a forest that had been cleared of all leaves and wildlife, we were heading for a death trap.

'Only with thine eyes shalt thou behold and see the reward of the wicked.'

I turned and looked back at Leach as his eyes opened.

'Brace!' Carrera screamed like a banshee, and I thought to myself, *I can't brace any more.*

As the frame of the WACO shuddered and was torn apart on Rommel's asparagus, Leach's prayer stuck in my mind as the world erupted in the hell of battle around me.

2

The silence of the flight was a distant memory and almost a sorry one. As the faint sounds of the C-47's engines faded in my mind, they were replaced by the agony, fire, and the wrenching sound of crumpling alloy and crashing timber. The wind tore through the fabric of not only the WACO's skin, but my mind. My heart thudded in my chest, as if trying to match the impossible rhythm of the distant German machine gun fire. The timber posts whirred past, like the memories of everything I had done up to this point in my life.

The remaining pilot held his hands in front of his face, as if that would save him. The frame lurched, and as if it was a blanket torn from a sleeping child, the hide of the WACO was ripped away and the world outside was revealed to me as I fell. My M1 was torn from my grasp. In my horror, weightlessness came over me as I saw hell imprinted on the world outside.

The sky above me was as red as the fires of hell. Black shapes moved slowly above like carrion birds circling above a dying animal. More fell to earth, engulfed in flames as if they had caught the burning plague from the sky itself. Tracers lined the sky, peppering the fire as if to throw fuel on it.

The deep thudding of the heavy cannons echoed through my soul and trembled the foundations of every happy day. As if each was a knell that beckoned me to my death. And the message that each sound carried with it, was written in the blood of the allies that had come before: 'You will die here, alone.'

Nothing made sense, nothing seemed right. Although I knew my team was close, I felt alone. My fear rattled through my chest as I trembled through an exhale.

My back slammed into the mud below. Although cushioning my fall, any breath that had remained left me in a rush, as if fleeing for its life. The remains of the WACO twisted in on itself as its momentum carried it away. More men fell from the wreck as it was thrown from pillar to post, until it finally snagged and stopped dead in its tracks. More were thrown at that point – viciously torn from their shell like the life is torn from trapped vermin as it's shaken in the maw of a rabid dog. I lost sight of all of them in the naked forest of timber posts. I lost sight of any objective; all I needed was to stay alive.

I clung to the nearest post as I tried to suck air into my lungs. The mud caked my clothes and hampered my ascension. As my feet slid and I fell back to the earth, stars formed before my eyes. They danced like the tracers that etched their way across the sky. My hands grasped the rough timber, and I felt small strands bite into the flesh of my fingers. I opened my mouth again as a dark spot began to form in the centre of my vision. I gasped, and gasped and gasped… and finally the kiss of air filled my lungs as I collapsed again, resigned to recover. As I sucked air and mud and shit into my mouth, the world above me erupted in fire and a horrible sound of a screaming turbo prop as a flaming C-47 ripped passed, at an altitude so low that the ground shook in fear. The heat of the fire warmed my skin as it passed. Through the forest of poles, I saw it vanish over a small rise, along with the glow from its fire, and suddenly it seemed like the brightest of all lights shone from that point. Brilliant and intense, and then it was gone. No doubt with the lives of all on board.

'God,' I pleaded as I finally dragged myself to my feet. 'I… am not…

going to die… in this field,' I said each segment on an exhale as I continued to suck air into my body. Whether spoken to myself, or to the God above, the determination was there. I needed to move.

Staggering at first, I supported my weight on each post in my path. I scoured the ground around me for anyone. My heart wanted to head toward the WACO, to regroup. But in my panic, I had lost all sense of direction. Anywhere was better than here.

Machine gun fire opened up close by and I threw myself to the ground, expecting a wave of death to erupt around me. But the fire wasn't directed at me. As I rolled over, I saw another WACO skim above the posts, the fabric skin torn to shreds by the withering fire.

'Dear God,' I muttered as I regained my feet quickly this time and moved forward, changing my angle slightly to move away from the ripping sound of the machine gun.

Below that sound was nothing. I didn't hear the commands of Americans; I didn't hear the groans of pain. It unsettled me and cemented the isolated feeling in my gut with every step. Some at least had to survive. 'Jackson,' I said. 'You have to be alive.'

Before me, the naked forest thinned, and I threw myself to the ground once more as I pushed myself to the edge of my cover. There looked to be a culvert, or maybe it used to be a stream, that ran alongside the field. I had no idea; there was no guarantee that we'd landed anywhere near our target area. There was no landmark for reference – nothing that I could see, in any case.

I chewed at the inside of my cheek as I scanned the ground before me. Thirty feet to the drop, but what waited over there? Was it safer to wait for assistance? Would that ever come?

The decision was taken from my hands when a whistle ripped through the air – short, fast, and abruptly cut off by an explosion fifty feet behind me. Mortar fire. I lowered my head to the earth as another ripped in and another. Dirt, mud, timber shards and steel shrapnel filled the air to my rear. I regained my feet and ran for the culvert.

With each thudding footstep, my short ragged breathes echoed in my head as the field behind me rippled under the mortar fire. The sound as each of my mud-sodden boots slapped against the earth was drowned out under the waves of aeroengines, explosions, and cannon fire. I waited for a shout of alarm, a call in some foreign tongue to bring the wrath down on me, but it never came. Exposed as I was, the lack of direct fire did not settle me. Every whistle, every clatter of fire, I thought was destined for me.

I slid into the culvert as if I was sliding to home base, my feet out in front of me. The mud that caked my pants helped my momentum. The darkness consumed me as I fell below the line of cover and became instantly tangled in foliage. Branches snapped under my weight as slender boughs waved their arms in alarm. I thought even the land had surrendered to the Reich, afraid to offer any cover to the liberators. But again, nothing came of the movement – there was no shout and no direct fire.

There was no stream in the culvert, no water to offer me any succour. It was as if the ditch was just an overgrown remnant of an ancient structure, moat, or wall that had been lost to history. Nevertheless, I untangled myself and moved to my right, not bothering to check my compass as there was still no landmark to use as reference. I followed the ditch for a few hundred feet, sporadically lifting my head above the line of cover to investigate the naked forest and the field where my comrades may lay.

Eventually, I saw the remains of my WACO. It had been completely destroyed by the final impact that had ended its short descent to hell. The hide had been torn from its frame, exposing the twisted wreckage below. The front clip that contained the pilots remained, but the Perspex on the right side was gone, blown out by the impact of the pilot's body as he was thrown forward into it. It seemed that his final defence of holding his hands before his face didn't save him. Those same hands were now stretched out before him down the nose of the WACO, lifeless as they hung from his slumped body. Even in this darkness, I could see the blood that smeared the nose of the WACO – bright red over matte green.

Another body was tangled up in what remained of the tail section. His limbs were twisted in angles that were unnatural. Even as I watched, some German probed the body with far-reaching fire. A single shot punctured the soldier's torso. Red mist appeared around the body for a short while, then like the life that had already left the man, it too vanished, settling on the mess below. I lowered my eyes to the dirt before me and the watch that still clung to my wrist. Time of death, 6:18, so many days ago.

As the shelling of the field continued, another WACO attempted a landing and pulled up hard at the sight of the asparagus. Its air speed washed away as its nose rose into the air. As its underbelly was exposed, the airframe was struck by anti-aircraft cannon fire. The light frame disintegrated in mid-air, and showered the ground below with shrapnel, and corpses. Another failed attempt.

The field came to an end at a road that was bordered by a small stone wall. The light that rippled in the air above illuminated the men that cowered behind it. I saw rifles and the familiar shape of GI helmets, and my heart fluttered into motion once more. Some had survived. Now I needed to get towards them without exposing myself again. Somewhere there was a machine gun nest, somewhere there was a radio. There had to be if they were able to call in mortar fire.

To the rear of my position, the sound of an engine broke through the din of battle. I carefully lowered myself back into the base of the ditch and lifted my head above the other bank. The small stone wall extended on that side of the ditch and seemed to follow a narrow road. Two hundred and fifty feet beyond my cover was a T junction, and directly opposite the road, a cottage loomed in the darkness.

An old lorry, as the English would call it, worked its way up the narrow road. Only its bulk and the suggestion of a canvas back was what identified it to me, as no light shone from its fenders. Even the road itself must have been reduced to mud, as the lorry seemed to wander from side to side while its engine bellowed through its strangled exhaust. The lorry ambled its way beyond the cottage when it seemed to lose all traction. The engine revved, revved again, then quit.

I shifted my position behind the cover of foliage as men began to climb out of the truck. They looked briefly at the rear tyres, as all their comrades came out. Twenty at least. Armed soldiers, not men. I slid my bayonet out of its sheath as I continued to watch them.

Behind me came the rapid semi-automatic fire of an M1. It was obviously not trained on this group of soldiers, but they all stopped and looked in the direction of the fire.

One addressed the others; he pointed down the road in the American's direction and eighteen of the soldiers headed off in that direction after curt nods. There was no salute, no clicking of heels. Just action. At this distance I still could not identify them. All I could do was wait. As the eighteen advanced, they fanned out as they neared my ditch. Some came to my side of the road, others went beyond. I laid still and waited for them to enter.

They made a lot of noise as they did, the actions of their weapons clattering as they readied themselves for fire. One man loomed in the darkness, twenty feet from my position. He created no silhouette, and still, I couldn't identify him. I shifted towards him but my shirt snagged on the foliage and I was forced to stop at my first movement.

'Scheisse,' the soldier muttered as he stirred in his position. I froze. I couldn't tell if he was looking at me, or still at the other Americans. Their flank was completely exposed, that was obvious to me now. I held my breath as I waited to be spotted. But my luck had not run out.

As the Germans that had moved into the ditch beyond the road moved forward, the Americans saw them and began to organise themselves in preparation to attack them, obviously believing they were still safe behind the wall. All at once the Germans on my side of the ditch began to open fire.

I watched as the closest man to me was struck high in the chest as he brought his M1 up to fire. The rifle muzzle lifted high into the air as it went off and he collapsed backwards. A shout of surprise escaped his mouth as he went down. The others, panicked by the ambush, stood up.

It all went south from there. All I could do was hope that none of those men were from my squad, as the last one was cut down trying to escape back to the naked forest. His Thompson fell before him as he collapsed, barely thirty feet from the stone wall.

At a quick snap of a command, the Germans advanced. The one closest to me muttered something as he left; I only caught the tail end of it. 'Amerikan.'

Still unarmed, I had lost my chance of striking while the German remained in the trench with me. The field where the GIs had fallen was lost to me. I turned to my rear again, swallowed a dry mouthful and left the ditch, as I made a beeline for the cottage. Four against one were not good odds, but it was a fair shot better than one against eighteen.

3

The sounds of horror and murder filled my ears as I left the safety of the culvert and exposed myself to the night again. The sky continued to run red with fire and blood, as if painted by those that had fallen. With nothing to focus on but the cottage, my head swam with the sounds of the carnage that unfolded behind me. Of all the sounds that filled me while I made that journey, only one stood out to me. Above the warble of the aeroengines, the staccato of the cannons and the old final roar of German rifles as wounded GIs were put down, I heard one man laugh. The obscene image was planted within me as the shrill, hysterical nature came to me below the roar of death. Within all of this, how could anything be humorous? How could anyone find the will to laugh ever again? Yet, as I found myself hunched over in the middle of an English paddock, rushing toward an unknown objective, that laugh clawed through to assault the last of my sanity.

Anger boiled inside of me as an image was painted in my mind. With each report of a rifle, I imagined the Germans firing into the GIs as they lay dead or dying. There were no screams, no pleading for life, and I could only hope that each one of those rounds were wasted on dead flesh. Each one they wasted, was surely one less they could use against us.

Throughout my anger, my sorrow and fear, that thought shone

somewhat briefly as a glimmer of hope. My fist clenched around the haft of my bayonet as the cottage loomed closer and closer. Soon I'd get my own back. Either that, or the war would be over for me. I didn't care which came first. I wanted to laugh down at them and see how they felt hearing that. I wanted that so much that I was prepared to die for it if need be.

Fifty yards and counting. Each step brought me nearer. Within the cottage, a faint glow began to emit from the windows and I doubled my pace. I couldn't be caught in the open. As my back slammed against the stone outer walls, I had to stop myself from gasping for air. My body shook as all my will went into slowing my heart rate. My mouth opened, disobeyed my mind's command, trying to suck air in to keep the pace that my lungs wanted. Fast still, the breaths came and went.

I shifted along the wall as I listened to what was happening inside. Slower and slower my breaths became, and just as I neared one of the windowsills, the glass panes were hastily thrown outwards.

I paused and laid myself flat against the stones. I pressed a hand against my mouth to muffle my still semi-heaving breaths. Meanwhile inside, a German began to speak. Another one coughed, then sniffed; I could imagine the man dragging the grey of his Wehrmacht coat across his nose with the sound that he made. There were footsteps and below it all, the sound of slow, wet breaths.

A match was struck and even from outside, I heard the first draws of a cigarette. The man that lit the match exhaled as he leant against the window sill.

'My friends find the smell in here extremely toxic, old man.' The man spoke in accented English. 'I hope you don't mind.'

The wet breathes continued from the other side of the room, as another German spoke in his native tongue. The smoking man replied, and shortly after there was the sound of chairs sliding on hardwood floor. They screeched as they moved, then I heard the weight of men collapsing into them.

'To be honest, I am surprised to see someone still here,' the smoker began again. 'I thought the SS went right through this place.'

The wet breathing changed its pitch at this, and hitched. Then came the crackling sound of an old, sick, rattling voice: 'They took… my daughter… she…' The old Englishman was racked by a cough at this point. There were impatient sounds from the Germans, who obviously felt uncomfortable being around illness. 'Was looking… after me…'

The German tutted before he took another drag of his cigarette. 'No doubt your daughter will be of great service to the Reich.'

'Fuck the Reich…' The sick man said before he erupted in a bone-rattling cough.

The smoker laughed. 'Be careful old man, if I were an SS man, that cough would have been cut short. I wouldn't take solace in what is happening outside.' The man's voice became cold at this point. 'You're not liberated.'

'Yet…' The old man croaked at the tail end of his cough.

As I sat there, trying to ascertain what move I should make next, the smoker's cigarette butt was thrown out of the window before me.

'It seems that it's not just your smell that is toxic, but your words as well, old man.' The German's tone had gone sour, a petulant and dangerous tone. 'I'll be sure to pass on your regards to your daughter, if, by chance, she is still in England.' The smoker raised himself from his seated position on the windowsill and moved into the cottage. Before leaving the building, he barked something at the others in the room, who replied with a curt affirmative, 'Jawohl!'

I frowned at the situation I was left with. One outside, three inside. The obvious choice would be to move against the man outside – to do that I needed to move beneath the open window, silently. At this point I had barely gotten my breathing under control, so the thought of moving silently was impossible. I lifted my weight from the stone wall as the old man inside was rattled by another stream of coughs that were full of corruption. I took my chance, and finally made my move.

I dared not steal a glimpse of the view inside – the sight of my helmet would no doubt send the Germans into alarm. So far, they seemed not even slightly concerned by the events taking place just down the road. I wanted to keep it that way. As I moved past the window, a German grumbled in annoyance as I heard papers shuffle. Another man somewhere else in the room grunted and spoke something almost inaudible. There was a click, and a short time later a radio began to play; the sound was faint enough from where I stood, but the music seemed Bavarian. I stole a breath as I moved past, my breath ragged with anticipation.

I neared the corner of the stonework and kept my bayonet at the ready. I leant my weight on the corner stones and peered out beyond. The lorry loomed twenty feet away. The officer was standing before it, looking down at the rear tyres once more, another lit cigarette smouldering away in his right hand. I saw my chance.

Leaving the relative safety of the stone corner piece, I moved out into open and kept myself low. The loose earth crunched under my feet, but the sound was drowned out of existence by the combat that echoed throughout the countryside. As I neared the officer, I noticed that he was dressed similarly to any other Wehrmacht man. His grey trousers vanished just below his knees, consumed by high leather boots. A leather holster was perched on his hip, still fastened shut; there would be no easy access to his sidearm. The man didn't wear a helmet, but what looked to be a soft cap. As I neared, he removed the hat with his left hand and looked up to the red, war-weary sky, taking in the sight of the American planes on their treacherous journey.

No alarm was visible in his stance as I approached him from his rear; the man seemed to hold no concern whatsoever for the sight of the countless planes above him. Many were burning, falling through the air, their crew lost to the war machine. Yet, many more remained. Even as I approached and raised myself to my full height, I caught a glimpse of the side of the man's face – he was smiling. Perhaps that was what made it easy for me.

I waited for him to exhale one final plume of smoke before wrapping my left hand across his face, bringing him close to me. His body tensed against me, struggled, then paused as I drove the blade of my bayonet up under his ribcage. As his body twisted against me, the groans and gasps for life escaped between my fingers. In the struggle, we lost our footing in the same mud that had sucked all momentum from the lorry. We tumbled to the ground with him atop of my chest, but I managed to hold onto him and muffle his cries of alarm. Warm liquid coated the palm of my left hand as he coughed. I pushed his weight over into the mud and threw myself atop of him and reefed the blade from his side. He gasped as the steel left him and groaned as I drove it back in, again and again. I was covered in his gore, the blood that had left him faster than his life.

I fumbled at his holster and drew the Luger. Finally, I was armed.

I didn't hesitate this time, ensuring the German sidearm was loaded and ready to fire. I didn't sneak to the door of the cottage, but walked as calmly as I could. As I placed my hand on the timber door, I saw the blood that coated it, the red that smeared across the weathered slats, and I remember having the strangest thought at that point. It was like the blood of the lamb, to protect the inhabitants against the Passover. But more than first sons would die today.

The thought was dismissed as I pushed the door open; there was no God here. Just men.

I stepped inside and took in the single room of the small cottage in an instant. Two Germans sat across from each other at a small, square table positioned by the window that I had cowered under a moment before. They were pouring over a map, their noses close to the paper as their eyes struggled in the dim light. The only source of illumination came from an oil lamp on the tabletop. Another man stood further away, sifting through the owner's belongings in a small kitchen area, a small woodfire stove nearby. Up on a shelf nearby the stove, was a small radio that crackled its tune. Finally, two cots sat head to toe along the right-hand side of the small dwelling; only one of them contained a soul.

The sick Englishman looked at me with the same red-eyed hatred that he had given the Germans. I suppose he was right to – I was just another soldier entering his home uninvited, dragging the war along with me.

I moved for the men at the table. My pace remained as calm as it could be. I carried my bayonet in my left hand, and the Luger in my right. As I walked towards them, the man across the table raised his helmeted head and saw me.

His eyes widened as he saw the blood that covered my front. He sat back, his mouth opened to yell. His hand moved. I raised the Luger and pulled the trigger. The Luger crashed in my hand; its report magnified in the small cottage. A hole appeared in the forehead of the German who had sighted me. The force of the impact drove him backwards on the chair, his feet clipping the table and upended it in his momentum to the floor.

The German at the kitchen spun around, his eyes wide as they fell on me. This man had a Schmeisser slung across his front. His hands went for it as I turned on him. The Luger crashed again, and a glass bottle exploded next to his head. He recoiled, screaming as he brought his MP 40 up to bear. Thunder bellowed for a third time, and I hit him high in the shoulder, twisting him as he fired the Schmeisser in a long wide burst.

The sound of it was horrible within the small confines. Suddenly, I was struck hard by the remaining man, who had now overcome his fright. I felt myself lift into the air, then I was slammed down hard on my back. For the second time today, the air rushed out of me. My hands were thrown out by the impact. The Luger crashed again, but uselessly this time. The Schmeisser's wild burst was cut as its wielder screamed at me. I brought the pistol up to bear again, but a hand seized my arm, and a German threw himself on top of me in a struggle for the pistol.

We struggled for a second, our bodies tangled in a fight for life, before I realised he only had one of my hands captive. I swung out with my left arm and drove my bayonet into his side. He screamed but didn't relent, so I stabbed him again. He pulled away, leaving the fight for the Luger to stop the pain at his side.

Now the Schmeisser was turned on me, but the soldier who sat atop of me still covered most of my body. I raised the Luger, and it thundered again as another bottle exploded.

'Scheisser!' the wielder of the Schmeisser screamed as he tried to find some sort of cover.

The Luger crashed a final time, and the round tore a gaping hole in his chest. He yelled as he fell back, his demise etched on his face. I tried to shoot him again, but in my concentration, I had neglected the other attacker. My left wrist exploded in pain as he twisted it. The bayonet clattered as it fell to the floor. The German exclaimed something as he reached for it, extending himself out to my side. I placed the barrel of the Luger into his stomach and fired twice. The groan that escaped the man was sickening. All the fight ran out of him as he crumpled to the floor.

I sat up and raised the pistol again as the Schmeisser wielder slid himself up against the stove. The muzzle of the Luger swayed, then steadied as I trained it on him. I pulled the trigger again and nothing happened. *Out.* The toggle of the pistol was locked open.

The German saw this and grimaced against the stove as he lifted the MP 40 from his lap.

With nothing left to do, I hurled the pistol as hard as I could before I regained my feet. Although the throw went wide, it was enough to make the man flinch and he covered his face with left hand. Not having the strength to support the Schmeisser one handed, it fell back to his lap. He realised his mistake as I rushed towards him. He struggled to lift the weapon again. I threw myself into him before he had the chance to fire. He groaned something I didn't understand, either due to the language or the blood that filled his mouth. Despite my weakened wrist, I overpowered him easily, and drove him to the floor. We both grasped the Schmeisser, but he did little to stop me as I brought the top of its receiver down across his throat and pushed hard. He never broke eye contact with me as I choked the life out of him with his own weapon. He seemed resigned, but the hate never left him until it flitted away, along with his life.

Exhausted, I collapsed, finally allowing my body to gasp and suck in all the air that it needed. The smell of decay and illness hit me, and it took everything I had to stop myself from retching.

As I raised myself from the ground, I held my form as my eyes fell on the source.

The dying Englishman held his hand out to me. His fingers waved in the air as he looked at me. My stomach fell, and while the radio played a German waltz, I raised myself to my feet and went to his side. His hands were weak, trembling wastes of flesh that wrapped themselves around the one that I had offered him. The breaths that had now turned to shallow gasps shook him with each attempt to prolong his life.

'It's ok,' I whispered to him as I knelt by his bed. 'They're gone.'

He tried to talk but fell into another racking spasm of coughs that sent saliva spraying from his open mouth. I turned away but didn't relent my grasp on his hands.

'Can I do anything for you?' I asked as the coughs finally subsided.

He glanced over at the radio before his bloodshot, bleary eyes fell back on me. 'Please,' he groaned as he closed his eyes for a long while and concentrated on his struggled breathes. 'Turn… it off.'

I could understand why he wanted that. He may very well be one of the first to be liberated, and anything that sounded German would surely be an affront to his patriotic senses.

'Sure thing,' I said softly as I pulled my hand from between his trembling grasp. Before I moved away, I fixed the hessian blanket that he withered under and pulled it up close to his chin. He nodded as his breath hitched again, so I left him and headed to the radio that still sang the Bavarian ballad up on its perch above the stove.

I was surprised to see that the radio was not of English manufacture. The small squat, timber vinier box consisted mostly of its speaker, whose fabric covering consumed most of the upper section. Three small knobs were spaced out in the lower section and while I struggled to see in the low light which knob would switch it off, I couldn't help but notice the plaque that displayed its name. Volksempfanger. A German radio in a small English cottage. This did not make sense. How could this man have something like this? Finally, the Bavarian ballad ended, and a fanfare of trumpets blared in my face, followed by the German's words, and their English translation: 'Achtung! Attention!'

4

'We interrupt this program to bring you an important address from our Führer,' the tinny voice translated after the guttural barks of the German announcer. Part of me wanted to leave. Fair enough, the words of a half-crazed Austrian Nazi would have effect on the war. But how much effect would they have on my war, the here and now? As I reached for the knobs to cease the racket, the Führer spoke for the first time, through the small speaker of the Volksempfanger.

'Mein Volk,' the mesmeric voice of Adolf Hitler projected through the night, and I found myself halted in my progress to cease its rattling. I wanted to hear what he had to say. How would he explain the mess that was on the doorstep of the Greater Reich now?

'My people,' the translator confirmed as Hitler's speech continued. 'We find ourselves this morning faced with a challenge. A struggle that will test our resolve as a people, as we have had time and time again over the past five years of this war. Their pincers claw at our sides as if to test our mettle, but each time they are found lacking as they face the might of the Third Reich.'

I half expected to hear a fanfare or a wave of claps and cheers as I had often heard in one of the Führer's speeches, but this time there was nothing. Perhaps this was a genuine reaction to our invasion?

'Our adversary is a cunning one,' the Führer's translator continued, cutting my thought off mid-stream. 'And those of you in the region where they are in operation may feel differently, but I assure you that this operation of theirs is nothing more than a ruse. An attempt to lure us into a trap, to commit all our forces in one area, when they will land in another. Trust in the Wehrmacht high command, the leadership of our officers, and the development of our engineers. Together, we will throw them back into the sea where they belong!' I frowned at this. Hitler had become more than energetic as he delivered this speech, whereas the translator seemed somewhat monotone.

'The defence of the Greater Reich is the responsibility of all. From the smallest child, to the highest-ranking officer in the Wehrmacht or SS, it is expected that all the Reich's people will inform the authorities of any allied activity. If not, indeed, take arms up against them. The Reich is eternal; its people owe it a sacred vow – which will be upheld. Remember that there is only one people. One Reich. One leader.' This last section needed no translation for me, as I had heard the slogan many times before. Ein Volk, Ein Reich, Ein Führer. The Nazi slogan of the thirties as they rose to power, now used to unify the vastness of the Third Reich and the cross section of its people. As the voice of the Führer gave way to '*Raise the Flag*', the Nazi anthem, I heard something behind me.

'Please…' The old man groaned, 'turn that blasted thing off. I can't stand it any longer.'

The old wretch stared at me. I dropped my eyes from his poor state and turned back to the radio, which had now resumed playing music. I turned both knobs to the left until the racket finally died.

The atmosphere in the dwelling had become cold and claustrophobic. The corpses of the German men that littered the floor only further darkened the room, as their blood slowly coated the stone floor. The only saving grace was that no matter how bad their bodies may start to smell, punctured by the wounds I had given them, they could never hope to match the stench of death and decay that lingered around the old man.

I returned to him at that point, kneeling by his bedside. 'Will you be alright?' I asked softly. Again, he took my hand, the withered flesh that clung with its last dying breath to the old bones beneath, clutched at the firmness of my own. I almost recoiled at his desperation, his neediness.

'You need to help me,' he gasped as he wrapped my hand in his own.

'I–' I started, taken aback. 'I can't stay with you.'

He closed his eyes as he shook his head, then he was racked by a cough that shook his whole, withered body. Spittle flew from his mouth as he did so and I turned my head back to the window. Outside, my friends were either dead or dying. I went to stand, but he clutched at my shirt with whatever strength he had left, and dragged me closer.

'Not me,' he gasped, breathing shallowly now as he attempted to rein in his coughs. 'My daughter.' My eyes drifted off to the other cot that lined the wall of the dwelling. 'They took her,' he gasped as his eyes burnt into me with such sadness and desperation.

'I… can't …' I don't know what I was trying to say, or what I possibly could do, but he didn't let me finish in any case.

'They've taken so many of our young. Everyone's, not just mine.' I placed my hand over the back of the wrist that trembled at my shirt cuff. 'Everyone fit and able. To work for the Reich.'

'Everyone?' I asked, somewhat doubting the implication. 'They'll…'

'All of them!' he barked before falling back into a wheeze. 'All of them…' He collapsed back into the bed and pulled the covers up to his chin. He breathed in and shuddered with his exhale. 'God, it's cold in here,' he muttered as he looked around the room. 'Before you go, can you please start a fire in the old stove for me? That's a good boy.' He patted my hand, and feeling obliged I regained my feet and turned for the stove, but again, one of his weak trembling hands stopped me by clutching at the sleeve of my coat.

As I looked back down at him, tears had begun to well up in his bleary eyes. He sobbed as he wiped at his face with the raspy blanket. 'Bristol…' he sobbed.

'Bristol?' I repeated, my brow furrowing once more. 'Is that–'

'There's a sea port there.' He sniffed again, and reached below his blanket to retrieve something. 'That's where they took my Bonnie.' He sobbed as he handed me a small square photograph. 'You stop them.' He pushed the photograph into my hand, and closed my fingers around it with his own. 'Don't let them take our children.'

'Ok,' I said softly and settled him back in the bed. I covered him as best as I could. 'We'll get the bastards, and save all we can,' I promised him, having no idea where this war would take us – not understanding the implications of what he just told me, and what it would mean for the rest of my life.

I left him and moved to the stove to start a fire for the old man. Then it would be back to the war, back to my friends. With some effort, I opened the old cast iron door of the stove; it ground on its hinges as it did. There was no fuel inside, and it looked as though no fuel had been burnt in there for a long time. I looked below the stove and around, but didn't see any timber, so I used the broken remnant of one of the chairs that had shattered in my fight with the Germans. For kindling, I tore strips of cloth from a German tunic that I lit with my windproof lighter. I had no idea whether the tattered rags would be enough to get the chunks of hardwood to catch, but it would have to do. With a sigh, I raised myself from the stove and returned to the old man to say my goodbyes, but in the time it had taken me to light the pitiful flame, he had already passed.

Another deep sigh filled my lungs as I looked down into his old face for the last time. His bleary eyes were still watering, but the pain within them had vanished. I ran my fingers down his face, closing his eyes for good.

'Bristol,' I whispered, a reaffirmation of my earlier promise. No other words needed to be said. I covered the lifeless face with the raspy blanket that he clung to in death. I retrieved the Schmeisser along with any fresh magazines that I could carry, then left the scene behind me.

As I exited the dwelling, the freshness of the outside air hit me in a wave. I took a moment to breathe deeply as I considered my next movements. Beneath the still burning sky, aircraft still littered the sky like a plague. It was awe inspiring. There were still hundreds of aircraft in the sky, spewing thousands of men from their sides, their parachutes blooming in the burning air.

No matter where I looked, the sight of the allied war machine was now apparent. All I was left with were the words of Adolf Hitler: that this was only a ruse, an attempt to draw the German forces away from the full assault. How could all of this ever be considered a mere distraction?

My thoughts were cut from my mind as a new sound became apparent. It started low and drowned out everything that had existed before. Shrieking, whatever it was rushed over the horizon towards the fields and the forest of Rommel's asparagus that I had left behind. At first it was just one. A single line of smoke, and hell fire that wailed as it flew across the air before it disappeared behind the tree line and exploded in such a furious force, that even at this distance the ground trembled beneath me.

Then another came, and another and another, more and more.

The world was filled with the horrible screams, smoke trail, and fire of the rockets that were unleashed upon the American position. Fear filled my soul, as the lands before me turned to fields of fire as each rocket screamed in and detonated. They moved slowly enough that you could see them, but fast enough that it made little difference. The barrage continued, and still I had been helpless but to stand and watch – that was until the field of fire shifted toward my position.

One of the screaming rockets took a wider arc than the others; it skimmed just over the roof of the lorry that was parked before me and missed the old man's dwelling by no more than an inch. It exploded in the field behind the cottage, sending a flurry of fire and dirt up hundreds of feet into the air. That single rocket was enough to get me into motion. I ran for my life, away from the structure, away from the death that fell behind me.

As I passed the lorry, I slipped in the mud again and went tumbling to the soft ground. Meanwhile, hell continued to shriek above and around me as even the mud trembled beneath the wrath of the new German weapon. A scream escaped my mouth as I tried to keep moving. Unable to stand, I crawled through the mud, dragging the Schmeisser with me as the world seemed to be overcome by the smoke of the rockets.

Every inch I pushed took me further away from the lorry, further from anything that could detonate and end my life with its shrapnel. But for every inch, there was another wailing bomb that ripped through the air. I regained my feet just as an American P-47 fighter roared past at a low altitude. My spirits lifted as I saw the white stars painted on its tail. The Germans didn't just have the bombers and infantry to contend with, but now ground attack aircraft. As the fighter vanished into the distance along the smoke trails of the rockets, I hoped that would mark the end of their batteries.

As I quickened my pace, one final rocket wailed in, lower than the rest. The white smoke buffeted the air around me and choked my lungs as the lorry exploded behind me and I was thrown from the force. I landed on hard earth and felt my teeth chatter as the air was again knocked from my lungs. Through ringing ears and stars that danced before my eyes, I turned back to see the cottage destroyed. The force of the explosion had thrown the lorry through the structure. Fire consumed it all. All that remained in the mess was one tyre that slowly rotated on its axle, as the fires that licked at its hide cooked it like a pig on a spit.

I gaped at the wreckage of the structure that I had just been in. Barely a minute had passed since I left its relative safety. With the fires of destruction raging all around me, I turned back to the field to try and find what remained of my unit. Following the same route that the Germans from the lorry had taken, I veered left into the fields to try and assault their position from the rear. The smoke from the barrage hung low, the white of their exhaust mixed with the black smoke that plumed from the fires of their high-explosive charges, to make a dense wall of cover, not only for the Germans, but for myself.

Pausing in the ditch that I'd once cowered in, I peered out into the open field, now seeing the other side of the small stone wall where the GIs had been gunned down. Shapes of men loomed through the smoke, dark and only identifiable by the direction in which they aimed their rifles. They were defending that position, not assaulting it, therefore they had to be German. There were four men that I could see, the rest must have moved beyond the wall or further down the road – all of that was lost to me in the smoke.

I checked the action of the Schmeisser and replaced the magazine to be sure that it was full, then stepped out into the open, as calm as I had when I entered the cottage. As I walked towards these four men, I remembered the German that had laughed as he shot down the GIs, probably my friends. The way he had shrieked the word 'Amerikan' ate at the walls of my stomach. The bitterness of war was ever consuming and as I came within twenty feet of the men, I repeated the phrase in the best representation of a German accent that I could muster.

'Amerikan!' I shrieked as I positioned the wire butt of the Schmeisser against my hip.

The Germans all jumped at the sound and turned. I saw their movements, but the features of their faces were still lost to the smoke. I squeezed the trigger of the Schmeisser and felt its rocking motion begin. The men screamed as I gunned them down. The slow, melodic rhythm of the machine pistol was like a heartbeat. The steady stammering of a machine that was alive. It felt as if it breathed in my hands.

Its fire ran up the men, hurting them. Putting them into such agony that even standing became too much for them. One man covered the wound made in his belly with his hands, only to lose his fingers by the next round that hit the same spot.

Yet still the machine hungered.

It took their lives next. I watched this happen to the four men before me. I saw one man's legs stretch out as his nerve endings fired, his face frozen as his life left him. It was never going to be enough.

I quickly scoured the area around me. Not seeing any figures moving toward me, I turned my gaze onto the forest of Rommel's Asparagus, and stopped. It seemed that each of the posts that had been driven into the ground were now on fire. Set ablaze by the high-explosive charges of the rockets. My heart sunk again; how could anyone survive what I saw before me? The bad thoughts began again at the sight, the expectation, of the death of my friends, my brothers. With each twisted thought that came into my mind, the bitterness within me swelled.

Ramming another magazine into the Schmeisser's forward grip, I turned down the road and continued. Somewhere ahead lay an MG position, and hopefully a radio. Not that I had anyone to contact – I only wanted to kill the bastards that had called in first the mortar strikes and then finally, the rockets. Looking back, I have to say that I was resigned to death at that point. I made no effort to conceal myself as I advanced down the road; I merely walked proud and straight-backed, the Schmeisser low at my side.

Eventually, more silhouettes revealed themselves through the heavy smoke, and again I had little doubt to what they represented. They were Germans, on my side of the wall.

One of them saw my advance and pointed to me. The man raised himself from his backside to a kneeling position and shouted, 'Halt!'

Without slowing my pace, I turned the Schmeisser onto him and opened up. The soldier fell backwards; the Schmeisser had thrown four or five rounds into the area of his face or throat. No words left his mouth, only the wet gurgles of a man that was resigned to drown on his own life.

The others reacted faster than the first group. A Mauser rifle was fired, but the shot went wide and the steady heartbeat of the Schmeisser cut through them before another aimed shot could be raised. Groans and cries filled the air from the dead and dying. I felt like laughing, as they had. I felt like spitting on their faces and rubbing my feet across their mouths. But I didn't. No words of mine could have replaced the words of the Schmeisser, as I placed the muzzle against their temples and fired singularly into each of them.

I knew I couldn't continue like this. I had killed seven men in this short assault, but the element of surprise was now surely lost. I turned to the field of fire that lay beyond the wall, and thought, *someone must be alive.*

With hope lingering in my stomach, I leapt over the stone wall, and lowered myself behind some cover. I bellowed the words of identification that had been drilled into all of us at basic training.

'Thunder!' I screamed, with both of my hands cupped around my mouth. 'Thunder!'

The words washed over the fields of fire, a whisper through the smoke. There was only a single-word response that I rested all my hopes on. I held my breath. I scoured the smoke, as the seconds passed like hours. I was just about to raise my cupped hands for another call, when before me, a silhouette in the smoke appeared.

One at first, then another, and two more. I raised the Schmeisser, and trained it on the figures that approached slowly in their uncertainty. 'Thunder,' I called again, but softer this time. 'Thunder or I will fire.'

The figures stopped. I squeezed the trigger.

'Flash.' The single word that I was waiting for.

I dropped the Schmeisser as I exhaled. The men rushed forward, revealing themselves finally as they took position to my sides.

'Cody,' Bill Carrera said as he placed a hand on my shoulder. 'It is good to see you alive, my boy.'

I looked up to him and squeezed his hand as I smiled and nodded.

'Private,' another voice, familiar and joking. I embraced Jackson briefly, relieved to see my friend again.

'Come on,' a gruff, bitter voice grumbled and I turned to see Little peering over the edge of the rock wall. 'Where are these assholes? It's time to get our own back.' His BAR rested in a position so that he could bring it up to fire quickly. I didn't know the answer to his questions and didn't reply. All I could do was see who the last person was. Jeff Gordon, the recruit, one of the replacements.

'Is this all?' I asked as Bill Carrera ran his hands over me looking for wounds. He was obviously worried by my dazed state. He met my eyes briefly, his nod was one of the faintest I had ever seen.

'Nebelwerfers killed us,' Carrera muttered.

'Nebel?' I tried but couldn't finish the word.

'The rockets,' Little grunted. 'Those fuckin' screaming things. That's how Skinner bought it. Motherfuckers, I'll be happy to ram one of those—'

'Enough, Little,' Carrera said calmly. 'We'll all get our chance.'

'Right,' said Jackson as he replaced the clip in his M1.

Carrera looked above the stone wall, considering our next move. I thought back to the old man in the cottage, and realised I had never looked at the photograph that he gave me. I took it out now and considered it. The grey likeness showed a young lady, photographed in a white background. Her features stood sharp against the softness of her hair that fell over her shoulders. Her smile was faint but it parted her lips enough to spread the beauty of it across her face. I was careful to brush a small section of mud away from the photograph's edge, and placed it safely in my breast pocket.

'Sarge,' I said as I fastened the pocket closed.

'Private?' He replied, not turning his face away from the concern at hand.

'I…' unsure of what to say, I hesitated for a few seconds.

'The war won't wait forever, Private,' Carrera prompted.

'I have a report to make.'

'It can't wait?'

'No sir, I do not think it can.'

PART THREE

North of Bristol – Occupied Wales

December 31st 1944

1

The camp fire crackled before me in the limited light of the morning. The winter cold soaked into our bones as we surrounded ourselves with blankets and fire in a sorry attempt to push it from our minds. Embers danced and flittered up into the air, carried by the heat of their bodies away from the fire that had given them life. Like souls leaving the vessels of their mortal lives, the embers rose and first glowed with the intensity of what their lives had been. Yet, the further they rose, the faster they faded, until nothing but a smudge of ash was left on the flesh of those that remained. What would happen then? Would the wielder of that smudge hold it there, protect it from the weather, realising the symbolic meaning of that mark and everything that it represented? Or would they brush it away with the ball of their thumb, casting it to the nothingness along with the soul that was now lost forever?

I sighed as I gazed into the flames and frowned as the memories of those past days sank into me. A week in England, four months in the war, how much longer would it go for? How much longer would I last? With so many dead now, there had to be no doubt of my imminent end. The question just had to be when, where, and how?

I sat with my back against a stack of ammunition tins as I pondered this. I looked down at the photograph that rested in my open palm. A smudge of ash had formed on her cheek, covering her beauty spots that I had come to adore. Worried about the longevity of the photograph that I now seemed to cling to, I brushed the smudge away.

In the seven long days since our landing at Liverpool, I had seen enough of war. After I had given my report to Sgt Carrera, we had set about taking the German command post and the damned radio position that had continuously rained mortar fire and rocket artillery on our heads. Thankfully, we lost no further men. We were lucky enough to head off another patchy unit of men from various patrols that were either turned around or separated. We folded them into our small squad and together we formed our foothold on the English isle.

The after action was the worst. Sifting back through all the ground we had made, looking for our friends, our brothers.

It was me who found Skinner, or what was left of him.

As Little had said, he had fallen victim to the rocket barrage, and there wasn't much left of him. His torso lay there in the mud; he had been torn in two by the explosion and his guts hung out below him. What was left of his abdomen was an empty bloodied sack that only held its shape because of the bones that remained. I looked into his eyes as I removed the linked section from his dog tags with trembling hands. I remembered the way he used to joke about everything, the way he seemed not to care about living or dying. Well, if I had the chance to ask him now, I wonder if he would still feel the same.

Leach, Walker and more, so many more from the other WACO that was decimated above the field of fire. By the end of it, Carrera had a small bag filled with dog tags that he carried everywhere with him. Each tag like an ember from the fire, the metal tab getting colder and colder, the further Bill walked from their bodies.

Beyond the first day, we linked up with Charlie Company to take the town of Liverpool itself. After two days with long vicious fighting, it was the first elements of the Second Armoured division that won us the battle, those that had landed on the beaches of Southport. With a port won, we rested in the city that had a population of a small town. Those that remained, although grateful for their liberation, were concerned for those that were taken. This reinforced my story about Bonnie and it didn't take long for the brass to take note and send us to Bristol with all haste, in search of these people that had been taken to 'serve the Reich'.

Until then, we'd pressed the Wehrmacht hard in their retreat, facing dogged resistance from a battle-hardened enemy that seemed to lack direction and armoured support. Progress was slow, and it frustrated me to the point of insanity. Each day that passed meant more time for the SS to pull out of Bristol. Despite Carrera's assurance that the fly boys were doing everything in their power to destroy the ports and remaining vessels to prevent such action, I still had my doubts. So instead of worrying about something I didn't know or couldn't help, my mind decided it was a good substitute to dwell on the loss of my friends instead.

Across the fire from me, Jackson was sifting through his mess kit, no doubt looking for some sort of ration to ease his never-ending hunger. Flash Gordon lay to his left, stretched out to some obscene length, his helmet covering his face. Assuming that Flash was asleep and there was no one else to over hear us, I swallowed and spoke to my friend without looking at him. My eyes were fixed on her and the place on her cheek where the smudge had been a moment before.

'What happens to us?' I asked softly.

Jackson paused and shot me a sideways glance. He considered me for a second, then looked over his shoulder at Flash.

'When we bite it. What happens after?' I elaborated on my question.

Out of my peripherals, I saw Jackson return his gaze to me. He sighed and relinquished his pack and settled himself on his backside. His shoulders slumped like a parent that was about to have "that talk" with their eldest kid; the first time was always the hardest.

'That's a heavy question for this time of the morning,' he said glumly. 'What time is it anyway?'

'6:18,' I said without looking at my watch and laughed.

Jackson didn't laugh with me, instead he removed a flask from his pack and took a long swig. He grimaced slightly at the taste, and sucked in air as he fastened the top and tossed it to me over the fire. It landed in my open palm, breaking the eye contact I held with her. It made me blink and stopped me from laughing. Suddenly, all I wanted to do was cry. I looked at him, the embers seeming to dance more ferociously than ever as I watched them through my tears.

'Where are they now?' My voice broke slightly as I asked the question and I fought the urge to break down.

'Where do you want them to be?'

'Here... alive...'

He smiled softly at that. 'That can't be.' He broke his eye contact with me and looked down at his hands. 'Drink.'

I took his advice, and fumbled with the cap on the flask. Jackson waited patiently for me to take my first sip. The whisky burnt my throat as it passed; it tasted foul but I wasn't going to complain. The sip was short, fiery sweet. I exhaled and felt the warmth of my breath against my now running nose. I took another swig and refastened the cap.

'So where then?' Jackson asked as he held his hand out to me, asking for his flask.

I tossed it back to him as I pondered his question. 'I don't know. Heaven, I guess.'

Jackson took a swig, exhaled heavily, and smiled again. 'Then that's where they are.'

'But who is heaven for?' The new voice startled me, as it echoed beneath Flash's helmet. He lifted the helmet from his face and placed it on the ground next to him. He folded his hands behind his head and looked up at the place in question. 'Is it for us, or them?'

'Heaven's for everyone,' I said bleakly.

Jeff laughed softly. 'Yes that's right, but who does it benefit more? Those that supposedly go there or us that are left behind to say "they have gone to a better place."'

'Flash, I don't think you're helping here,' Jackson muttered.

'No…' I said to Jackson before I sniffed the snot back into my nostrils. 'He's ok.'

'The other question is: were they called by God, or were they taken?' Flash continued.

'Taken?' I questioned him.

'Who killed them, who took their souls?'

'The Germans killed them,' I answered.

'That's not what he means,' Jackson said. The soft smile returned to his face. 'If God be for us, who be against us?'

Flash lifted a hand and clicked as he pointed at Jackson. 'Gold star. If God be for us, then who could ever stand against us?'

I sat in silence for a moment, pondering the words. 'Are you saying we're fighting the devil?' I remember asking this question. I don't know where it came from or what I even thought at that point in time, it was all so long ago. But I'll never forget what he said back to me.

'How could God be in any of this?' he said it coldly. 'Can you see God in the way the sky turned to fire when we dropped in? Were those Nebelwerfer rockets created by God's hand? Where was he when the mortars hit? Are we soldiers of God? Because those men we killed, they were Christian too.'

'I would say all of those things were the devil's work.'

'What's the difference?' he said with no emotion whatsoever. 'From what I've seen, there is none. Just crap that people preach to make themselves feel better. So, to answer your question, Skinner, Leach, all those boys back in that fucking mess of a landing, they're where we left them. Buried, with their rifles dug into the ground above them to signify their grave. There's nothing after this, there's just us and them. If God ever existed, he turned his back on us long ago.'

'I see God in us,' Jackson said bitterly and Flash laughed softly. 'Hey don't fuckin' laugh at me, everyone has their choice in this. You don't get to laugh about it.'

Flash held up his hands. 'Hey, peace! I just didn't expect that to come out of your mouth.'

'It's easy to think about what's happening to us. But think about the poor Tommies that have had their lives torn apart, being dragged from their homes to do God knows what for the people that have conquered them. How do you think they see us?'

'Tell me,' Flash gave in.

'With white fuckin' wings hanging from our shoulders. That's how, you blasphemous son of a bitch.'

Flash laughed again. 'What, and you got that opinion from the handful of shell-shocked vessels that we saw in Liverpool? What about the rest of them?'

'The Nazis took them, that was all that was left,' I interjected.

'Garbage,' Flash dismissed it. 'Think about it, what would they do with them? They've got Germany, Austria, Czech, Poland, Italy, Belgium, France, Norway, not to mention whatever the hell happened with the Russians. What about all those people? They can't have put the entire continent of Europe to work, what the hell would they be making?'

'Ok. If it's not true, then where are they?'

'Hiding in their cellars. Too damned worried about protecting what they've hidden from the Germans, to come and say thank you. That's what I think.' The emotion had now come out well and truly in his voice, and he almost shouted this entire statement.

'You're a bitter, bitter man, Gordon,' Jackson muttered as he took another swig from his flask. I watched him as he drank. His eyes cast about the camp, then stopped and doubled in size. He quickly took the flask away from his mouth and fastened the cap as he stood.

'Private, that better not be what I think it is,' Carrera grunted as he stormed into camp carrying a BAR.

'No sir, cough syrup sir,' Jackson spluttered as he stood and saluted.

'Uh-huh, and I'm Doug McArthur.' He rolled his eyes and tossed the BAR to me. I caught it with both hands, the weight of it considerably more than my M1. 'On your feet soldiers, time to haul ass.'

'What's the word from the brass?' Flash said as he raised himself from the dirt and kicked out the fire.

'Us and two other squads are punching ahead of the column. Seems Cody here was right.' He nodded to me.

'Don't say that too loud, his head's already big enough.' Jackson laughed.

'Right, about what?' I asked.

'Surveillance photographs have come in. The Germans have amassed a large number of civilians at the port; it's our job to go in there and stop their export.'

Jackson and I exchanged a glance.

'Little's already at the Jeeps. We pull out oh-six-thirty. Collect your gear.' With that, Carrera left.

Going to rescue the civilians, I couldn't believe it. I stole one last glance at Bonnie's photo before I collected my things. With no fire, the light had now diminished considerably, but I could still see her smile. The way her lips parted and the small cluster of beauty spots that sat next to her left eye. I ran my thumb over her likeness again and a soft smile crept across my face.

Jackson clapped me on the shoulder. 'Hey lover boy,' he said as he laughed, 'put that away. You're going to get your chance to meet her in person. So don't wear the photo out, you'll need it to identify her from all the other gorgeous dames we're about to rescue.'

Flash laughed as he picked up his M1. 'I thought you would have had them all to yourself, Jackson?'

Jackson smiled. 'Not sure what you're worried about, all your dames are back in Liverpool hiding from you. You sure we're heading in the right direction?'

I laughed as I shouldered my pack and stole one final glance at Bonnie. Soon I would rescue her, soon I would uphold my promise to her father.

2

The three of us spoke barely a word as we made our way to the motor pool. We passed the lines of camps and the scatterings of men that huddled next to their fires in their blessed period of rest, no doubt thankful that the rain had relented. I looked at the faces of some of them as I passed. Remembering the faces of the dead I had seen back in Millisle, it struck me as curious how similar some of them looked. With the sheer weight of exhaustion overcoming them, they slept like they were dead. If it wasn't for the rise and the fall of their chests, I would even believe it. All the pain was gone, washed from their bodies by the grace of unconsciousness. All the worries – past, present, and future – couldn't touch them there. It was like being granted a fabled recreation pass. Everyone had problems but they could wait until you were back, or in this case, awake.

As soon as this thought crossed my mind, it was eviscerated by the screams of a man close by. Flash, Jackson, and I whipped our heads about as we unslung our rifles. To be honest, I didn't know what to expect as I thumbed the Browning off safe and ran towards the hysterical shrieks. As we ran, men were rousing around us.

'What's going on?' one man asked.

'Is it the fuckin' Nazis?' Another screamed as he scrambled to his feet.

We didn't answer any of them as we ran towards the screams that seemed to fill with pain and anguish the more they drew out. My heart hammered in my chest with anticipation; my body readied itself for the fight in front.

'No, fuckin' no!' was barely audible in the hysterics of it and I was left thinking how could they hit us here, after everything? How could they get so far in? As I rounded a canvas sheet that had been hung over a rope, I saw the man who was screaming. He lay by himself, his pack and M1 nestled on the ground next to him, ready for action. Tufts of grass were torn from the ground as his fingers clutched at anything to shield himself... but from what? More men gathered as Jackson moved forward and knelt beside him.

'What happened?' one asked, but not a soul answered.

Jackson placed a firm hand on the screamer's shoulder and shook him. The screams of horror intensified somewhat as the man's hands went from the dirt to Jackson's, and his efforts to kick himself free were doubled. Then he opened his eyes. They darted around as the barks of horror continued to escape his mouth, but became less and less as he saw the countless American faces looking down on him, and that the hand on his shoulder belonged to another.

'It's ok, Private,' Jackson said softly, 'it was just a dream'.

'Are you sure?'

'Positive.' Jackson smiled as he ran his hand through the young soldier's hair and stood to return to us. No one said anything about the false alarm, not one grumble escaped a GI's lips. I continued to look at the Private as Jackson returned to my side, and watched as he took in his surroundings and his breaths slowed.

I patted Jackson on his back as we turned back to the motor pool, my mind returning to my fears. How could they get us? Well, that was easy, wasn't it? They got into our heads. If they could do that, then even the gift of sleep meant nothing to a man. The comparison to a rec pass was null and void. Instead, one was stuck living the same hell, every second of every day.

I wondered how good the muzzle of the M1 would look; I wondered how it would taste.

The motor pool seemed unperturbed by the events of the dreaming screamer. Soldiers moved around the eight Jeeps that sat in the limited light. The scene made me think of a book that I had read once upon a time – some European knights readying their horses for a final charge. So much had changed in the world, but when you thought about it, it was only the small things that differed. In the story, men watered the horses, and checked the armour that they donned.

As I looked around our steel pack mules as they sat silently in wait, I saw one soldier checking the fuel supply in each vehicle. Instead of the clatter of wooden arrows as the archers readied themselves, steel tins crammed full of fifty-calibre were loaded into the back of each Jeep. The smell of piss and horse shit had given way to fuel and motor oil, while the clanking of knights' armour was replaced by the racking of slides and the jingle of the machine gun belts that were thrown into the pintle-mounted machines.

Little stood in the back of one of the Jeeps as he single-handedly raised a fifty-calibre machine gun into the pintle mount that rose up from the centre of the floor pan. His arms and shoulders bulged with the strain of lifting the monster, and when he locked it into place he turned and spat to the ground. The Willys Jeep was not a large machine, but held four men well enough. Although with the bulk of the fifty now taking up so much space, I couldn't see how four men would be practical.

I moved to the Jeep that Little stood in and threw my pack into the back, atop of the ammunition crates. Little looked down to the pack, then slowly raised his eyes to mine. Without a word, he slid his foot under the pack and hoisted it out onto the ground with one of his large feet.

I watched it fall to the ground. 'Slept well, I see?'

Little glowered down at me, then bent down and retrieved one of the ammunition tins that I had covered with my pack. He lifted the lid and withdrew the belt of ammunition inside and proceeded to load the fifty without another word.

I looked to Jackson, who raised his eyebrows to me and slowly mouthed the word 'ok' as he turned his back to Little. A smile spread across my face as I bent and retrieved my pack. I considered placing it into the back of the Jeep again, but thought better of antagonising the big man. Men had started to clamber into the Jeeps, and I couldn't help but feel there was some direction that I was missing.

'Should we get into a Jeep?' I asked Flash and Jackson as I leant my newly acquired BAR against the front fender, far enough away from Little to not upset him.

'I don't know,' Flash said, 'I supp–'

'Top's coming now.' Jackson cut him off as he gestured to the rear of the Jeep. 'Who's that with him?'

I looked over my shoulder and saw Bill Carrera heading towards us. His helmet was strapped on and his Thompson was ready at his side. Following him was a slender man with a child's stubble. He carried a carbine that looked proportionately the same size as my usual rifle, the M1. 'Fresh meat,' I muttered and Jackson made a sound of agreeance.

'Men,' Carrera said with a little more authority than usual. 'We've got a replacement here for Skinner.' He gestured to the boy, who looked to the three of us and nodded his head. 'Private Perry, meet the squad: Jackson, Gordon, Cody.'

We all shook hands briefly. He seemed ok, but it always took time for newcomers to settle into the squad. Hell, if we kept dying at the rate that we were, I don't think any of us could see much point in getting to know a man.

'Little here is our BAR man, so you'll stick with him no matter where he goes.'

Perry moved to the side of the Jeep and extended his hand as far as he could to match Little's height. Little turned his back on him to secure his BAR in the back of the Jeep, without offering him even a glance.

Carrera continued without addressing Little's obvious mood. 'We will be under Captain Watkins for this mission. We're being folded into a makeshift raiding party to try and stop the Nazis from exporting the locals that they've taken prisoner. I want three men per Jeep. Gordon, you and Perry stay here with Little. Jackson, Cody, you're with me in the radio vehicle.' He gave Little, Flash and Perry a short look each and finished with 'good luck' before he walked off.

Flash gave us a smile and clapped Perry on the back. 'Welcome to the squad. Come sit in the front with me and we'll leave big Little back here to himself. Or is it Little big? I always get those mixed up.'

Jackson laughed under his breath as he followed Carrera to one of the Jeeps near the front of the small group. Carrera clambered into the passenger seat and without question, Jackson jumped behind the wheel. I sighed as I again threw my pack into the back of the Jeep and leapt up behind the machine gun. I didn't mind manning the fifty, but I rubbed my lower back in anticipation of the bumps and the jarring it would receive sitting above the rear axle. Everyone seemed to get themselves settled. I checked the fifty and made sure it was ready, locking its pintle so it didn't swing as we were driving.

I had just racked the machine for the second time, feeding the belt into the breech, as an officer spoke up from where he stood on the passenger seat of the lead Jeep. 'Men, it has come down from top brass that the Germans are attempting to deport a quantity of the civilian population. We have no idea what that might be for, but the order has come down for a small detachment to break out and put a stop to it. As there is little strategic importance in civilians, we expect that resistance will be minimal. Follow your section heads, stay together, and look out for armour that may be lying in ambush.'

The officer that I imagined to be Watkins gave Carrera a nod and turned to reclaim his seat.

'Start her up,' Bill said to Jackson as he readjusted his Thompson. I sat down amongst the tins of ammunition, resting my weight on my pack to save my back. As the sun finally broke over the horizon, the Jeeps fired up and revved their engines. I looked over to the captain and saw him scouring over a map and talking to his driver. I thought about some of the things he had said as he addressed us. Armour lying in wait, the lack of strategic importance, even the way he spoke about this mission. I got the impression that he felt like the mission was a waste of time.

'Lack of strategic importance,' I muttered to myself. In one way, I was offended by the implication that Bonnie's life lacked importance and a scowl spread across my face as I glared at him. But on the other hand, I liked the sound of little resistance.

As the eight Jeeps revved their engines and the men settled in and readied themselves for their raid, Watkins signalled his driver and like that, we were off.

Jackson worked the Jeep through its gears as the sun rose. Mud and shit flicked up from the tyres of Watkins' Jeep and spattered us as we tailed it.

'Back off,' Bill said as he lowered his head against the spray. Jackson eased up on the throttle and soon enough, we were cruising at about twenty-five miles per hour and the bumps didn't seem that bad. Carrera had pulled a letter from his breast pocket and was reading over it, while I occupied myself by looking at Bonnie's photo once more. I don't know how much time passed as I became lost in the drone of the Jeep's engine and the beauty of the woman in the photograph pressed between my fingers. I focused hard on the three beauty spots that I could barely make out in the photo, perhaps because no matter how smooth the road was, my hand moved in front of my face with each pebble the Jeep rolled over. Nevertheless, I knew they were there, and when I closed my eyes, I could see them on her face. Three small dots a quarter inch from the corner of her eye.

I imagined meeting her for the first time. The tears that no doubt would well up and run down her cheeks in her joy of liberation and the knowledge that she was safe from her captors. I imagined telling her that I was sent from her father. Again, I could see the similarities in that story of the knights. It would be I who was the shining hero, who would sweep her off her feet. Of course, more tears would form as she learnt about the passing of her father and I would rub them away with the ball of my thumb across her cheek. My thumb would linger there, and rub at those beauty spots as if they were a piece of ash.

A familiar sound echoed in the din, rolling over the monotonous howl of the Jeeps. Blinking, I looked down to her face and realised the pain that was in my finger and thumb from clutching her likeness for so long. I secured her in my breast pocket and looked around. All eight Jeeps drove in a line; the sky above was clear, yet somewhere another vehicle was lurking.

No – there were two or three. I sat up and turned my head as the rolling sound of aeroengines drifted over the Jeep again. Bill had heard it as well. He turned around in his chair and we both saw them at the same time.

'Friendly?' I asked hopefully as the three sleek planes began to bank.

Bill didn't say a word, he just continued to squint into the air.

As the planes banked, they were silhouetted against the glow of the rising sun, and a peculiar shape was presented to us.

Bill laughed as he pointed over to Watkins. We all looked and saw the captain bellowing into the radio handset. As he stood up, he waved his arm, pointing forward of his position. 'Lightnings,' Bill said. 'Nothing else could be that ungainly and be in the air.'

Jackson and I exchanged a glance, unsure what he meant, but both of us relaxed a little at his laugh. I doubted very much that Bill would act that way if they were German. Still, I clung to the spade grips of the fifty.

The Lightnings came low over the top of us, and I saw what Bill meant when he regarded the aircraft as ungainly. The Lightnings were a twin-engine plane that didn't have a conventional fuselage. The cockpit that sat in the usual place between the two engines did not connect to the tail. Instead, two separate bodies stretched back from both engines to their tails, where a further connection was made at the rear of the plane. Through the air they screamed, faster than any Stuka. The three Lightnings roared overhead to the cheers of the men in the Jeeps.

Having three aircraft acting as angels on our shoulders, meant we would at least feel safe. We watched as the Lightnings rose up into the air, washing off speed as they gained altitude. All of our eyes were on them, as they gracefully twisted through the air. I don't even think we reacted when the first black gouts of smoke erupted around them. In the distance, even over the howls of the Jeeps and the whines of the Lightnings' superchargers, I heard the distance thunder of FLAK.

3

I watched in horror as one of the P-38s rose up into the air, spiralling in an effort to evade the black death that erupted around it.

'FLAK! Everyone get ready,' Carrera called out as he took his focus back to Watkins, who held his head closer to the radio's speaker.

Watkins' Jeep stopped on the road abruptly, as the captain continued to bellow into the handset. I watched as the Lightnings desperately tried to avoid the FLAK. Two of the planes banked off, diving low to the countryside. One kept on its rising course, spinning and turning in all directions, as if lost in the black clouds. It was like watching a bird flee for its life. At times the concentration of FLAK was that great, that I even lost sight of the aircraft. Then finally, black smoke began to trail behind it, pouring from its right engine.

As the rest of the Jeeps came to a halt behind Watkins, we groaned as the black clouds engulfed the Lightning and it was torn apart. One engine was torn free from the body, and it coughed briefly as it was starved of fuel in its final moments, before it began its plummet to the ground. The wings were snapped as if they were small twigs and the fuselage burst open. Among the debris that fell to the ground, I saw a lifeless figure. Legs and arms flapped uncontrollably as the pilot's broken body tumbled over and over.

'Christ Almighty,' I groaned as I followed the pilot's body to the ground.

'Christ has got nothing to do with it, son,' Carrera growled as he forced the letter he was reading back into his pocket. 'You two stay here,' he said as he leapt from the Jeep and ran to Watkins' side.

The two spoke briefly. I watched Carrera's face intensely, looking for a sign of what was to come, but he hadn't changed. He had been looking sullen for the last few days now, and I could understand why. With all the death that we had seen, hell, I supposed even I looked sullen.

The two remaining Lightnings roared back overhead, but this time they were not met with cries of joy, but cries of anger, from the soldiers beneath as they fled in the face of the FLAK.

'Where are they going?' one soldier screamed.

'Where do you think? Away from the FLAK,' another called back.

'Cowards!'

'Enough!' Carrera bellowed, startling me as I hadn't seen him return to the Jeep. 'You want those planes back? Then mount up and let's go knock out those FLAK units.'

'With what?'

'With your hands, your teeth. Your lives, soldier. Now I'm going down that road, to our objective. Who's coming with me?'

Among the commotion and the calls of support that the other soldiers were throwing behind Bill, I looked over and saw Flash in his Jeep. There was no smile on the man's face this time. He had his head low and was talking softly to an ashen-faced Perry as he sat in the passenger seat. Little glowered from his position in the rear, as he twisted his massive fists on the grips of the fifty.

While Watkins continued his back and forth on the radio, Carrera was running his eyes over the Jeeps. He gave each vehicle a direction, telling some to branch left once they hit the town; others were told to skirt right or to follow us on our charge through the middle. Throughout this, I never stopped to ask why Bill seemed to be running the entire section. I saw him as my superior, so it didn't feel strange to me, but I remembered the way Watkins spoke to the men back at the motor pool. He didn't seem like a leader. As I watched him pore over the map while he spoke to his driver, to me he seemed more like a planner. I felt a tremendous amount of pride for Bill in that moment.

Eventually, as every seemed to harden themselves for what was to come, Bill clambered back into the Jeep. 'Hard,' Bill said as he pointed forward. 'Drive hard, Jackson. Ready yourselves, this isn't going to be easy.'

Together as one, the Jeeps charged forward, their transmissions whining as the drivers pushed them through their gears.

'Before we left, Watkins said light resistance!' Jackson shouted over the increasing roar of the American mules.

Carrera looked at him with a dark face. 'No reconnaissance. All I know is what Watkins told me after he spoke to that pilot.'

'Uh-huh,' I grunted. 'And what is that?'

'Armour.'

'Christ,' Jackson said and he backed off the throttle.

'Drive hard. No backing off, Jackson,' Carrera said sternly. 'Speed is what's going to keep us alive here. We're need to keep mobile, take out the FLAK emplacements, then keep the Panzers busy till the tank busters can come and rocket a typhoon up their ass.'

'Jesus,' I said as the Jeep bounced over a culvert in the road. 'And that's the plan? The flyboys know their role in this?'

Bill nodded. 'The flyboys will do their part, we just need to do ours.'

Jackson shifted up a gear, and I glanced over my shoulder at the column of Jeeps that followed us. The men in the back readied their M2s, while the men in the passenger seats checked their weapons. In the distance, the FLAK had fallen silent. I wondered if the Germans knew we were coming. I wondered how many of us would make it out of this.

'Top, why would the Wehrmacht have FLAK, and armour guarding civilians?' Jackson asked as he turned his eye away from the road.

Bill cocked his Thompson as the road narrowed into a small path that led between two hedges. 'I wouldn't say that they're Wehrmacht.

Wehrmacht is their army; guys like you and me. They wouldn't care about this, it's their job to fight us.'

'So, who are we fighting?'

'SS,' I answered from the rear, thinking about the words of the Wehrmacht officer back in Bristol.

Bill looked back over his shoulder at me and nodded. 'Does it matter?' he asked as he looked back to Jackson.

'No. I suppose it doesn't.'

'That's right, soldier. Now pick up some speed, we're almost in town.'

Bill was not wrong, and the rapidity in which everything went south was astounding. The Jeeps broke out of cover at almost top speed and instantly the world was filled with a buzzing and a stream of incoming small arms fire. From where we broke out, the road led straight to the town, with open paddocks either side of the road. Carrera dropped his Thompson, as he leant over hard and pushed the steering wheel.

'Off the road!' he screamed as the Jeep swerved off the raised section of road and down into the paddock below.

I screamed as I was thrown around, and almost off the Jeep entirely.

'Christ, Top. I thought you said we needed to have speed; we can't do that down here!' Jackson screamed as bullets panged off the steel.

I turned and saw Flash and Little disappear down the other side of the road, their Jeep's drive train howling in the process, while Watkins charged straight ahead, down the middle, and exploded in a massive fireball. The frame of the Jeep shot up into the air as the bodies of the men that occupied it were thrown like ragdolls. The mine that had claimed it had no doubt been intended for a tank.

I ducked my head as the flaming wreck came down on the road, while the bodies of the men that had been in the Jeep were thrown even further. That was a horrible sight, and one that I will never forget.

'Cody!' Carrera screamed my name as he turned around. 'Do you need to be shown how to use that damned gun?'

'No sir,' I said as I took his hint. There is a saying about the Browning M2s, or as they are affectionately called, 'Ma Deuce', that when old

Ma speaks, everyone listens. And now for the first time, Ma Deuce spoke. This was what it was meant for. Heavy machine gun fire ripped out at the Germans from at least four of the Jeeps. Tracer now filled the air both ways, but with the heavy thunder of the fifty calibres, the German fire became more sporadic. I saw tracer fire fill the air from a first-storey window of a brick house and turned Ma Deuce's fire onto the position. With the bucking motion of the Jeep's progression across the paddock, it was difficult to hold a steady aim, but I stopped worrying about aiming and just followed the tracer fire. Soon enough, a good beaten fire was hammering the side of the house. The big difference between the thirty and the fifty calibre machine guns is power. A thirty calibre will pepper a brick wall and eventually do some considerable damage. A fifty calibre will destroy it. Eventually, the section of wall below the window collapsed and the German machine gun and its operator fell forward out of the window.

More fire raked up the Jeep from our right and a pain seared up my arm. I didn't even check it; I just swung the fifty around and continued to fire at this new raised German position. This position was on the flat roof of a structure. Drifts of sand shot up in the air as heavy rounds impacted on the extra bags that had been placed to strengthen it.

Only a hundred feet remained until the town itself. A stone wall guarded it, with openings only at the major sections of streets. Beyond, black smoke rose from the stack of a ship. The ship that was our objective – where no doubt, as we spoke, Bonnie was being loaded like cattle for export. Another Jeep from our convoy rushed past us, its occupants bouncing to hell as the gunner tried his best to steady the gun. I watched in horror as two German MG 42s focused their wrath on the men. The sight was abhorrent. The Jeeps, although steel, were completely open and offered no protection against small arms fire, especially when it came from an elevated position.

The fire swept over the men. The driver was hit so many times his body convulsed with the impacts. Blood filled the air as he slumped backward, forgoing any control of the vehicle. The gunner was hit hard and thrown from the back, his hands stretched out as if trying to reach for the spade grips of the fifty that he had once clung to. The barrel swung madly and the passenger, the only man left alive, reached for the wheel as the Jeep swerved, then overturned. The vehicle rolled multiple times, forcing us to change our route. As it went, the crippled body of the passenger was thrown through the air.

On the other side of the road, down where we couldn't see, more smoke and fire billowed up from what I could imagine were other Jeeps that met a similar fate. I thought about Flash, Little, and even Perry in that moment, and hoped that they made it through.

Fifty feet now, the German machine guns sounded as though they were right on top of us.

'Hold on!' Jackson called as he turned the wheel hard and the Jeep careered up the slope to the road and became airborne with its momentum. We crashed back to the ground as most of the ammunition tins went soaring through the air, leaving the Jeep for good.

I saw German machine guns positioned on the roofs of houses that now became unusable as we burst into the town itself. As the stone boundary walls shot past, I saw ten men, dressed in black with white piping on their uniform. Even at this speed, the SS runes on their collars shone out to me as Ma Deuce spoke once more. The SS men had been surprised and were left with no cover. They dove for the ground nonetheless, as fifty calibre rounds hammered into and around them. A shot of red mist dusted the air, as one man was cut almost in two. Then they were gone, vanishing behind the wall of a structure with the progression of the vehicle.

The scene in the town was chaotic. Germans ran everywhere in a scattered defence; some shot at us from alleyways, others leant out through the open windows of upper levels and shot down at us. A round from a German Schmeisser hit me square in the shoulder and rocked me back. The pain was horrendous but I gritted my teeth and pushed through it.

Ma Deuce spoke briefly once more, before running dry.

'Shit!' I exclaimed as I threw the top cover open. I reached down and found a fresh tin of ammunition and as I brought it up, I saw Jackson get hit in the side of the face. He screamed and the Jeep lurched as he let go of the wheel to press at the searing pain. As the vehicle lunged, I was hit again in the backside and my left leg gave out on me. I fell from the side of the fifty, and I watched as the tin of ammunition sailed over the side of the Jeep and vanished.

Well, we're fucked now, was the thought that crossed my mind as Bill took control of the steering wheel.

The fifty swung wildly on its pintle mount as Bill struggled to bring the Jeep under control. Jackson still clung to his face as he rocked his head back and forth. There was no chance I was going to risk standing at this point, so instead I grabbed my BAR and continued fighting. With a lower profile, I felt a lot safer. The BAR, although a large weapon, was easy enough to use in the position I was in. Another SS man leant out of a window toward the end of the street, which seemed to open onto a significant courtyard. The SS man let fly with his Schmeisser and as the course of fire fell over the Jeep, I heard Bill groan as a nine-millimetre slug hit him somewhere. I swung the Browning around and with three slow, mechanical thumps, the SS man was gone.

The Jeep shot into the courtyard and I saw the first FLAK guns. Having heard the commotion, the crew had levelled the barrels, but luckily for us another Jeep had entered the courtyard from the right side before us. I watched as the power of four twenty-millimetre guns ripped through the light steel. The small American mule was dismantled. Larger again than the fifty calibres, when a man is hit by cannon fire, he is literally torn apart. The Jeep propped with impacts, and the men fell apart.

'Top!' I screamed as all three of us now were in a world of hurt. 'On your right!'

Bill, having witnessed the fate of this first Jeep, turned ours straight for it. With his other hand he pushed down hard on Jackson's right leg.

'Brace yourselves!' Bill screamed as the Jeep rocketed toward the FLAK crew. I remember seeing the faces of the men who sat with the guns as they spun the adjustment wheels as fast as they could to bring the fire onto us, but to no avail. When the Jeep slammed into the gun emplacement, the four men that supported the gunner were all thrown from their positions. I was thrown forward and landed on the cobbled street on my side. The air rushed out of me as I landed but I wasn't crippled. I managed to bring the Browning up and I shot the gunner where he sat, four times. The support crew were all scrambling and trying to run – two of them I shot in the back, while Carrera got the other two with his Thompson.

'Cody, to your left!' Carrera screamed and I rolled over to bring the Browning around to my other side. This crew only had a single-barrelled gun, and they were quicker, but less protected by armour. I brought the Browning around onto them and fired. The gun rocked methodically, then ran dry. The loader put both of his hands to his gut and began to convulse as torrents of red flowed down his front in a horrific flow. But the gunner was not even touched. The gun swung around and slowly, the barrel dropped down and down and down, until I was left looking up its bore.

Suddenly, across the other side of the courtyard, another US Jeep roared onto the scene with its fifty-calibre booming. The sound of it made me look away from the FLAK emplacement, but when I returned, the gunner was gone, running for cover from this new threat. 'Top, call the fly boys!' I screamed as I watched the newcomers gun down the fleeing German. 'FLAK emplacements are knocked out!'

4

I laid there, on the cobblestones, exhausted. The thud of the other Jeep's fifty cal rippled through my chest, my heart spasming against the concussion. Skipping through a dissonant rhythm, unsure whether to laugh, cry or to turn around and pack it all in. FUBAR. Fucked Up Beyond All Recognition. I watched as Jackson writhed in the driver's seat as he clutched his disfigured face. Blood and what looked to be flesh hung down through his fingers, his mouth open in a silent scream of horror. I watched the other Jeep, as it bounced over the body of the flee-ing FLAK gunner, and its body hitched with the unexpected obstacle within the road. The faces of the two men that remained in that Jeep were cold, and pale. Although some victory could be claimed with the feat we had just undertaken, there was no joy in my expression. Finally, I watched Bill Carrera, as he screamed into the mouthpiece of the radio, while his left hand kneaded at Jackson's shoulder. His eyes darted from Jackson to the other Jeep, and finally came to rest on myself, where they lingered as a concerned expression lined his face.

I have no reason to know why Bill would have been concerned by looking at me, after all these years I can only imagine that I looked dead as I lay there in utter agony and complete exhaustion. As my chest rose and fell, I rolled onto my side and let the Browning fall out of my hands, empty and useless to me now. The Jeep gunned its engine sporadically as it made its way around the perimeter, making noise that was senseless and unnecessary. As Bill continued to shout over the radio, I thought *what next?* Would we wait for the flyboys to offer us cover, in the confines of this village, before we pushed forward to the ship? Would we let the flyboys take care of the rest?

As if to answer all my questions, as if to solidify any doubt that had ever crossed my mind, the boisterous Jeep bounced over the German's body once more and exploded in a flurry of fire, shrapnel and flesh that shot up into the air like a pillar to the Lord.

Something heavy slammed into me but it didn't hurt, nor did I react as I was transfixed, completely stunned, and helpless but to follow the Jeep's journey through the air as it twisted over and over and tumbled slowly back to the earth, a ruined shadow of what it had once been. The wheels had all buckled under the fall and the white star of the US armed forces shone out between the flames. Slowly the paint bubbled and wept, until the flames licked at the steel once more and removed it from memory. Nothing else remained but darkness, ash, and death.

I tried to get up and something firm shifted on my legs. As I looked down, my eyes bulged at the sight of what laid on my lap, leaking its life all through my clothes. It was one of the men from the Jeep, or part thereof; his head and at least most of one shoulder was all that remained, as if someone had tried to cast a bust, but instead of bronze or brass, this was dead flesh. It became paler the more I looked, the more that the blood that remained inside wasted itself against my greens.

As the ground began to shake, I pushed the head off me. The vacant eyes cast their sight across all the world and saw nothing as they went. The mouth remained open, relaxed now as if emitting the final sigh as the breath was taken out of his lungs. Face down it fell, as I moved on, gritting my teeth as my muscles screamed in protest against the orders to *move* and *move now*. My shoulder waned at the weight of the Browning as it came back into my grasp, the left side of my ass shrieked as my legs scrambled to move me back toward Carrera and the safety of our Jeep.

Black smoke filled the air from the burning Jeep, which filled my senses with its cancer. The fires crackled around the steel, rubber, fuel, and flesh, but somewhere below there was something else. Something mechanical, something guttural that belched and gurgled and roared, but it was behind the veil. Carrera was up and moving, a grimace on his face as he dragged the now semi-conscious Jackson into the passenger seat of the Jeep. He looked up at me as he finally dragged his legs over and let Jackson slump into the seat. As Bill's eyes met mine, he froze and he focused over my left shoulder.

'Cody, get in the Jeep,' was all he said as he rushed forward to the driver's seat and tried the starter, but the sound was drowned out by something else. A monstrous engine roared behind me, and through the smoke and the fire I smelt the richness of its exhaust. As I moved, the ground seemed to shake beneath my feet and even as I mounted the back of the Jeep and laid my hands on the M2 once more, I could feel the vibration through my soul.

Steel screamed and even the flames that had engulfed the Jeep shook in protest as the frame of the vehicle was crushed. Black smoke billowed up and around the monster as it surged forward and growled as it did. The muzzle brake of its gun was all I could see through the smoke at first. Then the barrel, and how long it was, kept coming and coming until the Jeep was gone and only the sides of the monster were shrouded in smoke, as it billowed out through its interleaving road wheels.

The King Tiger accelerated when its vision ports were cleared of the smoke and we were finally seen. It lunged forward with surprising agility, given its size. As its ultra-wide tracks spat out the ruined Jeep behind it, our own Jeep shot forward. There was a grind as Bill shifted gears and then we were off again, fleeing once more for our lives.

The Tiger's main cannon erupted as Bill hit second gear. The concussion was absolutely devastating and awe inspiring at the same time, but what scared me the most was the moment that all the air was sucked from the world as the eighty-eight passed within a foot of us. To our right, a building fell in on itself, the undeserving victim of the high-explosive shell that was meant for us. As if the Germans had given up on trying to shoot a rabbit with a howitzer, the captain's cupola swung open, and a capped SS man raised his head out of cover.

'Get that fifty ready to fire!' Bill shrieked at me as he shifted into third.

'Sir!' I replied as I again threw open the top cover and fixed the M2 on its pintle. There was one can left. Barely a hundred rounds. Fifty calibre against hardened steel that was two hundred and eighty millimetres thick at the strongest point, meant nothing. I may as well be shooting spit wads. Still, if there was an opportunity, I needed to be ready and so did the gun. As I slammed the top cover down, Bill shot us out of the courtyard as another building exploded from a last-ditch, high-explosive effort. I shielded my eyes as the Jeep bounced and was showered by broken brick, silt, and plaster.

'What's the plan, Top?' I screamed down as I unpinned the pintle and the M2's weight fell into my hands.

'Let's keep him busy until the air support gets here; they'll turn that thing into mincemeat.'

'Roger,' I said as I swung myself around. The Tiger was quick for its size, but it wasn't as nimble as the Jeep. As we raced down the street that ran adjacent to the courtyard, the Tiger's barrel was only coming into sight now. As the monster clipped its edge, the building crumbled and collapsed in on itself. Part of the building fell onto the tank itself, which was enough to send the commander back down to safety.

'Hope the rubble jams its turret,' I muttered to myself just before Bill jammed on the brake and swore.

'Hold on!' he screamed as I almost fell backwards over the hood again. I looked over my shoulder and saw another long barrel like the King Tigers emerge out of an alleyway.

'Not two of them,' I said to myself. But it wasn't another King, not even a Tiger itself. It was an opened-backed tank hunter, using the chassis of something old. It had one of the German high-velocity guns on a fixed forward-facing mount. Unlike a normal tank, this was open at the top, leaving the crew somewhat exposed.

'Marder!' Bill screamed as he turned the wheel hard and brought the Jeep around the Panzer Jager. The crew lifted their heads above the armour to peer out at us. I racked the fifty and as the side of the tank hunter became exposed, I aimed for the very top lip and sent a wild volley their way, a small reminder to keep their heads down.

Bill looked back over his shoulder briefly as he turned left down another side street on his way back to the courtyard.

'Change of plans, conserve that ammunition,' he called back as he worked the Jeep through its gears.

I locked the M2 on its pintle again and knelt beside him, grimacing at the fresh pain shooting up my backside.

'Call it,' I grumbled once I was next to him.

'We need to get behind that tank hunter. Their armour is paper thin at the rear, glorified car doors. That fifty should be enough to cut through.'

'Uh-huh,' I nodded. 'Then what?'

'You'll see.'

The tyres of the Jeep screamed as Bill turned another left, bringing us back into the courtyard once more. The flattened Jeep laid almost at its centre, while the anti-aircraft cannons laid dormant and in wait. It was a shame they were all twenty millimetres; even they would be too small to even scratch the Tiger's armour.

I stood up behind the M2 again and let its weight come back under my control. My heart was in my throat – it was bad enough racing into a wall of lead on the back of this Jeep, but to chase down armoured fighting vehicles and attack them with pea shooters was to the point of suicide. Nevertheless, Bill was a man you would follow until the end. Either his or mine.

As Bill eased the Jeep into the alley that the Marder had nosed out of, he let the speed wash off. He leant over the steering wheel as he tried to listen for the sound of either enemy vehicle. My mouth had gone dry, and my hands that clasped the spade grips of the fifty were filmed with sweat. As we came to the end of the alleyway, Bill stopped the Jeep short and left to cover the rest of the distance on foot. He snuck up to the edge of the brick wall and leant his head out and looked both ways. Left then right, where he paused and considered for a second.

After a moment, he ran back to the Jeep. With an outstretched finger, he raised his eyebrows at the M2. 'Ready?'

I nodded and unlocked the pintle. Without a word, he leapt into the driver's seat. We roared forward into the intersection and turned right.

It didn't take long for me to understand the situation at hand. Once we had passed the Marder, its crew had taken a right turn, to head down to where the Tiger had crushed the building. The Tiger crew had moved forward, unperturbed by the debris on its hull, and had completed another right turn to take them back to the courtyard. As we raced up behind the Marder, the tail pipes and hot jets of the Tiger's exhaust vanished down the side street.

'Now!' Carrera screamed at me as the back end of the Marder loomed a hundred feet in front of us. I lined up the barrel of Ma Deuce on the Marder's back end, and just as I squeezed the fire control, I saw a German helmeted head raise up to look at us over the thin, rear armour. Again, Ma Deuce spoke that day, in short, controlled bursts at first so that I could ensure that my shots were hitting home. But as Bill drew us closer, I gave it everything that I had.

Sparks flew from the back end of the Marder, and some shots visibly ricocheted off the steel plate. But more went through. I watched as one man tried to jump out of the death trap and over the side of the armour skirt, but I cut him down before he was able, and left a good part of him running down the side of the tank hunter.

Bill locked up the brakes as we neared, and threw himself out of the Jeep. 'Hurry, we don't have much time!' he screamed as he leapt for the rear doors of the Panzer jaeger. I leapt off the Jeep to follow him, and each step that brought me closer to my target, also brought me closer to the carnage of what I had done. The rear barn doors of that machine were cut into Swiss cheese. Big, half-inch holes peppered the entire rear section of that machine. The holes that were lower to the floor were filled with the blood of the crew, which oozed out and down the rear of the machine's hull. Carrera threw open the doors and leapt up into the mess. I opened my mouth and quickly shut it again, against the vomit that wanted to surge forward and out.

'Get up here!' Carrera screamed at me as he tossed a portion of a German soldier out of the open barn doors behind him.

With a trembling hand, I grasped the hand rail and hoisted myself up. The sound my foot made when I stepped into the back of the machine was the same as I remembered as a child when I ran through a puddle. The floor of the machine was ankle deep in blood. The carnage of the M2 was horrific. Having nowhere to go, the bullets broke through the weak armour at the rear and were contained within the cage that they broke into. The men were torn apart by the spalling effect the ammunition had. It was abhorrent.

Carrera bent down and seized the remains of a man that was slumped against the main gun's elevation controls. As he pulled him away, only parts of him came out in his hands.

'Ah, fuckin' Christ,' Bill groaned as he resorted to just dragging what he could away from the gun controls. He stepped over the rest and looked down the sights. 'Get ready!'

I moved to the left side of the gun, almost falling as I gingerly stepped on one of the crew. I looked up over the armour as I heard an engine revving hard before us. It was the Tiger; the commander had heard the racket of the fifty calibre and had reversed the monstrous fighting machine back into the intersection. As I looked over, it came to a halt and the turret began to swing toward us.

'I'll handle the fire controls,' Bill yelled, 'you just be ready to jam another shell in when I shoot'.

I looked down and saw a rack of shells next to my left leg. I bent down and picked one up and it slipped out of my hands. It clanged against the armour, the blood that lined its casing shining in the low light. As I retrieved the shell, I looked up over the armour once more, and began to panic at how quick the Tiger's turret was coming about.

'Hurry u–' I got cut off when the Marder's main gun erupted right next to me. The concussion made me almost jump out of the tank. A line of white fire shot the sixty yards from the muzzle to the Tiger's turret, where the shot glanced and sailed off into the horizon. 'Holy fuck!' I screamed as the turret stopped.

'Load!' Carrera screamed as he began to adjust on the wheel. I stepped back and slammed the shell as hard as I could into the rear of the breech and felt my hand get pushed to the side as the breech snapped shut.

I opened my mouth to comment, but no sooner had the breech snapped shut had Bill pushed me to the side. I fell when he did and banged my head on the side armour so hard that I thought we had been hit. I looked up at Bill, but no sooner had I opened my mouth, the Marder's main gun fired and recoiled three feet back into the fighting compartment. If I had stayed where I was and Bill had fired, it would have caved my chest in. I leapt to my feet and seized another shell. I rammed it home and moved forward so that I could peer over the frontal armour once more. Our second shot had hit the Tiger on the side armour, above the road wheels. There was a hole there. A glowing hole. Bill fired again and another hole appeared about a foot to the right. The Tiger's cupola swung open and I could already see fire coming out of the man-sized hole.

The same commander became visible, but his flesh was black. I reached down to see if there was any sort of sidearm that I could use to put the man down, but a hand fell on my shoulder. I turned and looked at Bill.

'Leave him, son.' In his eyes were the dead from the road, the ones that were chewed up by the Messerschmitts. The boys that didn't make it out of the gliders; the GIs that fell in the trenches of Northern Ireland. 'Leave him be.'

I turned back and watched as the German officer tried to pull himself out of the burning tank, as inside rounds started to detonate from the heat. He lifted his head to the sky, and as he opened his blackened mouth, his skin split from the pressure and blood and pus ran down the corners of his lips. He screamed as he slowly vanished back inside the burning tank, the war machine so prestigious that it acted as his tomb.

5

The smell of burning fuel, steel and flesh filled the air along with the sounds of the crackling fire and detonation as eighty-eight-millimetre shells cooked off inside the steel coffin. Oddly enough, the sounds reminded me of popcorn. A strange vision swept through my brain of miniature shells, the same as what we just used to kill the monster, rolling around in a frying pan soaking up the heat. Slowly but surely, they would pop, just ones and twos at the beginning, then large clumps all letting go as if encouraged to do so by their neighbours. But when they popped, they didn't leave behind a fluffy centre, they left the limbs and rotting torsos of American GIs. The heads separated from the shoulders, their eyes long plucked by the carrion that waited to feed after every battle. Vacant of life, their souls stolen by the shells that had once remained. As if to feed the hungry machine that kept on churning, using, and consuming.

The steel of my helmet clanged against the armour of the Marder as I slumped down next to the gun. Smoke listed out of the open breech and waved in the still air before my face. Carrera stood on the other side of the gun, just staring at the burning Tiger, his mouth open as if in disbelief that we were still alive. We had killed the best machine that Hitler had to offer.

'Das Reich,' Carrera said softly as he continued to stare at the burning, big cat. I turned and shot him a questioning look. He never looked at me but must have understood that an explanation was required for what he said.

'The Wolfsangel painted on the front,' he pointed. 'That runic N symbol in the shield.' I continued to look up at him. I couldn't bring myself to look back at the burning officer. 'It's the sign of the 2nd SS Panzer Division. They call themselves Das Reich.' He spat over the edge of the Marder's armour, a subliminal action that almost made me smile. The inside of the Tank Hunter was covered in blood, shit, dirt, and unburnt gunpowder, yet still the man tried not to spit inside. 'I told you we weren't fighting Wehrmacht men,' he said finally with a grimace on his face.

The sound of the burning steel and the popcorn shells were suddenly drowned out by the familiar sound of aeroengines. Bill craned his head back to look at the sky as the P-38s made their presence known once more. I joined Bill, standing next to the breech of the Marder's gun as we looked up to watch the P-38s cut through the air and loop and turn, as if proclaiming our victory to the German foot soldiers that were still scattered throughout the village.

Behind us, the tell-tale sound of a Jeep's engine was heard whirring up the street. Both of us turned as Flash Perry and Little pulled up beside us. All of them looked as though they had copped hell. Little sat in the back of the Jeep, the M2 locked on its pintle. He cradled his arm while blood oozed from his legs from multiple wounds. Flash likewise had been hit in his hip and he grimaced as he brought the Jeep to a halt. Perry just sat there silently, his eyes unfocused. He seemed unwounded, but as we would come to understand, wounds can sink deeper than the flesh.

None of us said anything as we sat there and looked over each other and assessed what hell each of us had gone through. They looked over the Marder, the King Tiger and our battered Jeep, which idled roughly. Jackson was slumped in the passenger seat. We returned the gesture.

Flash was the first to break the silence. He gestured at Jackson, his jovial demeanour gone. 'Alive?'

'Yeah,' I said, 'he's alive.'

Flash nodded and looked back over the Tiger, with an expressionless look. 'Well, it's just us. Two lots of boys caught it on the way in and I gather either one of these two' – he gestured at the Tiger and the Marder – 'got the other boys in the square back there.'

'Yeah,' I said again. 'Watkins caught it on the road, and another in the paddock.'

Flash nodded. 'Yeah.'

I looked over at Little, who brooded silently in the passenger seat, his eyes downcast and vacant. Perry looked worse. All the colour had run out of him. Only God knew what they had gone through, but as God knew that, he also knew what Bill, Jackson and I had suffered as well. Each of us suffered together, alone.

A rattle of German sub-machine gun fire broke the silence, but it wasn't directed at us. I figured more than likely one of the foot soldiers had become sick of seeing American air power above his head and fired without any effect at the P-38s.

Bill, Flash and I looked around at the sound of the small arms fire, while Little remained fixed on his own personal battle.

'It's time to move,' Bill growled as he stepped to the rear of the Marder and dropped down. 'Flash, patch up Little as best as you can, then yourself. Let's go liberate some civilians.'

After all of that, I had forgotten about Bonnie. I was amazed I could. At the mention of the word civilians, I threw my hand to the pocket where her photo was, as if in panic that I had lost it in the commotion. I sighed when my fingers brushed the edges of her likeness. I didn't need to look at her, not while I was so covered in filth. And anyway, it was needless, as now that my mind was centred on her again, all I had to do was shut my eyes to see her face.

My thoughts raced, clouded by the image of her in my brain as we clambered back into the Jeep, strips of overcoat covering our wounds.

While the fabric did little to stem the pain, at least the sulphur would prevent infection. As we drove again through the streets of the village, I stood behind the M2 as Jackson's head lolled loosely on his neck with the movements of the Jeep. My eyes skittered over open windows, dark alleys, and door jambs, not sure whether I would see an angry SS man, intent on ending my life, or the flowing brown hair that hung around her shoulders, and the three small beauty spots that sat next to her eye.

It wasn't long before we saw the black smoke from the ship's stacks rising into the air. Bill surged the Jeep's engine at the sight, and we broke into a mad dash to reach our goal. I racked the fifty calibre. I had barely thirty rounds left to fire, but if I needed them, they were there. The planes would have to do their part.

Closer and closer we came, and the black cloud of the ships exhaust became larger and larger until I could almost smell it.

We rounded a corner, passed a brick factory that had seen fighting as one wall had collapsed and rubble littered the streets. A German half-track sat across the street, fifty yards before us in a makeshift barricade. As soon as we entered the street, the air was filled with machine gun fire. I squeezed the M2's firing paddles and the weapon thudded into motion, but I was torn from the handles by a heavy force that struck me high in the shoulder, throwing me backwards. I took one step, then another, and my foot fell into nothingness. As I fell backwards off the Jeep, I looked up in the air and saw one of the P-38s coming in hard, and I closed my eyes.

The Jeep hurtled off the road and I landed hard on my back in the rubble that littered the streets. I lost my breath but I wasn't sure if it was the fall or the bullet that had stolen it. None of it mattered as the ground shook under the force of four fifty calibres and the thunder of the aeroengines.

Thankfully, the pilot's aim was better than mine, as he didn't hit me. I had no idea if he had hit the Germans and I didn't even care – if I was alive that was all that mattered. I opened my mouth and tried to breathe. At first nothing came. Finally, my airways opened and I breathed exhaust and dust into my lungs, and it never tasted sweeter. I coughed and rolled over. Extreme pain burned in my shoulder, but still I moved. I looked up at the halftrack, and saw a few dead men lying nearby. I wasn't sure if they were all gone, but I was hopeful that the first strafing run would have been enough to make them turn on their heels and run.

The Jeep reversed up to me, and Bill looked down at me from the driver's seat. 'You ok, son?'

I didn't speak but I looked at him, as I held my hand to my shoulder. I nodded.

'Come on,' he said softly as he clambered out of the Jeep and helped me to my feet. 'We're almost there. Just another mile or so.'

I nodded and another cough escaped me, which sent rivulets of pain shooting down my chest, through my shoulder and up my back from the wound in my backside.

Bill patted me on the back. 'You'll be fine. Just a few more streets.'

He wasn't wrong. Resistance was minimal the rest of the way. Most of the SS men seemed uncommitted to stopping us. Some barricades were even abandoned. I understood why when we finally reached the pier. Flash had rejoined us at this stage and the six of us sat in our Jeeps, exhausted and half dead as we watched the ship sail away.

Tears ran down my face as I watched the women and the men rush to the back of the boat, screaming and reaching out for us as we pulled up to the pier. There were SS men there too, but they didn't even try to calm the people or hold them back from the rail; they just stood and watched as our Jeeps came to a defeated halt.

One man leapt from the railing; we watched his descent, which was more of a fall than a dive, as did the Germans. He hit the water and as he rose and began to swim towards us, machine gun fire erupted from the rear deck of the ship. The water around the man churned white and we had to duck our heads for the sheer number of ricochets that hurtled our way. Eventually, after a few short bursts, the bullets found the man and soon, the water became calm again, no longer disturbed by the rippling bullets nor the thrashing swimmer.

It was some distance between us and the ship, so it was difficult to make out people's faces. I scanned each of them, trying to find her as I held the photograph in my hand. I'm not sure why, as if from the distance she would see it and know what it was and call out to me, to say 'hey, that's me. How did you get that?' But it never happened; we were too late. Two Jeeps remained out of ten, six people out of thirty. And we were too late.

Then the water was churned up once more as the sound of eight fifty calibres cut through the din and the aeroengines of both P-38s screamed as the planes cut down through the sky. I screamed as fifty calibre rounds swept the deck and even from this distance, I saw the red mist lift from the crowd of civilians. I held my hands to my face as the horror of what I just witnessed sunk in. Carrera was on the radio instantly, screaming through the receiver for them to pull off, but one run was bad enough.

The ship trudged along, unperturbed by the fifty-calibre strafing run, and sure, a fifty calibre was nothing to a ship, but to the people standing on the ship it was devastating. As Carrera continued to talk to the pilots, I watched as the Germans began to throw the dead and the mortally wounded from the back of the ship. One after the other.

'Pull off, the ship is full of civilians,' he said as they threw another. 'Let them go boys. We were too late.'

PART FOUR

The Ruhr Region – Germany

November 5th 1945

1

The tracks of the halftrack rattled beneath me, just a single vehicle in a line of hundreds. And I was just a single man, one amongst thousands and thousands that made Omar Bradley's push to the east. I was a man that had seen four seasons of war now. Most of those from a hospital bed. I found it somewhat fitting that I had entered the war in autumn, and now as the soles of our boots stepped finally into the Fatherland, those days of summer and rest were long behind me now. I couldn't tell if it was the hint of the oncoming winter or all those that we had left behind, that had sent the chills running up my spine.

The men that surrounded me chatted to themselves. Jackson spoke to Perry, and Carrera – a lieutenant now – spoke to command on the radio that was mounted behind the driver. Flash and Little joked and laughed with the replacements of replacements. Endless worlds that flowed out like water out of an empty cup. They carried no meaning as they drifted away across the Westerlies, carrying my hopes and dreams along with them.

Trees haunted the sides of the road, their limbs stretched out in silent salutes to the men that were invading their land. I let my head rest against the lightly armoured side of the halftrack and felt the vibration of the churning tracks run down my spine. The things that these trees would have seen. The men of the Wehrmacht and the Waffen SS, proud and stalwart as they marched by, five years before. Then the same men, still strong, but fewer, as they came back the other way, not yet defeated but still fighting and closer to home. Now us, the men that had been sent halfway across the globe to destroy the Third Reich, to crush the Nazi Regime and to liberate the people it had conquered.

I laughed to myself at those words, as they ran through my mind. *Liberation.* Indeed, we had liberated England, we had thrown them out, and they had made us pay for every inch of occupied land that we took. But in the end, I personally never liberated a soul. Sure, some people were found in the cellars of pubs, or hidden in the attics. Cowering, even afraid to show themselves to us, for the fear… for the fear of what? We still do not know.

I remember that day, as we all sat there exhausted on the Jeeps that had carried us through to Bristol. The shell casings that swallowed our blood as it pooled in the footwells. While the people we had come to liberate sailed away under the flag of the imperial eagle, as it clutched the swastika in its talons. I can only remember how fitting that flag seemed to be, as if the eagle had come and stolen the litter from the nest, carrying its prey away from us, and we were like field mice watching as it whisked itself out of our grasp.

We missed the final assault on the German positions, all five of us that remained. All but Perry required surgery to right the wrongs the SS small arms fire had inflicted on our bodies. We may have missed the fighting, but we all suffered the retaliatory fire of the Vengeance series weapons. The V1s that warbled their way through air, each one sounding like an armada of Lancasters. The pulse jet warble that rattled not only the windows within their frames, but the souls of all the men that laid helpless in their beds, waiting for the cut off. Then it would come – the sound of the jet engine would cut, starved of fuel, its supply calculated meticulously to allow the flying bomb to fall at precisely the right time. Once it cut, all you could do was close your eyes and wait in silence to find out if it was your turn to eat the ash.

The V series rockets fell in their thousands across England as the US and the Canadians, and now the first elements of the Australians who were no longer in a fight for their lives against the Japanese, began to ready themselves for a fight for France.

I have said it before: the Nazi Germany that we fought in our time-line was not the same misled, disintegrating force that the soldiers of your time fought. In your time, the men fought bravely, bolstered by the love of their Führer and of their homeland. The men we fought were adamant for new lands. Desperate, even. Once obtained, they fought to the death to hold them, even though it wasn't a land that was of a strategic importance, apart from being a place to live.

'Lebensraum' was a word that was thrown about often. Living space. This, we thought, had to be the reason why they fought so hard for these places. At first when we looked at the clearing of the population of England, it made sense. For the German race to spread, room needed to be created. But that all went out the window when Paris was liberated. One of the things that sat in the minds of the men that I served with as we marched on Paris, was not the Eiffel Tower, but the French women who would welcome us with open arms, open mouths, and most importantly, open legs. I recall that we had a similar discussion on the road to Bristol, but the sight that we faced in France was worse.

It was empty. I cannot say it any clearer. No one was left. Not an old man in a bed, not a child hiding under one. No family hiding in the cellar, no couple and their baby lurking in the catacombs. They were all gone.

Every house had been searched. There was evidence of this no matter where the eyes were turned. Doors had been torn off their hinges, great gouges cut into ceilings to expose any stowaways. Beds were overturned, floorboards torn up. In every damned house. And not one German set-tler. You wouldn't do this to every building if your own people were settled there. You would only go to this extent if you needed to find people, and from everything I could see, they had succeeded excep-tionally well. First Carentan, then Cherbourg, Saint-Lo, and eventually

Paris itself. Not a single soul did I liberate. There were no women, or even men for that matter, waving flags as our Shermans and halftracks rolled down the streets. No one to help us mourn for the men slain. We were liberating a ghost town, and it took the biggest toll on our morale.

Why were we sacrificing ourselves to save people that didn't even seem to exist?

But that was where we were wrong; they did exist. I knew that they did. She did. There was no way they took her from her home, all this way for nothing. She had to be alive. She was alive, and I was going to find her, no matter what it took.

To be truthful, it wasn't just me that drove this, it wasn't just her photo that gave me the drive to continue. It was the direction from the top brass itself. Even they weren't blind enough to not see what was happening. All the extra resources that had been prepared to feed a city of starving people and not a single ration was required. That was enough to raise some eyebrows.

Soon it became military doctrine that it was the air force's job to scout out prisoner-of-war camps, labour camps or anything to do with manufacturing. Hell, if there were people there that didn't fit the Wehrmacht bill, they wanted to know. Then it was our job to go and get them. Facility after facility we took. One such was an underground bunker that looked to be the launching pads for the V1 series rockets. But by the time our halftracks ground to a halt nearby, the place was deserted.

Fencing and barbed wire surrounded every train station, to the point that the transport hubs looked as though they were designed to cart cattle rather than human beings. Each time, we were too slow. In the meantime, the clash between our main front line and the Germans saw different tactics being played.

The Germans didn't want to smash our lines, it was as though each day they tried to engineer different circumstances that would allow them to take prisoners. One such example I heard of was a raid led by a man named Otto Skorzeny, an SS officer who was only given the jobs that no one else wanted. He dressed himself as a US Major and waltzed close to an American camp one night in March. He managed to get himself alone with a young private, whom he convinced that he was a defector of the Third Reich and now serving in the United States Army. The private helped him round up forty men whom were excited by the story, which entailed German Intelligence of an outpost nearby.

Quick and quiet was what they needed to be. Skorzeny led them into an ambush where not a single shot was fired. All men were captured, never to be seen again. The only word, if any, were found in the letters that were written to loved ones. Piles upon piles of them, amongst other personal items. Letters along a trail that led nowhere. A trail, which we followed aimlessly through the chaos.

Yet, as Omar Bradley's war machine began to pick up speed and our boys gained the strength of countless supply shipments and the backing of entire armoured divisions, we began to catch up. Although powerful and well supplied, the German forces couldn't withstand millions of men pushing on their boundaries. Once they started moving backwards, it wasn't easy for them to stop. And finally, it looked as though we were apt to have our first chance at true liberation.

The pitch of the halftrack's engine changed as we pulled away from the convoy. Flash's head peaked over the side armour as we made a left turn, while the main fighting force rolled on to Oberhausen.

'Hey, Lieutenant,' Jackson wailed above the din of the convoy. The scar on his cheek had turned his smirk into a snarl. 'What gives? Why we pulling out?'

Carrera was standing behind the driver, leaving his body woefully exposed as he ran his eyes over a letter that he held in his hands. It made me uneasy to see him standing like that. We couldn't be invincible, at least not forever. I turned my head to watch the progress of the convoy behind us and saw that another halftrack had followed us.

'They've found something,' I said to myself as I turned back to Carrera.

Bill gave the letter a final look, before he folded it neatly and stowed it away. He raised his eyes to the sky. What looked to be a hundred B17 Liberators were flying in boxed groups, the sounds of their aeroengines only now just washing over us, drowning out the rattle of the halftrack's running gear. P-51 Mustangs and the oversized fighters, P-47 Thunderbolts, gracefully danced in between the bomber groups, as if taunting any would-be attacker to try their luck.

'Presents to Berlin,' one of the replacements called out and the others laughed.

'Addressed to 147 Kiss My Ass Road, Courtesy Adolf Hitler,' another crowed in a Boston accent.

'No return address.' Flash laughed.

'It's beyond that now.' The Boston replacement laughed. He was a squat fellow, broad shouldered and barrel chested. His hair was cut close to his head, and he was unshaven, which was apt to get him his ass kicked by Bill if he wasn't careful. His name was Robert Biancini, typical Italian of that city. Loud and outspoken. 'With what we got? They ain't got a chance in hell at hitting back at us with those guys' – he pointed back at the column of vehicles – 'and our boys in the air.' He pointed up to the flying fortresses at this point and everyone's eyes followed. As he spoke, another sound occurred. One that reminded me somewhat of the warbling roar of the V1 series, except this was no roar, but a shriek.

Six streaks of smoke shot out from nowhere and slammed into the backs of B-17s as they rolled slowly across the sky. Three of them exploded mid-air, sending shrapnel, engine components, and the shockwave from their entire payload into the other Liberators from their box section.

More planes went down, either smoking or on fire from the explosions. Then cannon fire was heard and the P-51s banked hard to come about, but it was too late. Three black streaks shot through the formation of planes and continued their path of flight.

'Holy shit!' I shouted as I watched the path of the bombers falling through the skies. The bombers exploded upon impact, somewhere out of sight.

'See that?!' Bill shouted as he turned back to his men. A scowl was spread across his face as he pointed vigorously at the scene of the action.

'The minute you under estimate your enemy is the minute they will prove you wrong.'

Biancini put his head down in shame, which drew Carrera's anger.

'Look at them!' he bellowed.

Biancini raised his eyes to Bill's – they were red and almost bursting from the tears that had welled, I imagined from his shame. But he didn't say a word, and his eyes left Bill's to watch the dog fight, where outclassed American P-51s and P-47s tried to keep up with the blisteringly fast ME 262 Jet fighters. We watched in silence while the fight remained above us, but it wasn't long before the canopy of the forest that we drove through cut the sight from our eyes.

With the events of the aero battle gone from our eyes but not our ears, Bill lowered his gaze to us again. He swayed at the front of the halftrack's cargo area, one hand still in the pocket where he had placed the letter. Each of us just stared back in silence, waiting for him to answer the original question, 'why are we here?'

'Early elements of that bombing run radioed in to us,' Bill said as the halftrack ambled up a small rock step. 'Looks to be a prisoner of war camp a few miles north of here. A Kampfgruppe of heavy Panzers and infantry guarding it. No doubt our friends from the Waffen SS.' He looked at me when he said that.

'What are we going to do against tanks?' one of the replacements, Franco, asked. 'We haven't even got bazookas.'

Bills eyes rested on him. 'If you'd shut up, you'd know by now.' He stared until Franco broke his eye contact. Carrera continued to stare at him for five more seconds, then resumed. 'There's a half shot to shit armoured division that's going to meet us there; most of their tanks are gone, but they've managed to reappropriate some German armour, so we have the rare opportunity to hit them back with the same tools they've used to hammer us.'

The GIs all cheered at that.

'Fuckin aye!' the youngest, Phillips, crowed as a cigarette hung out the side of his mouth.

'We will meet up with the armour two miles out, then we will draw the plan and launch the attack before dawn.'

Everyone acknowledged.

'Get used to standing by German armour boys, because it's going to be our job to support them.'

That was an interesting thought to be left with. I remember the sight of the King Tiger, as it brewed up. The sheer size of the machine, the width of it more so than the height. The length of its barrel, its high-velocity eighty-eight, and the sound of its monstrous engine as it roared in the square. I shuddered at the thought of it. US armour was 'GI issue'; it did the job and did it well. German armour was almost like the Stuka, built in a way that the very idea of the machine was enough to strike fear in the enemy. The Tiger did that for me. I have no idea what seeing their own armour turned on them would do to the Germans, but soon enough I would find out.

It took us three hours to get to the rendezvous location. The sun had finally set, and the crew took a well-deserved rest from the ambling shunting motions of the halftrack. I lay on the ground some thirty feet away from the halftrack, next to a line of bushes. The idea was so that if any German decided to succumb to their curiosity and look at what an American halftrack was doing miles away from the line of advance, I would be safe.

2

I remember the dream I had that night. Perhaps because it was the first of many times I'd had one of those dreams. They varied over the years. The time, the place, the people I was with. But two things always remained the same: she was there, and something always went wrong. I have a very good reason to remember the exact details of this dream – it was because all the situations that occurred in the dreams to follow hadn't happened yet, so this, this terrible memory, had to be the first.

The bristling walls of the WACO glider surrounded me. Presumably, I was on the way to England, but I suppose none of that really mattered. The white knuckles of my hand shone in the darkness as I grasped the stock of my M1 while it rattled against my helmet, as I sat there in a prayer that I had never known.

'He that dwelleth in the place of the most High shall abide under the shadow of the Almighty.' The prayer escaped my lips and it felt at home there amongst the rest.

I would like to say it was my brothers that sat around me, and really, they were, at one point. But these things that lined the edges of the WACO's frame were corpses. Their rotten clothes hung off their wasted bodies in sheets of rags. Bones poked through the wasted flesh like fresh mountain peaks bursting through the crust of the earth. Rust speckled their helmets, and the whole cabin stunk like the dirt they had now been buried in and over the rushing air that flowed around the WACO's frame. Single dog tags clinked noisy around their wasted necks.

'He is my refuge and my fortress: my God, in him will I trust.'

Skinner's upper torso sat to my left. One of the smaller men was made even smaller by the lack of the lower half of his body. He clutched his Thompson to his chest. No other features of his face remained, just the gaunt skull with flesh pressed over it. I looked at the man that sat across from me; his helmet had fallen over his eyes and I could hear tendons cracking as his jaw moved but no other sound escaped it.

My voice started to quiver as I continued, but even I knew that the sight had shaken me as the words began to falter on my lips. 'Thou shalt not be afraid for the terror by night, nor for the arrow that flieth by day.'

Something clapped on my shoulder and I turned to see the hand of a skeleton. The white fingertips clenched and dug into my shoulder, pressing harder and harder as my mouth opened and I tried to scream. Only one eye remained in Clark's head, the other gone, lost somewhere in the chaos of the beach in Northern Ireland. I couldn't tell if he was grinning at me or if it was just the way the flesh had pulled back from his mouth in its rot and decay, and the most horrible thing was that the sand that had rested on his lips was still there. As he smiled at me, sand that was wet with the decay from his body fell and I felt it tumble across the back of my hand. The one remaining eye swivelled loosely in its socket and bore into me as a beetle crawled out of the other socket.

Clark's mouth opened and he spoke in a dry, crackling voice. 'Nor the pestilence that walketh in darkness, nor the destruction that wasteth at noonday.'

I pulled myself away from his grasp and stood. I backed up away from Clark but was stopped when the man that had sat across from me reached out and clutched at my leg. As he lifted his helmeted head, I saw that most of the man's chest was gone. Nothing remained but tattered rags and shards of bone.

It was Leach, and in a voice that was remnant of something demonic, he crackled, 'A thousand shall fall at thy side, ten thousand at thy right hand. But it shall not come nigh thee.'

Finally, I screamed and battered Leach's hand away. As I struck his arm, the entire limb came out of the socket of his shoulder and clattered to the ground. I screamed as I turned and I screamed as the rest of the men, all of them fallen brothers in arms, tried to drag me down with them. The WACO began to shudder. The sky outside turned red with the fires of hell and even below out in the distance I could see that the ground was burning. A world in flames. A world in flames and nothing could ever live there again. I stood there horrified at what I was seeing, and as fleshless fingers clutched at my body and the smell of rot and death overcame me, I saw that there were two figures in the cockpit. Full figures, full of life.

As the force that shook the WACO tripled in its ferocity, one of them turned and looked at me. Bonnie. The fires of the world glittered in her eyes and her lips matched the redness of the earth. She smiled softly at me, as over her shoulder I saw the C-47 that was towing us burst into flames, and the body yaw upwards in a slow death roll as it hurtled toward us.

I tried to shout; I tried to scream again or bring my hands up before my eyes. But I did nothing. I stood there as the WACO shuddered around me, and I noticed the three small beauty spots by her left eye.

Just before the flaming hull of the C-47 crashed through the cockpit, she said to me almost inaudibly. 'Only with thine eyes shalt thou behold and see the reward of the wicked.'

There was something missing, and it was never spoken. The final words of the prayer that meant everything. But she was gone, consumed by the fires and the crushed steel.

The trembling became unbearable and the final phrase that escaped my mind before I was torn from the dream was the single thing that I clung to in that moment: 'He shall call upon me, and I will answer him.'

*

I burst out of the depths of sleep and sat up breathing heavily. But something was wrong. The clawing hands and fires of hell were gone, but the trembling sensation that had shaken me to my bones was still there, as was something else. At first I thought it was just the fear that lived inside of me, awoken by the dream that made me shake, but it wasn't that at all. The world seemed to rattle around me and the ground shook beneath my fingers. I could hear the clanking of steel tracks as the bushes started to give way before me, and in the darkness something massive trundled towards me.

Somewhere deep inside of me, there was a voice. Something small and timid, that wanted me to stay still and allow the rolling steel to plunge me into the depths. To crush the life out of me; the world had become too much to bear.

More of the brush subsided, offering no resistance to the monster that crushed its way forward. Then I remembered her and the reason why I was pushing on through all this misery, and I leapt to my feet and scrambled out of the way.

The beast that came forward was enormous. Larger and more imposing than any American tank I had ever seen. Its flat armoured plate screamed absolute brute force and the length of its main gun meant that the muzzle brake that sat at the end of its long barrel was already behind me. Mud flew up from its ultra-wide tracks as the earth churned beneath them, and the spare tracks that were stowed to the front lower section of the armour shot out forward, like the teeth of a tiger.

The German Tiger came to a halt just before me, and although I recalled that Bill Carrera had said that we would be using captured German armour, I was instilled with fear. I reached down and seized my M1. It came to my shoulder like an old friend and I shrieked to my brothers in arms that we were not alone.

A hand fell on my shoulder and I couldn't help but think of those white bones that had pressed into my flesh in my dream only moments before, and I screamed and fired. The round struck the flat plate of the Tiger and the world was filled with the roar of the M1 and whizzing bur as the round sailed harmlessly off the heavy armour and into the distance.

The M1's barrel was reefed out of my hands, while I was spun with force. I expected to see the rotten face of Clark, the beetle that worked its way into his eye cavity, the horror. But what I saw was the angry face of Bill Carrera.

He threw the M1 to the ground and cocked his arm to strike me. I stood there, surprised, one for the fact that it was Bill before me and two for the rage that was evident on his face. But he held himself there, poised to lay me down.

Finally his arm fell to his side as he grumbled, 'You need to pull yourself together if we're going to get through this'.

He stared at me for some time, before he turned to the Tiger as the commander's cupola swung open and a man clambered out.

'Jesus Christ!' the American said as his head appeared above the tank. He yelled to be heard over the tank's massive petrol engine. 'Thanks for the welcome, asshole!' He directed his anger at me and rightfully so.

I didn't say anything as Carrera turned his back to me and moved to the side of the Tiger to talk to the commander. My attention returned to the tank as another hatch opened on the left-hand side. The engine stopped and everyone was able to lower the tone of their voice as the Maybach finally ceased its purring. Another man emerged from the hull before the turret and stretched his back as he stood above me.

The man was of average height. Grease and oil stained his clothes while his white flesh stood out under a black smear that spread itself across his face. He looked down at me and smiled wearily before he leapt down and stood beside me.

'They may be big on the outside but there ain't a whole heap of room for the driver. I'll give you the mail.' He laughed as he held his hand out. 'Wright,' he said as he grinned lopsidedly.

I shook his hand and introduced myself. 'How did you come to be the driver of this?'

'We captured this big cat at Bastogne. Hell, I don't know if they had run out of ammo or fuel. Both most likely, but they must have fought like screaming banshees – the old girl's got some scars.'

He pointed a few out to me, some I had looked right at and never even noticed. Pock marks like a teenager's acne, divots in the metal where Sherman 75mm shells had simply bounced off. There was a tremendous scar down the right-hand side of the hull, which Wright proudly told me was from an American 105mm field gun that had been turned on the monster in hopes to stop it, but seemingly only the lack of supplies had stopped this Tiger.

'I know she's obsolete, but I've got a tender spot for her,' he said, sighing. 'There was two others, but I see why they replaced them. We've had a hell of a time keeping her running. We had two others in worse shape, and they barely made it fifty miles before they came to a grinding halt. But if it wasn't for them, and the parts we salvaged from them, we wouldn't have this old girl,' he said as he patted the heavy armour affectionately.

The Tiger I was an imposing monster. The King Tiger that we had faced in Bristol was its replacement and even now it was a relic. The Germans had standardised their tank production and we had started to see the even larger, more fearsome creations come forward, like the dreaded MKVIII Maus.

'So why are you the driver?'

'They picked us for various reasons,' he sighed as he leant on the front end. 'I was a truck driver back home. Sparks over there' – he gestured to the commander – 'commanded Shermans through England and France, plus he speaks fluent German as well, so maybe they thought it was fitting.'

As he said this, Sparks clambered down the front of the tank while two other tank men, presumably the gunner and the loader, started to hand down bundles of something to infantrymen that had started to gather around the tank.

Carrera walked back around to the front to join myself and the driver as Sparks dropped down before me. I noticed for the first time that he dressed in the black of a Nazi Panzer officer with pink piping. White stood out from the corners of his collar, the SS runes emblazoned on the black. That, and a silver Death's Head skull, glinted madly. A Luger was strapped to his hip as well as a beautiful ornate dagger. He noticed me looking at him and he smiled.

'Was hältst du von mein Panzer?' He said it as if he was Heinrich Himmler himself.

I didn't say a word, having no idea what he said. Seconds passed and Sparks smiled widely as he laughed and slapped my shoulder, and the Bavarian accent was replaced by a New York twang. 'Just kidding with you, I'm dressed this way for a reason.'

Carrera barked at Little, Perry, and Flash to join us. He ordered all of us to help remove some crates that had been stacked down the centre of the rear deck of the Tiger. We followed orders as Wright and the rest of the tank crew had some chow, while Carrera and Sparks discussed their plan. Both crates were heavy; we heard metal clank within and the audible rattle of ammunition.

Curious, we broke open one of the crates while some of the other infantrymen tore open the bundles that had been passed down before. What stood before us were the uniforms, helmets, and weaponry of a Waffen SS Kampfgruppe. The new Sturm rifles looked almost like something depicted in a fantasy novel: short with a long magazine and a pistol grip. They were stacked high in the crate, mixed with the common Mauser rifles and a few Schmeisser sub-machine guns.

Little held up one of the great coats before him – it looked like a child's blanket in comparison to the size of the man. 'Do they make them in men's sizes?' he asked and guffawed at his own humour.

Flash was wearing one of the German helmets and had rubbed dirt above his top lip in a poor imitation of Hitler. 'Ahh but this one' – he slapped Little on the back – 'will be great for pulling the wagons when we have to eat the horses.' Some of the men laughed at this.

'We aren't here to play dress ups,' Carrera barked as he and Sparks ventured over to the commotion. 'You're looking at your new uniforms.'

There was some silence at this. I believe that some of the men considered that we were being asked to defect, but Bill continued, 'Replace your M1s with the rifles in the crates. Use the guns that are closest to what you use now. Cody, Jackson, I want you two on the new battle rifles. Gordon, Perry, on the sub-machine guns. The rest of you on the bolt actions.'

'And why are we doing this?' Gordon asked.

I could see anger swelling in Carrera again. Over the last few months his temper had been running thin. 'If you would let me talk, you would find out,' he snarled through gritted teeth. A few seconds of silence passed and he continued, 'The camp is only a few miles away. We are aware of heavy tanks defending the camp. HQ doesn't want to risk collateral damage by sending in the air force to deal with them, and there is nothing we have on hand to take them out, apart from this.' He pointed to the Tiger.

Sparks took over, walking straight-backed with his hands clasped together behind him. He walked around us as he spoke. 'The new German armour is much better than ours, you know this. The eighty-eight on this Tiger is powerful, but we will need to fire at almost point-blank range if we hope to kill a MKVIII Maus, if there is one there.'

'Do we know what we are going up against here?'

'We know that there are heavy tanks,' Carrera said.

'But not which ones exactly.' Sparks smiled. 'If there is a MKVIII, we will know once we get closer. They are over a hundred tonnes; they will be different to anything you have ever seen before and they will outclass us by far.'

'So, we need to dress up as Krauts so that–' Little started.

'So that we can fit in, get right up to their heavy tanks and fire on them when they don't expect it,' Sparks finished for him. 'Hopefully there will be enough of a commotion that we can knock out all their tanks before we are killed, and then we can move on to liberate the camp.'

'I don't like the sound of this,' Flash said. For a man that was normally jovial, he looked dark and concerned. 'What support do we have?'

'None,' Carrera said coldly.

'What plan do we have if they work out we're not German?'

'None,' he said again.

'This is why you all need to let me do the talking,' Sparks said coolly. 'Stay behind the tank, that's where you should be. When we stop, come to the sides, but take it easy and be ready.'

'I still don't like the sound of this,' Gordon repeated.

'Do us all a favour,' Carrera grunted, 'get into character and shut your mouth'.

We all took that advice, changed uniform, and prepared for what was to come.

3

The early morning was grim, everything felt surreal. The clothes that touched my flesh, the helmet that weighed down upon my head, even the feel of the Sturmgewehr in my hands. None of it seemed right. The world seemed to have taken some odd upside-down twist and I wasn't sure if it was the way I was dressed, or the dread of what lay ahead. Even her photo pressed to my chest inside my Waffen SS tunic was not enough to dispel the disquiet that had settled within my bones.

The earth itself trembled in fear as the Tiger churned forward. An unrelenting rattle of power and might filled the air as if to hold contention with the thick fumes that bellowed from its exhaust. Mud flew into the air to my right, flicked up by the tracks as they raced around the numerous road wheels and into the past like the lives of those that had haunted me in my dreams. Thunder cracked overhead as a line of lightning etched its way downward into the distance.

'The gods are angry,' Flash said timidly, but still loud enough to be heard above the din of the Tiger.

'Gods?' Perry asked him. 'What sort of Pagan are you?'

Flash smiled below the brim of his Stahlhelm. 'I'm no Pagan.'

'Well, if you say gods, then you can't–'

'He's a philosopher,' I said, cutting the young man off.

Flash laughed at this. 'I wouldn't even say I'm that.' He looked to Perry and considered. 'You weren't there by the fire outside of Bristol, were you?'

Flash was right, Perry wasn't. He had joined us for that mission, but not before. So, he wasn't privy to the conversation that we had about the gods. Perry reminded us all of this and then continued his questioning. 'Are you telling me that you bunch of hard men sat around the fire one night, contemplating the Almighty?' He laughed as he said it.

'We didn't contemplate God, but rather he who stands against him,' Flash replied solemnly.

'If God be for us, then who be against us?' Jackson muttered. 'Or something like that anyway.'

'Yeah,' Flash said. 'Something like that.'

'But god's hand is in everything,' Perry said, becoming more serious in his tone.

'In everything?' I asked. 'So, He's in the steel of that Tiger, the FLAK that tore us to shreds in that square? In the screaming Mimi's that still freak the shit out of me?'

'No, not those,' he said defensively.

'But you said everything.' I was getting upset, but it was too late for me to stop now. 'In the hands of those fucking bastards that dragged everyone from their homes, and sent them to this place? In the deaths of all our men?'

'I worship that God.' Perry said.

'Cody, enough,' Jackson said.

'No, it's not enough. I don't think he understands what he's saying, because if he does, he's an idiot.'

Perry flared up at this. 'So, I'm an idiot now? Is that it?'

'Yeah, sure you are.' I stopped walking, allowing the Tiger to move away from me.

'Do we have a problem?'

'Yeah, I think we do,' I said coldly as I let the Sturmgewehr fall to the ground. "Cause you're telling me that you worship a God that would allow all this shit to happen. Worse yet, you proudly say that his hand is in all of it, and you want to get upset with me when I call it out.' I pushed him. 'Then yeah, I think we got a fucking problem on our hands. Don't you?'

As if in an exact replication of his namesake, Flash was between us. A hand pressed on my chest as he pushed both of us apart.

'Hey, hey. Come now. We don't need this shit. Do we fellas?'

'I don't need–' I started.

'You don't need to keep talking,' Jackson said as he placed his hand on my shoulder.

Jackson, of all people, was against me in this. I finally started to think that I'd gone too far.

'I was just trying to say, that His hands are in us being here. Yeah, there's bad shit happening, but that's not Him. He's us, and we're Him.'

I spat on the ground.

'Hey, if you don't believe me then tell me what this says.' He turned and took four steps to the side of the road. He leant down and fought with something in the mud; swearing, he finally dragged up a post that had been pressed into the ground by some passing vehicle. Nailed to that post were two planks of timber, both cracked by the force of whatever had laid the post down, but still the words were legible, even through the darkness of the mud that splattered them. Nonetheless, Perry wiped his hand over the planks to ensure that I could read the words clearly:

MÜLHEIM AN DER RUHR

JUDENFREI

'Do you understand what this says?'

Those words had been plastered everywhere in France. Painted on the walls of empty streets, etched into crosses, and nailed to trees. Not the town name, just the last part. I didn't know what it meant, all I knew was that this place, this whole continent, seemed to be stripped of the one essential thing that gave it its name. The people. They were all gone, nothing remained. Not like in England, not a sick man to tell the story.

Not even a diary, from what I could tell.

'Jewish free.' Perry enunciated it slowly to ensure that I understood.

'You know what else it says?' Carrera's voice came from nowhere. We all turned and saw that the Tiger had come to a halt up ahead. Sparks was standing way above everyone, looking back at us impatiently. 'It says if you don't get your Yankee asses back behind that armour, then I get to kick your ass all the way to Berlin.'

'I don't see where it says that,' Flash said as he looked closer at the sign.

Carrera looked at him coldly.

'Sorry sir,' Flash said softly and shot us all a betrayed look as he walked past the lieutenant and back to the Tiger. We all followed suit and the squad fell into silence as we marched onward to Mülheim.

I don't know how long we walked in silence. I was still nursing my temper that had seemed to swell from nowhere and now lingered just below the surface; the others all seemed to contemplate the words that had been exchanged. It was the person I least expected that broke the silence.

'My mother always said that it was the devil's hand that was in everything, not God's,' the big man said as he trudged onward.

We all looked at him; none of us said anything. Perhaps we knew that he wasn't finished and we all gave him the time to find the words.

'Maybe it was because my old man beat her all the time. That drunk used to beat us kids too and laugh as he did it. Used to call me hoss, and say "I whip you like the hoss you are boy and don't you go crying to your mamma, cause then she'll get it too."'

Little straightened his back, as if in pride. 'I ran him out of town myself. I said to him that if I ever saw his drunk self again then I'd kill him, and he turned and ran like the coward he had always been. When I think of him, I think my mamma was right. It was the devil that was in that man, just like it's the devil that was in the words on that sign. I don't know if I believe that God's in us, but I know this isn't God's work and I damn well know that the devil exists, because I think I met him in that drunk old bastard.'

I nodded. I couldn't disagree with anything he said. To be honest, the big man echoed my sentiments exactly. If there had been any transcending presence in the last year or so of my life, it had been Satan. No matter how hard I tried to believe, no matter how hard I thought of all the prayers from childhood and the nights spent kneeling next to my bed with eyes pressed shut as I spoke to our Heavenly Father, I could draw no solace. Nor could I believe that those men that I saw in that dream were in His great halls, feasting at His grand banquet. They were rotten shadows of what they once were, left to decay in the pine boxes that they were laid in.

All the hopes, all the faith that I had, were gone. Nothing remained now but the constant swell of sorrow, anger, and disappointment. I hadn't saved her last time. I had failed her father, who still lay in his cot, rotting like the rest. With that final thought, I understood my position on this whole thing. If that's where these men laid, rotting, not living their absolution, then none of it was real. None of it ever was, and none of it ever could be. We were all just dirt in the end, we came from the earth and back to it we would go, just like some damned dog laying at the curb, its guts squashed out by the tyres of some old Buick.

'If the Krauts put up Jewish free signs everywhere, then why did they take everyone? Not just the Jews?' Perry asked, disturbing my train of thought and dispelling any musings of gods and their antis along with the rest.

It was a damned good question. Everyone had been taken by the damned Nazis, not even the old and infirmed remained any more. We even searched the cellars, the attics, every damned place had been stripped. Only Germans remained.

'You're right,' Flash said as he looked to the younger man. 'All of them.'

'Why didn't they say "foreigner free"? Or something else along those lines?' Jackson asked.

Flash shrugged. 'Maybe it just doesn't roll off the tongue the way that Judenfrei does. Who knows?'

'I suppose we can ask them when we see them,' I said as I saw the town just ahead.

'Cut the shit,' Carrera barked as he came up on us. 'Everyone into positions. Little, you take your damned shirt off.'

Little hesitated, then stripped down to his bare chest.

'Sorry to do this to you, son. But it needs to look real.' Carrera said with some remnant apparition of his old self before he shoved Little hard in the back, and sent the big man sprawling in the mud.

Little slid on his face, and slowly raised himself up. Sparks raised himself out of the Cupola of the steel monster before us, and threw down a length of rope. 'Tie him up. We aren't far now. We need to get through this town, then the camp is on the far side. Keep your mouths shut and good luck.'

We started to tie up Little, binding his hands behind his back as Sparks started to yell at us in German, bellowing at the top of his lungs. Single words stood out to me, like the all too familiar "Juden", in conjunction with "Amerikan". As Jackson and Perry pushed Little toward the front of the squad, I stepped out from behind the Tiger and saw that the town was coming alive.

The tank started to crawl forward. Sparks continued to spray what I could only imagine were orders down below to us before he faced the town and took a deep breath.

There was a checkpoint before us. Two SS soldiers stood somewhat relaxed at the barricade, looking out as the lights on the front of Tiger illuminated them in the darkness. The revs of the tank's motor slowed as we neared and I stepped to the edge of the Tiger's tracks to see what was happening.

One of the SS men had moved to the middle of the road and held his hand up in halt gesture. Sparks was yelling down to him as he waved his hands in furious motions.

'Christ,' I said to myself. Sparks was going to get us into trouble, why was he yelling at them? I looked out again and saw that the SS man didn't even bat an eye lid at the commotion raised by the supposed officer above him. He held his hand out in motion until the Tiger came to a halt. Sparks continued for a short while to hurl abuse down at the imposing force before him, then finally fell quiet.

I fell back behind the sheer bulk of the Tiger and listened to the muffled back and forth between Sparks and this man before us. It was hard to hear them with the rumble of the exhaust in my ears and the fact that the men were standing on the other side of sixty tonnes of steel. After some time, I heard something change in Spark's voice. He turned back and pointed down to us and I heard the word "Amerikan", and he started ranting all over again, hurling abuse down at the SS man, whom held the rank of Rottenführer.

Suddenly Sparks turned around and spoke in very clear, German-accented English. 'Hey, Amerikan. You better make yourself look pretty. Mein kameraden is coming to visit.'

We all looked at each other.

'Shit,' Flash muttered.

'Shut the fuck up.' Carrera grunted as he pushed forward and latched his hands onto Little's shoulders.

'Hey Amerikan, you smell so bad that my friends don't even want to stand next to you.' Sparks laughed as he yelled down again.

We all took the hint and stepped back as Carrera trudged forward with Little, the muzzle of his Schmeisser waving around on its sling, battering against his hip. As Carrera came about the tank, he hooked his foot under Little's and pushed him savagely. Again, Little went sprawling into the mud. He tried to clamber up on his knees, but Carrera kicked him hard in the ass and sent him crashing back onto his face.

As Little swore and spat curses from the ground, the Rottenführer came about the side of the Tiger. He stood before him, looking down on Little like he was a piece of shit stuck to the sole of his immaculately polished boots.

The SS man didn't say a word for some time, he just considered the man lying on his back, his arms twisted behind him, panting, mud strewn across his face.

'What unit are you from?' The Rottenführer asked him.

'Go fuck yourself, Nazi,' Little spat.

'Now, now. My Amerikan friend,' Sparks yelled down. 'You should at least stand before your superiors.'

Carrera grunted as he hooked his arm under one of Little's. He gritted his teeth as he hoisted the big man while Little's feet scrambled in the mud in a hopeless gesture. Finally, he succeeded and Little not only stood before the Rottenführer, he towered above the Nazi. The big, proud American looked down his nose at the German, who was forced to lift his weak chin so that he could look the man in the eye.

'What unit are you from and where -' He pronounced his Ws with a V. 'Were you captured?'

Little looked at us, and spat on the ground rather than answering. The Rottenführer followed the spit with his eyes, all the way from his mouth to the mud at his feet. Slowly, he raised his head to look coldly back to Little.

'Go fuck yourself, Nazi,' Little repeated, slower this time, in case the German was hard of hearing.

The Rottenführer didn't react. He didn't nod or show any sign of being infuriated. He simply removed his pistol from the leather holster on his hip, held the pistol out and upward at arm's length so that it rested on the bridge of Little's nose and pulled the trigger.

The report was dull and barely even echoed in the night. Little's head rocked back, further, and further. I even thought at one point that he was going to stop, rock back to his original standing position and tell the German to go fuck himself again. But that didn't happen, not in this devil's world.

He just continued backward until his legs unhinged and he collapsed in a heap on the side of the road.

My hand clutched the Sturmgewehr at my hip. Rage boiled within me. I was just about to raise the barrel, and unload everything upon that son of a bitch when I felt steel clang off my helmet. It was Jackson, behind me. He had leant forward so this helmet touched mine. I felt downward force pushing the Sturmgewehr away from my shoulder.

'Don't do it, man,' he whispered. 'Keep it cool. We will get those fuckers.'

And he was right, but I cannot help but think it perhaps would have been better if he didn't stop me. If he didn't, I would have reacted – I would have shot that bastard and killed him where he stood. And then we would've all died. Perhaps that would have been better. Better than what followed in the months to come. But sadly, I didn't.

I stood there and watched as the Rottenführer looked down at Little's body. Finally, he turned back to the barricade and ordered us through, shouting commands in German to Sparks, obviously on the route we were meant to take by his hand gestures. Like any soldiers knew, there was no time for mourning. Orders came first.

4

Sparks cried out in German as the Maybach revved and the transmission clunked into gear. He continued to look down at Little's body as he gestured in a forward motion with his right hand, an action that seemed horrifyingly like the Arian salute that was synonymous with the Nazi party. We fell into line behind the Tiger as it trundled into Mülheim. The exhaust bellowed as the tracks began to crawl forward, flinging mud into the air. I watched as the chunks of dirt, silt and shit fell onto Little's body, as if to begin the burial before his body had even gotten cold. It took a lot for me to start walking, but a gentle shove from Jackson got me moving. As did the gentle whisper that floated forward, almost inaudible under the bellow of the Tiger's plant.

'We'll get them for this, just stay calm.'

And for the most part, I think I did. I kept my temper under wraps as we marched past Little. I held my tongue as other SS men ventured out to clean up the mess the Rottenführer had created. Although I turned and watched them begin to drag Little down the slope that led into the paddocks off the side of the road, I never said a word, nor showed any contempt. Even as his head bounced along the rocks, as the two men struggled with his mass.

I'm sorry Little, I thought. *You deserved a better end than that.*

That man's end was the beginning of the most terrifying moments in my life. It was this day that I got the first glimpse of what was to come.

The Tiger crawled through the slim gap that was created when they lifted the boom. A slender piece of timber that had no possible hope in hell of stopping such a monster like the Tiger I, yet the symbolism counted for everything. A horrible feeling sunk into my guts as we ventured through. As rain started to patter down on the lip of my stahlhelm, I thought that I had finally entered hell. Part of me now laughs at this thought – I wish hell was that tame.

The rain wet the stones that made up the structures to either side of the streets and they glistened in the low light. Flames danced on their smooth surface, a reflection from the fire that warmed the gatekeepers and echoed of the hell that waited for us all.

Come to me and feel my fire, my everlasting hunger and desire, it seemed to say. But a footfall followed each step as the gate fell behind and the flickering light died in my eyes, replaced by the spire of a church tower somewhere in the middle of the town. The arches that contained the bell loomed in the darkness, and formed two windows that looked down on us like the predatory eyes of a monstrous demon.

The rain became heavier as we passed men that smoked in doorways, all of them draped in the black of the Waffen SS. The burning ends of their cigarettes barely glinted in their vacant slate-stone eyes.

Not a single soul apart for the men of the SS seemed to inhabit this town. There were no merchants pushing their carts, no father walking home drunk from the local pub, not even a child's cautious glance from the upper windows of their stone villa as the Tiger rattled through the town. Perhaps they were no longer impressed by the daunting shape of the Tiger I?

No one accosted us as we walked; they just let us walk further into the town. Some didn't even acknowledge us. A side of me thought perhaps they were becoming used to seeing German forces march back to Berlin, rather than to the front. The front that seemed to inch closer to the German capital as each month went by. Each month that cost thousands of lives on each side. But worse yet, how many lives of those that were called Jews were lost in that time? I could never answer that. Although I feel I now know the answer, back then, this was all just the beginnings of something terrible.

The tower loomed as we neared it. The road before us opened into a sparse courtyard littered with canvas shelters that protected precious supplies of rations and ammunition. Men sat around a fire, the rain failing to dampen not only the fires that burnt, but the soldiers' desire to steal its warmth. Through the centre of the courtyard there was enough space for our Tiger to venture through. It led us beyond the canvas city and into the motor pool where, from behind the now questionable safety of the Tiger's hull, I saw a Maus for the only time in my life.

Larger in every dimension than the Tiger I, the rounded edges of the monster's turret lurked in the darkness. The rain pelted the sloped exterior of the camouflaged hull, and ran rivers down the lines of the Zimmerit coating. The one-hundred-and-twenty-eight-millimetre gun barrel dwarfed the shorter coax of the seventy-five-millimetre gun that sat to its side. Even in its silence, the monster dominated the courtyard.

Opposite the Maus sat two Panther tanks. Completely outclassed by the super heavy Panzer that sat across from them, the Panthers were still better than any Sherman. Their crews milled about them, adjusting the torsion of the nuts that held the interweaved road wheels to their axle hubs. Above them, men were rearming the turret with seventy-five millimetre, high-velocity rounds that, at this short range, would cut the Tiger's heavy plate to cheese.

I had no idea what Spark's initial course of fire would be, but I didn't think he would drive past this opportunity.

My heart began to flutter in my chest as we neared. I have no idea whether it was from the anticipation of the fight or if it was the rattle of the Tiger's tracks. I moved to the left so to edge closer to the men working on the Panthers; thirty feet remained from the muzzle of the Tiger to the Maus. Sparks looked down on us. His face was grim but his eyes danced with excitement. He didn't offer us any words but he didn't need to. Good luck was the sentiment that I received from his gaze, before he lowered himself into the turret of the ancient dinosaur. The Panzer repairmen didn't even offer the Tiger a second glance as it rumbled closer and all its hatches began to close in preparation for battle.

Closer and closer still, the Tiger edged. I gave myself a little space, not knowing if Sparks would use the turret traverse or shift the entire vehicle to fire on the MKVIII Panzer. Hell, I didn't even know if he would fire on the MKVIII first; the unmanned monster seemed to offer less threat than the Panthers that were being loaded as we spoke. Still, I shifted myself closer to the Panthers to try and dispel that threat. But I had to wait for Sparks. I had to wait for the eighty-eight to strike the first blow.

Just before the Tiger came into the sightline of the Panther's barrels, the Tiger slewed on its tracks forty-five degrees and the eighty-eight of the Tiger I spoke. The sound was deafening; the concussion that I felt throughout my entire body made me want to curl up and die. The heat of the charge and the instant reaction of the target when it was hit, was abhorrent. The Panther was struck at almost point-blank range just below its turret, which was lifted thirty feet into the air by the force of the hit.

The men that were standing on the back deck were obliterated by the explosive detonation of not only the eighty-eight's armour-piercing charge, but all the Panther's ammunition that was just loaded into the beast. The turret sailed through the air, tumbling as it twisted over and over and over, until finally it came crashing down behind us on one of the canvas structures.

The men that were working on the Panther's road wheels were completely stunned. They lay on the ground looking up at the jet of fire that was now spewing out of the top of what remained of its flaming hull. They offered no fight, yet I raised my Sturmgewehr and sent a volley of bullets into them, killing them before they realised what had happened.

The Tiger's engine revved and I heard the transmission clunk. I looked over and the Tiger begin to reverse as its turret came around.

'Reversing!' I screamed back to my men before I turned the Sturmgewehr onto another SS man who had exited one of the stone buildings in a daze.

Sparks was a smarter man than I. From inside the Tiger's armour, he had seen what I could not from the ground. The first Panther's main gun erupted out of nowhere and struck the front of the Tiger at an angle. The round skated off the flat armour of the Tiger's front and sailed off into the distance. I looked from Panther to Tiger, then back again as I heard the hydraulic whine of the Tiger's turret come to a halt – just as the Panther's bow machine gun swivelled in its socket to face me.

The eighty-eight roared once more and a blistering red hole appeared in the middle of the Panther's sloped frontal armour. The entire tank rocked with the force as even the steel that surrounded the entry wound seemed to melt at the force of the impact. Light shimmered inside of the tank, then flickered as fire began to lick up from the inside. Smoke billowed out of the entry wound, then out the back of the turret where the loaders must have entered.

I had just escaped death again, and it shook me to my bones.

I staggered behind the Tiger as around me a massacre ensued. German soldiers came running, not knowing who or why this was happening, and saw us as their kommeraden… until we raised our guns and shot them where they stood. Germans cowered as the sky above them turned red with the fires that now engulfed both Panther tanks and stilled the German guns, the sounds that once would have been comforting. The sounds of their brothers in arms fighting alongside them, now turned against them in the darkness and horror of the night.

In the din of the battle, I stood at the rear of the Tiger, breathing heavily as the fumes of exhaust and gunpowder filled my lungs. I felt sick to death until a sound filled the air and made my heart stop. At first, I didn't know what it was, something whirring and spooling. It was close but was muffled by everything else that was happening. I couldn't locate it until the engine of the silent monster caught, and the rumble that it echoed shook the ground. Black smoke shot into the air from the exhaust stacks of the Maus and it revved hard as if to proclaim that it was now in this fight to the death.

Somehow, men had gotten inside of the MKVIII without us realising it. I moved forward shakily to see if there was still some sort of hatch that remained open. But as if in answer to the sign of life emitted from this new threat, our Tiger pounced on it. Ripping fire came from its bow gun to ripple off heavy plate steel. Tracers whirred through the air and ricocheted wildly into the distance, as the rounds fell off the armour like the rain had done only moments before.

I raised my arm to shield my face as the spray of machine fire was sent in all directions and I was forced to fall back.

The Maus didn't roll on its tracks; perhaps that was not the intention of starting the monster's engine. But soon it all made sense – they needed power to traverse the immense weight of the turret. Hydraulics whined horribly in the night while small arms fire continued to rip through the flesh of men on the ground and the main gun of the monster began to swing.

The ground below the Tiger I rumbled as Sparks brought the body to face a similar forty-five degrees to the MKVIII. Meanwhile its own hydraulics howled as the eighty-eight came around, having moved the hull at the same time as the turret, that meant the Tiger's barrel would come on target before the Maus'.

All I could do was watch in awe as the race took place, and I held my hands over my face and screamed as again the eighty-eight ripped fire through the air and sent my ears into the depths of concussion. I couldn't hear anything but when I opened my eyes, I couldn't believe what I saw. The base of the armour piercing round that the Tiger had just fired, jutted out of the side armour of the Maus. At point-blank range, the eighty-eight – the round that no American armour could stop at almost any distance – could not penetrate the side armour of this new machine.

The cupola of the Tiger flew open and Sparks raised his head from the depths. He screamed and pointed as the main gun of the MKVIII slowly came around. The Tiger lunged forward; jets of black soot shot out of the rear as the Maybach engine bellowed under the strain. As it charged, the Tiger's barrel raised higher and higher.

In the heat of battle, men do things that can be defined as insane. But as the events unfolded and chaos fell upon us, I can't see how we could have survived if Sparks had not acted in the way that he had.

As the Tiger rushed forward, the muzzle break of the eighty-eight caught the barrel of the MKVIII and jammed the turret. As the Tiger slammed into the front corner of its successor, I could only remember the spare track links that jutted out of its frame. The jaws of the Tiger had snapped shut on the Maus.

With the Tiger right next to the bulking shape of the Maus, a much taller and wider tank than the dinosaur that Sparks drove, there was no way that the one-hundred-and-twenty-eight-millimetre could ever be brought onto it. I could hear the strain in the hydraulics of the monster, whining and whining as if it was a dog that pined for something that it would never have the hope of getting.

The Tiger's turret adjusted slowly and methodically to clear the mantlet of the MKVIII's main gun, so that it sat just an inch away from the front face of the armour.

The eighty-eight crashed and both monsters rocked with the impact. But nothing happened.

As if out of fear or ferocity or just the helpless want to do something, the one-hundred-and-twenty-eight-millimetre cannon of the Maus broke the din of the battle with its fire. A jet of flame illuminated the night and behind me I heard an explosion, but I never turned my head to see what had been destroyed.

Again, the Tiger I barked in fury, and soon after the Maus fired again, not just from its main gun but from its seventy-five-millimetre coax gun. With the effort of recoil, I saw the barrel of the Maus shift a few further inches to the right. How far had it moved?

I moved away from the two monsters as the Maus wore blow after blow while it continued to send shells out into the abyss. Cracks in the MKVIII's armour started to appear. One long shard of light was visible running from the top of the hull down to vanish behind the interweaving road wheels, but still the fight continued.

The Americans were almost finished enforcing their own "final solution", when with one final crash, all three cannons – the single eighty-eight and the two from the MKVIII – fired at the same time, and I finally saw what the Germans' target was. As two shells exploded at the base of the bell tower, I saw the entire foundation explode outward in a ball of fire. I looked up, hopeless, as the spire leant out over me.

'Cover!' I screamed as stone and brick and even the bell itself pitched outwards over us. I ran for my life. Stones the size of small cars slammed into the ground around me as I ran.

I saw one American or German, even I was confused now, get flattened in a sickening thud. But I couldn't stop, I couldn't hesitate. Pebbles and shards of mortar rained down on the Tiger and Maus, and the final thing I saw before I dove beneath the rear of the Tiger I, was Sparks close his hatch. And then hell fell around me.

5

Darkness consumed me. Unsure of where, when, or who I was, the world had taken a turn for the surreal. Mountains of fire etched up into skies and the earth was a cracked maelstrom of despair. The air I breathed was like poison and I couldn't help but think that this was it, this was the hell that was waiting for me after life. Everything I had worked for, was for nothing. Everything I had done, was for a God that had long since perished in this world of blood, death, and fire, and the only thing that remained was the Anti.

I remember that a compound stood before me. A wide but shallow structure of stone and brick with a peaked tower in its centre that had a gaping mouth below, where two gates rattled on their hinges as the fiery breeze whistled through its maw. There were words that I couldn't read through the silt that the wind carried, but they were wrought in iron above the gates. I have no idea what they said, but I knew that they were lies. That no matter what, if I walked through those gates, I would know nothing but death, despair and the Anti that ruled beyond. The one that rose victorious from the ashes. The one that waited, everlasting and unidimensional. The one whose hunger would never be staunched.

I felt a sensation across my face, as if my skin had started to crawl. I pressed my hands to my cheeks and everything felt wrong. I looked down and saw that my fingers were bones, strangled tendons still clinging in places. Dust fell from my joints as I clenched my fists and I opened my mouth to scream but nothing came out, as what I saw beyond my hands had stolen the breath from my lungs. Slowly, I tilted my head back and back to look up at what had risen beyond the open maw of the gates.

Clawed hands broke the tiles of the tower roof as its talons raked themselves across the surface. Shards of terracotta tumbled to the ground in heaps of broken dreams as the demon opened its mouth. Rotten flesh clung to teeth that were easily longer than I was tall. Two gnarled horns swept back from either side of its head, and I remember they were as black of the depths of hell and still, I could see the ridges and the lines of age that had eroded their surface. Its flesh was the dark grey of the German field uniform and hair clung to its hide and shoulders like sharp bristles that reminded me of the Rommel's asparagus back in England.

Its eyes were the worst; they glowed unnaturally from the pits of its skull. An amber so haunting that even to this day I cannot bear to think of this dream. Those eyes radiated above me and I knew that their gaze was on me. I felt it. I felt it in my mind, raping every corner of my consciousness. And as it roared a scream from another world, I finally found my voice, and I screamed in horror as its grasp locked my mind and seized control of my body.

I screamed as I felt my arm move. Powerless to stop it, I screamed as I felt my hand grasp the hilt of a pistol. Hoarser still I bellowed, a passenger in my own mind, as I finally learnt its intention and malice – projected into me, sweeping through the hallways of my mind like a drug.

'Die.' It spoke to me in no language at all. 'Die.' That was what it wanted. That was what it always wanted. For me… to… 'Die'.

My voice broke as the pistol's barrel touched my temple, and in my final seconds of life as my voice descended into a gargle of suffering, it spoke to me again, and again, and again, as if even after death I would never be rid of that insane voice that clutched my soul with its claws.

'Die.'

The sensation on my face came again, but it was real this time. My eyes opened as I felt stone and grit grind against my cheek. I blinked, and saw in the low light that the ground was shifting below me. But it wasn't. With each second my senses were coming back to me and I felt the grasp that someone had on my legs. I was being dragged out from under the Tiger, its massive engine quiet in the night. With a tremendous heave, I was sucked out from below the iron beast. I gasped, as it happened with such ferocity that I thought it had to be the monster from my dreams come to reality.

But it wasn't that at all. A man stood above me that I had never seen before. He was dressed in the same uniform that I was: black with the white SS insignia blazoned on his collar. He looked down at me, as if considering. I did the same. Was this man German or American? No doubt he was thinking the same about myself. Not a word was spoken as he shifted his hand and I saw a dagger clenched in his gloved hand. The blade was red with blood. Clots of life clung to the blade, covering almost all of it except one slither of shining steel that rung out clearly in the limited light. Silently, he knelt next to me and I felt the blade touch my throat.

I felt resigned to death at this stage. I looked into the eyes of the Waffen SS man above, eyes that seemed darker than that of our uniforms.

He uttered the only words that I heard him say, and the way he said it, sounded as if he was scared to death.

'Götterdämmerung.'

I closed my eyes and waited for death.

A shot rang out. I jumped at the report and I opened my eyes as the German collapsed on top of me. The blade clattered to the ground next to my head. I sucked a breath of air deep into my lungs and shuddered as I exhaled with the weight of a dead man on top of me. I didn't try and move, still paralysed from the dream. Even with the feeling of his life's blood saturating my tunic, I didn't move. I sucked another breath and shuddered again on the exhale as the soles of boots crunched on the ground beside me.

The German was dragged off my chest and a hand was extended to me. I took it, and Carrera again dragged me to my feet.

He looked sullen and exhausted as he looked me over and nodded before he moved on. The town square was destroyed by the collapse of the tower. Large chunks of brick and stone were scattered everywhere and complete houses had been flattened by the destructiveness of its fall. One of the Panthers was completely buried in rubble while the Tiger to my side was covered in debris.

It took us what seemed hours to remove enough of the rubble so that we could uncover the commander's hatch, and finally it swung open. Sparks sat inside, looking up at us. His face was covered in the soot from the powder of the massive eighty-eight and his eyes shone from the darkness in such contrast that it reminded me of the dream and the monster that waited in the depths of my sleep. I blinked to expel the thought from my mind and extended my own hand to Sparks.

We faced little resistance in the town beyond that. It seemed that with the destruction of their Panthers and the massive Maus, the Germans had lost their taste for battle and fled. Nonetheless, we remained on our guard as we walked the quiet streets of Mülheim, then beyond. We walked without the support of the German armour; the Tiger having suffered a broken final drive in its impact with the MKVIII. Although the rumbling beast was a machine of our enemies, I felt naked standing out in the open without its steel in front of me.

When we arrived at the concentration camp, it was likewise abandoned. The main gates of its boundary were open and they clanged against each other in the breeze of the early morning. A sound that chilled me to my bones in the otherwise silence.

Carrera, Jackson, Flash, Sparks, and his tank crew were now all that remained of our force. The others, it seemed, either perished in the collapse of the tower, or had their throats slit by that Waffen SS man. The part that also chilled me, was that we had also found Germans who had their throats slit in the same fashion. Whether it was the collapse of the tower, or seeing the destruction of Hitler's invincible armoured divisions, that man had descended into the depths of insanity. And I felt that I wasn't far behind him.

Clothes of civilians were scattered everywhere. A woman's coat lay in a heap next to a vacant block of buildings, its occupants gone perhaps only minutes before we got there. A child's shoe sat lonely on the destroyed railway that led out of the camp. Each of the timber supports for the rails had been ploughed so that we couldn't use them to follow the Germans in their escape.

The body of a man lay outside of another block. A US soldier, we identified him by his tags after being drawn to him by the shade of his fatigues. Perhaps this was one of the men that Skorzeny had kidnapped from the front lines. We took one of his tags before we searched the buildings and found letters to loved ones that would never be read by their intended recipients. Letters in French, English, even a few in Spanish. They all said similar things. "Don't cry for us, we're already dead."

The only thing that didn't fit in the whole place was a crate that sat out in the open. The imperial eagle was stamped on the crate in black paint; the edges of the swastika stood out like the teeth of the monster that refused to leave my mind. One word was hand-painted onto the crate in scrawling letters that had run before the paint could dry. Even in the limited light I could read what it said and the word chilled me to my bones.

Götterdämmerung.

'What do you think is inside?' Flash asked as he kicked the box.

Carrera grunted with his back to us. He was staring out at the railway, as if in contemplation of what to do next.

'I'll look around for a pry bar,' Jackson said as he stepped up into one of the dormitory blocks. I wasn't sure what he hoped to find in there. I had looked through two already and nothing much was left, beyond rows upon rows of empty bunks, from floor to ceiling.

I was sitting on one of the steps to another block, with her photo in my hand. Her face was almost gone now, almost faded into nothingness, but my memory held fast and as I ran my thumb over her fading likeness, I closed my eyes and saw her beauty renewing and in colour.

'I wonder why they would have that written on the side,' Sparks said and I opened my eyes to see that he was running his fingers across the painted words.

I was about to ask him what the word meant when all the loudspeakers in the camp crackled and the familiar Nazi anthem *Raise the Flag* started to play. Then something happened that scared the hell out of all of us. Something that horrifies me still to this day. Something inside the crate began to claw at the sides…

6

'Oh shit,' Flash uttered as he backed away from the crate, his mouth open and his eyes wide. The scratching sound that came from within the crate was loud enough to be heard over the static of the horns of the Nazi's anthem. Flash's Kar 98 still leant up against the crate, nestled in the corner against inch-thick timber supports.

'What is it?' I snarled, not knowing whether to advance or retreat, raise my rifle, or throw it to the ground.

'I don't know,' Jackson mumbled.

'Probably some damned dog,' Carrera barked as he walked by us, completely ignoring the crate as he looked up to the loud speakers that emitted the song of the Führer's forces. 'Sparks,' he snapped. 'Translate this bullshit for me when they start talking.'

Sparks slowly turned his head away from the crate, his eyes as wide as ours. Something didn't seem right. Sparks muttered a phrase in German beneath his breath and the word struck me. I turned my head away from the crate to look at him.

Why did he say that word? What was it? Why was it that the throat cutter in the courtyard had said the same thing?

Sparks walked toward Carrera as the scratching from the crate seemed to subdue. Then the words of the Führer himself filled the vacant assembly area, rattling the windows in their sills and making birds silent in their songs.

'My national compatriots, National Socialists!' Sparks repeated after the guttural words of the German leader. Some of the men kept their eyes focused on the crate. But none of us spoke, we all just listened.

'Twelve years ago, when as the leader of the strongest party, I was entrusted with the office of Chancellor, Germany found herself faced with the same situation internally as the one that faces it externally today.'

A breeze whisked through the assembly area, sending a chill down my spine. I shuddered as I held my Sturmgewehr close to my chest and wrapped my arms around myself as if in an embrace. All I wanted was to be warm. Something about that breeze made me feel that all the warmth in the world had disappeared and that there would never be light again, not for as long as I lived.

'The German ports were nothing but ship cemeteries,' Sparks continued, his face tight with concentration. 'The financial situation threatened at any moment to lead to a collapse not only of the state but also of the provinces and of the communities. The decisive thing, however, was this: Behind this methodical destruction of Germany's economy, there stood the spectre of the worldwide Jewry.'

'Humph,' Carrera grunted. 'This old horse and cart.'

'The horrid fate that is now taking shape in the west and that which eliminates hundreds of thousands in the villages and marketplaces, in the countries and in the cities, will be warded off in the end and mastered by us, with the utmost exertion and despite all setbacks and hard trials.'

'What and he's blaming us?' Jackson cried. 'They were the ones that left no one for us to save, how could we have—'

'Cram it and let him translate!' Carrera barked.

Sparks shot Jackson a distasteful look as he, obviously muddled now, tried to find his place in the Führer's words.

'Something like, if it was the old Germany facing us, they would be gone. Ahh yes, long since would we have been swept away by the hurricane of the international Jewish plot. Being armless and defenceless, we as victims would be helpless but to witness a reversal of all the laws of nature.'

Suddenly, the Kar 98 that Flash had left leaning on the crate fell to the ground. We all turned to look at it, except for Carrera and Sparks.

'But we are not that Germany. No, not at all.'

I took a step toward the crate, examining the place where the muzzle had been nestled, and where its butt had rested on the ground. There were no signs of slip; it could not have fallen by itself.

'Therefore, it is all the more necessary on this thirteenth anniversary of the rise to power, to strengthen the heart more than ever before.'

Something inside in the crate threw itself hard against the wall that the Kar 98 leant against. I saw the timber shake against its fastenings, like a door in a jamb being kicked from the inside.

'And to steel ourselves in the holy determination, to wield the sword, no matter where and under what circumstance.'

'Guys, I don't think this is a dog,' I muttered.

'Until the final victory crowns our efforts…'

'Cody, shut your trap.'

'When this final crisis is conquered by our unalterable will.'

It struck the side of the crate again, and timber shards shot out as there was a distinct crack of timber from one of the supporting beams.

'Top, this is serious.' I raised my rifle.

'By our readiness for sacrifice and our abilities.'

It struck the side again and timber splinters fell away again. The bracing sections across the centre of the crate would not hold for much longer.

'Let's just shoot the fucking crate!' Flash screamed.

'Hold your fire and shut your traps!' Carrera bellowed again.

'We shall overcome this calamity, and this fight.'

'Goddamned children scared of some damned dog in a crate.' Carrera had now lost interest in Sparks' words and he had returned to berate all of us now.

But Sparks continued, drowning out the words and the actions of our calamity behind him. 'And at its head will be the country that has represented Europe against the Jewry for fifteen hundred years.'

'Top, it ain't no damned dog,' Jackson spoke up and pointed.

'Just take a look at the crate.'

'And shall represent it for all times.'

Carrera burst into the centre of our group, his Schmeisser bouncing against his hip as he strode forward purposefully. 'I'm sick of you damned runts not stepping forward,' he muttered to himself.

'Our Greater German Reich.'

'Not a man amongst any of you,' he spat. 'All of them left on the fucking ground back there and I'm left with you damned green pups that are scared shitless of some fucking…' He kicked the crate hard.

'The German Nation.' Sparks lifted his head, returning to the current moment.

'Damned…' Carrera kicked the crate again.

Carrera and Sparks spoke these last words at the same time. Beyond that, everything happened so fast. But the clarity in what I saw remains, as well as the words that both men spoke, one in German and one in English, as the reality of the world gave way before me.

'Götterdämmerung' was the word that Sparks muttered again. The same word that he had said as he had left to walk toward Carrera and translate. The same word that the throat slitter had uttered before Sparks had shot him. The same word that was painted across the side of the crate that I was looking at, at that damned moment. The word that would haunt me forever.

'Dog!' Carrera cried has he brought his foot down hard in a forward kick against the same section of splintered timbers that had been weakened by whatever was concealed within the crate. As the fanfare of *Raise the Flag* died away in our ears, the world was filled with the final crack of timber as the support beams gave way. Carrera's foot disappeared inside of the crate, almost devoured by a black hole in its centre. He shuffled on his other foot as he tried to retrieve his boot, the anger showing on his face as the risk of being humiliated in front of his men became apparent.

Bill muttered as he struggled, then he froze. His eyes narrowed as they focused on the hole where his foot had vanished. Reflecting the terror in his mind, his mouth twisted as he fought to remove his foot from its snare. Carrera's arms flailed in the air as he hopped on his left leg, his eyes remaining focused on the crate. 'Son of a bitch has my foot, it's…' He considered. 'Holding it.' Then he turned to us, almost desperate now. 'Help me goddamn it, help me.'

Jackson and Wright – the Tiger's driver – rushed to his side. Each of them grabbed an arm to steady the man and together, all three of them pulled to remove Carrera's leg. Flash, in the meantime, had worked up the courage to retrieve his rifle. He slammed its butt into the side of the crate and screamed, 'Hey. Hey! Over this side. Let go you son of a bitch.'

Carrera had his left foot resting on the upper frame of the crate and he heaved with everything he had while the tankmen, Wright and Jackson, supported his weight.

Carrera screamed. I had no idea whether it was from his pain or his effort. But Flash doubled his efforts and slammed the butt of his Mauser into the side of the crate so hard and so fast that the butt broke through. Flash quickly knelt and peered through the opening in the crate.

'Can't see a damned….' he began before I saw his whole body tense as the words fell from his lips. Quickly he stood up and stepped backwards. 'Oh my God. Christ.' His hands covered his eyes as he muttered and back stepped from the crate. The Kar 98 fell again to the ground and clattered against the pebbles and the sand. 'Oh Jesus. What have they done?'

I stepped forward, my brow furrowed as I leant down to peer through the hole in the crate. I heard a crack and Carrera's screams intensified.

'Goddamn it. Pull!' he screamed again.

I stood up as finally the three men fell backwards to the ground in a mess. Carrera clutched at his leg, the colour quickly running from his face. His foot was completely facing the wrong way. No dog could have done that. I turned back to the hole and was about to peer through when a clawed hand came out.

'Oh fuck!' I screamed as I jumped to the rear and away from its reaching grasp.

'What in the hell?' Wright screamed as he too saw the grey, hairy flesh of the thing's hand and forearm wave in the air. Finally, it reached down and started to claw at the timber bracings on this side of the crate. The sound of it. The sound of those claws etching into the timber, the way each strand gave way under their force. It drove me insane.

'Kill the thing!' The other tankman bellowed as he stepped toward the crate and racked his Schmeisser. The scratching, clawing sound was replaced by the sweeping roar of the Schmeisser as the GI raked its power across the crate.

The hand withdrew with a horrible scream that made all my hairs stand on end. I held my hands to my ears and howled to try and block it out, to block out the pain that I not only heard in my ears, but felt in my mind. Just like in my dream, the thing was raping my thoughts. Like a dagger had been wedged down both of my ears and twisted, twisted, twisted until they reached the centre and touched each other.

The tank man wailed as his Schmeisser continued to roar, and finally, it all stopped. All of it. The digging in my mind, the screaming, the firing, everything.

I saw the tank man standing there, his body twitched and his head tilted slightly to the left. My eyes fell back to the crate and a cry of horror escaped my lips. I saw its face for the first time, looking out at the shooter. Its amber eyes glowed as it focused everything that it had on that man. That horrible sound that was flowing from my mouth continued as the GI turned the barrel of the Schmeisser around. I saw what it wanted through the grimace that it was in its eyes. The horror of it. The Schmeisser fired once more and the GI fell to the ground, in a heap of lifeless flesh, the upper back of his head blown out by his own weapon. It was here that I found my strength, somewhere deep within my fear. I raised my Sturmgewehr, trained it on the face, that horrible pallid face. And I fired.

For a second, its eyes fell on me and I felt the instant return of the stabbing pains inside my head. However, as the fire of the Sturmgewehr swept over the section of the crate where the eyes were, the pain stopped. The daggers inside of my mind stopped turning but they were replaced by the horrific screams of agony from that thing inside the crate. I didn't stop firing as the crate began to rock with the movement of the thrashing beast inside. Timber flew everywhere until finally, the side that Carrera had been ensnared in broke outwards in a flurry of timber and claws and blood. The beast rushed out.

Wright's mouth fell open in silent horror as he tried to bring his Kar 98 around on the monster, but he was far too slow. The grey, naked mass fell upon him. The monster closed the ground between the men and the crate in an instant. The size of the beast was another thing; for something that had been crammed inside a box that only stood chest high, the thing was enormously broad chested, but with slender, muscular limbs. Claws tipped the fingers of each hand and foot, which were more like the feet of apes than that of a man. All of them tore into Wright, as he writhed and screamed and tried to bring the Kar 98 between him and the monster that had latched onto him.

The creature reared back its head and howled as its bottom jaw split apart from its centre, exposing row after row of razor-sharp teeth that reached out like the claws on its hands. It sprung forward and wrapped its jaws around the face of the screaming American.

Jackson was white with fear as he dragged Carrera away. I reloaded my Sturmgewehr. Sparks was beside me now with a paratrooper's FG 42. The sound of Wright's face crunching and grinding beneath the power of this monster's jaws made me sick. His body flinched as his hands fell away from the Kar 98 that lay uselessly on his chest.

I heard the FG crack next to me and I joined my fire with Sparks. The grey flesh rippled as the eight-millimetre slugs hammered into it. Its face instantly turned to us; its jaws spread wide in a horrific scream of pain and anger that sent torn flesh at us in spray of blood and meat that was rivalled only by the lead and the fire that we sent back.

Through the recoil of my Sturmgewehr's optic, I saw that its left eye had been blinded and some sort of hope entered my mind. I tried to focus all my fire on its face, but with the strength of twenty men, I felt strong hands close over the barrel of my rifle and pull it hard to the left, where Sparks stood. The force of the pull reefed the grip out of my hand and as the barrel was brought to bear on Spark's head, the Sturmgewehr fell silent.

The creature screamed again as its mental hold over the rifle was dropped and the monster leapt up into the air, well above our heads.

'Holy shit!' I screamed as I brought the Sturmgewehr back into my control and looked at Sparks. He had no idea what had happened. His eyes were up, following the creature through the air, hands busy reloading the paratrooper's rifle. I should have taken the same advice, but I was too far taken by shock to have done anything.

I turned as I heard an awful thud behind me and a scream followed. I saw the monster on Jackson's back; Carrera was sprawled on the ground next to him, his face conquered by the pain from his foot. Jackson writhed beneath the monster, his face pressed into the ground as the creature leant down and ran one of its clawed hands slowly down his back. The screams that came from Jackson were insane with agony. Cloth and flesh parted beneath each pronged claw as the monster purposefully drew out the agony.

I raised my rifle, eager to support Jackson, but there was no shot I could take that didn't put Jackson at risk. I was forced to move and I did so as fast as I could.

My path took me away from Carrera. As I ran, I saw everything happen. I saw Carrera, groggy with pain and barely aware, look from his foot up to the monster. He didn't even really seem to acknowledge what this thing was. He just brought up the Schmeisser that still hung from his body and opened fire at almost point-blank range. Again, the monster's flesh rippled and this time, it stood up to its full height, somewhere short of ten feet tall. It turned its head viciously to Carrera, and took one lengthy stride so that it stood right above him. It leant down and placed one clawed hand onto my leader's shoulder. It was only then, that the Schmeisser stopped firing.

Carrera moaned in agony as the creature lifted him, four foot off the ground. Blood ran from this new wound and ran over the wiry hair and the grey clammy flesh of the creature as it held him before it, as if to consider him. The Schmeisser fell to the ground and with one trembling hand I saw Carrera pull a German potato masher grenade from the loop in his belt.

'Kill me!' Carrera screamed in its face. 'You goddamned ugly son of a bitch!' Kill me!' With a final cry, he spat in the thing's face.

I ran to Jackson's side; he was sobbing uncontrollably from the agony. I looked down at the ribbons of flesh and cloth and was forced to lay my Sturmgewehr down to drag him without touching his wounds. As I dragged him away, I looked up and saw the monster's lower jaw part just as Carrera pulled the fuse tab on the grenade.

'Oh shit,' I groaned. We were only ten feet from the pair. I gave two more hard yanks and threw myself down over Jackson as the screams and the horror were replaced by an earth-rending roar of power.

Jackson screamed in pain and in fright and I couldn't blame him at all. I felt shrapnel from the grenade graze my back and hammer the steel of the helmet on my head. My ears began to ring as I fell back off Jackson. My eyes closed to the world; surely this horror was finished. Surely the insanity of this day was over.

I took a breath, and felt the coolness of the breeze fill my lungs again. The beauty of that feeling, the same feeling that had made me feel as though all life was finished on this earth only moments before, now brought me relief. Was it because I too had died? Was it because I knew now that I could rest? Or was it the coldness of shock settling into my body?

Fingers rustled in the depths of my mind, and that was ok. I had just been through a horrible experience; I could honestly understand the feeling.

It came again and my hand twitched.

The coolness that I had just found soothing, turned sour along with every thought and memory that was close to the surface of my mind. I opened my eyes and saw the monster there, half of its face destroyed by the blast of the grenade but still its one remaining eye burnt into me. It could no longer control me, but it didn't want to. It just wanted to show me what was to come.

Pillars of fire reached up to the skies while the scorched earth below it was riddled with the bones of men. Titans roamed this world, aware and totally insane as they hungered eternally for the flesh of men. But not just men. The thought that was pressed into my mind with each beat of my heart struck fear into my soul, as each sign that I had seen raced past my eyes once more.

'Juden,' it cried. Desperately. 'Juden.'

And suddenly, I felt the most urgent hunger in my stomach as if my entire soul would vanish if I didn't eat soon, the ache, the vacantness of mind, the urging. The… the word stopped at the tip of my tongue, because it didn't make sense. None of it did.

As I looked up and into the depths of this creature's eyes, I saw the muzzle brake of Sparks' paratrooper's rifle nestle on the part of the creature's head, where I would expect my own temple to be. As it fired, the light vanished from the creature's eye and the hunger, the pain, and the sorrow, all stopped. The visions of the pillars of fire, the titans, and the bones vanished. I fell into the depths of unconsciousness, alone and afraid. And with only one word on my mind. The word the creature had used incorrectly.

'Juden.'

PART FIVE

Auschwitz – Occupied Poland

May 6th 1946

1

Dear Bill,

It's morning as I write this letter, the rains haven't stopped and I can only imagine that God is crying for us, as only He could know what I'm going through right now.

Daniel is still asleep, he's been hard to get to bed lately and maybe it's the fact that I'm not ok, that's causing it. Maybe he can tell? Your mother has offered to help but, I just can't have her here right now, I hope you will understand as the words I am going to say next are the hardest I will have to write.

Bill, I'm pregnant. I am so, so sorry. And I know that any words of apology that come from me, may seem so weak and fruitless to you. But I want you to know that I really mean it. I can't say how hard it has been for me. Every day the mail comes is a torture that I can't stand. Every day, I look at Daniel and I see your eyes in his, and I think, how will this boy turn out if his father doesn't come home? And I think that is honestly the hardest part — what would happen to Daniel?

It must be where it's come from and why this happened Bill, but you're only a chance Daniel needs a guarantee. I can't do this on my own.

I'm sorry Bill. This isn't your fault. But I won't be here when you come back. If you come back.

Susan

As the fingers of the wind gently caressed the letter in my hand, I sighed. How many times had those words been read? How many times had it been folded along the same lines that her fingers had pressed? The spring breeze cut through the field the way these words would have cut through Bill. Like German machine gun fire. The long grass and the hints of tussock whistled as the air rushed over them. A sound and a movement that made me think of all the souls in the world leaving their physical beings. And why not, after all? What could be a better sound than this? And here of all places. In the end, there is little difference between us and the grass in the fields when you get right down to it. We grow, get too tall for our own good until the weight of our success becomes too great and we are cut down by our peers. To fall and rot while those around us grow from our failure.

But no matter how hard I looked, I couldn't see where any growth could come from the failure that I was witnessing. The Germans certainly hadn't. Neither had we. The world seemed to shrink with every passing day. Like there was less of it to enjoy; either that, or no one left to enjoy it with. Perhaps that's what they wanted in the end. What their conquest, their dominion over Europe was all for. Hell, they wanted Lebensraum, they needed a place to expand. Well, there was no one left but us to stop them, so it seemed anyway…

Within the folds of Bill's final letter from his wife, I held her likeness as the breeze tried to take her from me. Just like they had. I ran the ball of my thumb across the photograph where her face used to be. Her features, one by one, had faded over the miles and months and seasons. Nothing remained now but the button of her blouse and the faintest hint of three small beauty spots at the corner of her eye. But perhaps they weren't there either. Perhaps it had just been my imagination that had clung to these things. Too damned stubborn to let them go as the photograph had. Still, I swore to myself that I would not forget what she looked like. Even as I looked at the vacant place where she had been, I could still see her there. The faint curl of her smile. Pinpricks of dimples that waited at the corners of her lips. Oceans for eyes, the depths of which could never be explored.

I knew from the moment that I laid eyes on her, that everything I was going to face was just a precursor to this moment. I never wondered where she had been all my life; I just knew that this intersection of time would come, and that eventually we would meet and everything would be worth it. Everything.

From the moment I passed out at the railway yard in the Ruhr Valley, my world had changed. Hell, it had almost ended. It sure had for Carrera.

With the death of our commander, I had received a field promotion, my second now, to a commissioned rank that I'd thought I would never attain. Second Lieutenant. I felt no pride in my ascension. How could I? What pride should I have felt, to have survived out of luck and to have filled a man's position out of necessity rather than desire? I know some would disagree, and perhaps I am wrong but that's just the way I see it.

The world seemed a darker place without Carrera in it, and it wasn't because of his humour. In all honesty, he had become unbearable towards the end, and now we know why. I wondered if there was anything I could have ever said to have helped him. The desperation in his eyes that swam just below the surface of anger. Bill was dead now. Maybe it would have been better if he never got the letter at all. All I know is that the crushing pressure that he felt, had no doubt contributed to his change into the toxic sufferance that he became. It was the same suffocating, nauseated illness that I carried since my promotion.

There wasn't anyone else anymore. There wasn't that mystical figure that sat above me that I could just depend on and say, "Hey, it doesn't matter what those damned Krauts throw at us, or what comes next. Because we've got Bill, and he had always seen us through". Bill was gone now, so was that safety net. For me anyway. Now I was the one they relied on, not that there was many left now, not the ones from the beginning. Just Jackson and I had suffered together since Northern Ireland. The rest – the ring-ins – had come and gone.

Of course Flash and Perry were there, and after the Ruhr even Sparks fell in after he understood the cause of what we were now tasked to deal with. The only thing worth fighting for now: the lives of those that were taken. If we lost that, what were we fighting for? There was no one left to claim the lands that we had liberated. If not for them and those that remained, what was the point of even carrying on? But still the major push was to Berlin, not south, where the trail led. The world demanded justice, and so the crushing defeat of the Third Reich was imminent.

Hamburg had burnt, as had Munich. From the photos I had seen of Berlin and the fighting that had just started in the streets of the German capital, there was nothing left to defend, and barely anyone to defend it. Hitlerjugend, the youth of the nation, inside of the massive hulls of the Tigers and MKVIIIs, not men. Adolescents manning the PAK 40 anti-tank guns. Women manning the MG 42s as the bodies of the men that were too afraid to man them, hung from the necks as if to decorate the streets they defended. The word Verräter or Traitor, hung from their chests for the world to see. But that was Berlin, and not where I went.

Like Hansel and Gretel, my squad and the group that were assigned to us, Easy Company from the Five Oh Third, with a small detachment of Shermans from the Second Armoured division, etched our way through central Germany. Following the trail of breadcrumbs, in the form of shoes and personal belongings of civilians.

But the disappointments came thick and fast, as they had for Bill. We were never quick enough to catch them. Letters piled up, the words that meant everything to the ones that wrote them, poured out now like water on the ground. How many fell to those things? Even now, I have avoided discussing "them" in this body of words because I don't know how to address what they are. Nothing alluded to them along the trail of breadcrumbs, nothing but that one damned word. "Götterdämmerung."

Somewhere between the Ruhr and this horrible, earth-ending place, I learnt the meaning of that word. It wasn't written on a crate this time, it was written across a derailed train car. One of its wheel bogeys had collapsed as the train and its convoy of cars were rounding a bend. The car had derailed and lay on its side, dragged far enough over to not hinder the passage of the remaining cars that were fit to travel. The word was painted on the roof of the car, above the bodies of six men and fourteen women. All six of the men were German soldiers; they had been branded with the word Verräter. The women were all civilians, of this there was no doubt. They must have been injured in the crash. Some of them had broken legs, obvious in the way they were unnaturally twisted. Others I could not say. All I know is that none of them were her. I checked each of them myself. What had happened with the so-called traitors, I will never know. Perhaps with the women being injured they were now no use to the Germans seeking Götterdämmerung, and hence they were no longer required. Perhaps those traitors tried to save them.'

I ran my hand over the word after I had checked the dead woman's face and rubbed the ball of my thumb over the flesh that lay next to her left eye. Rubbing away the blood, dirt, and grime in search for the signs of three small birthmarks. I tried the word on my tongue but it was clumsy and it didn't flow. It put a sour taste in my mouth just trying to speak that language that I now can speak almost fluently. Perhaps, all these wounds were too fresh. I noticed someone beside me and I turned my head to see Sparks there. He smiled at me briefly and pronounced the word emphatically.

'Gott-Er-Dam-Eh-Rung.' He emphasised each syllable.

I tried it again and it sounded better.

'Good,' Sparks said unemotionally. 'We'll make a Kraut out of you yet, Top.'

Top – the affectionate term we all used for Bill. Something I never became used to being called.

'This word,' I said, ignoring his statement, 'it was etched into the crate back in the Ruhr.'

Sparks looked at it again. 'Yeah, you're right.'

I turned to him. 'I remember you questioning why they had used it.'

Sparks met my eyes. 'I did…' he paused. 'And I still do.'

'What does it mean?' I asked, as some Easy Company men started picking through the pockets of the Nazi deserters.

Sparks considered this for some time. 'Twilight of the gods,' he said flatly.

'Twilight of the gods?' I repeated. 'What the hell does that mean?'

'Beats me.' He shrugged again as he met my eyes with his increasingly vacant ones. 'It was a piece of music as far as I'm aware, Beethoven perhaps. No. No, I'm sure it was Wagner.'

'Uh-huh,' I agreed, not particularly caring about the composer of a piece of music. 'And why would they write it seemingly everywhere we've been in the last few months?'

Sparks shrugged as he looked down at the railway tracks we had been following; these tracks likewise useless to us as their planks had been ploughed. 'Your guess is as good as mine.'

'Maybe it's their version of our prayer?' Perry said almost inaudibly, no doubt remembering the last time he had mentioned his religion was only moments before Little lost his life.

I shot him a questioning glance.

'If God be for us, then who be against us?' he repeated.

I didn't answer him. None of us did. It wasn't that we disagreed, I think it was enough to make us think.

All these thoughts ran through my mind as we neared what had to be our final destination. We had followed the trail all the way through the Rhineland, Bavaria and now we had left the Fatherland altogether. With Polish soil under my feet, we entered a town called Auschwitz, a name that meant nothing to me. Yet we knew this was it; I think we all had a feeling that this town was going to be the end of the journey for us. Soon we would be going home. One way or another.

2

The wind surged around us again, and in the field where we all lay, the blades of grass bristled as if a chill had run up their individual spines. Somehow, I knew how they felt. The cold seemed to devour everything in this place. Even the seasons didn't exist in this place. Summer was only a matter of days away, yet each time I exhaled I saw my breath escape my lungs. No warmth touched this place. It had left long ago, with those that had inhabited this land. Nothing was left but the vacancy of death and the cold wasteland that came with it.

I shifted in my position and took out my field binoculars. The complex ahead seemed abandoned; God knew that I had seen enough abandoned facilities in my time to know what they looked like. But something about this place seemed wrong. I scoured the perimeter inch by inch, across the lines of rubble and sandbags, up and down with the lay of the land until I settled on something that piqued my interest.

I held the binoculars away from my face and rubbed at my eyes before I brought them back up and focused.

'What you got, Top?' Flash whispered to my right and behind me.

'God doesn't work in straight lines,' I muttered as my eyes made out the sharp angles and edges of an early German Sturmgeschütz or StuG, as everyone un-affectionately called the low-profile tank destroyer.

The German armour was somewhat camouflaged as it nestled between the brickwork of the IG Farben facility and a large shrub. The muzzle brake of its high-velocity gun was what gave it away.

'Armour?' Jackson asked.

'Hmmm,' I considered as I adjusted the focus wheel of my binoculars, and a figure became visible in my field of view.

With its back leaning against the frontal armour of the StuG, the German stahlhelm was easily identifiable, as was the speckled white of the German winter uniform. I let the binoculars fall away from my face again as I furrowed my brow.

'Top?' Perry asked this time.

I didn't answer him with my words but my actions. I stood up in the clearing, and lit a cigarette. Each of them looked up at me alarmed.

'What are you doing?' Flash stammered.

'Get down!' Jackson hissed.

Again, I didn't say anything, I just raised my eyes to where the StuG was partially concealed and started towards it.

The rest of my squad and the leading elements of Easy stayed behind as I casually trudged across the field to the dormant armour. There was something about its paint that struck me as off when I viewed the armour through the lenses of my binoculars, and it wasn't until I was closer, did I understand what it was. The StuG looked as though it had been sitting in this field for years. The German yellow field paint was faded from the sunlight and no doubt the vicious wind that had blown sediment all over it. Of its six road wheels that lined each side of its tracks, only two were visible to me from the tangle of grass, weeds, and debris that had collected against the side of the vehicle. The other thing to consider was the soldier.

His uniform was heavy with dirt and rot. Even with the stiff breeze cutting straight through my own overcoat, the fabric that hung around the German didn't even quiver. Thick with age, the white was speckled with black mould that ran up his arm and down across his chest, beneath the gaping maw of what remained of his face. It was unclear what ended the German's life, as no flesh remained. The jaw had come loose at some point and lay in his lap amongst a mess of fingers that had likewise fallen apart.

I took another drag of my cigarette as I looked down at him. The remnants of what had once been SS runes stood like ghosts on the sides of his rusting helmet. Again, we were too late. I turned to the field and waved my hands and watched as forty men rose before me, cautiously at first.

'Come on, come on,' I said unenthusiastically. 'Nothing's going to hurt you. You all know the drill.' I spat my cigarette to the ground and looked back to the remnants of the SS man. 'Another camp, another facility. Another waste of fucking time!' I shouted as I kicked the soldier hard and my foot sailed through him, sending bones and rotting fabric into the air.

'Same again, huh, Top?' Perry said as he walked by, heading toward the main gates of the facility.

'You know what they say?' I muttered as I shifted the weight of my Thompson in my arms.

'Same shit, different day,' Flash and Jackson said at once, to the laughter of a few of the Easy Company boys.

'Yeah…' I grunted as I fell in. 'Same shit, different day.'

The gates to the complex were open. Unlike the ones from my dream, these were ornamental. Not meant to really keep anyone in or out, but to show pride in place of the facility, especially considering that it was a German facility in Poland. Brick buildings stood tall on the other side, like dark mountains that grew from the earth itself, standing stalwart against the cold. Signs in the Germanic language labelled each alley between the buildings and Nazi propaganda posters, faded with age, remained fixed to the walls. The face of the Führer and the God-like Aryan soldiers were doing a better job of standing up to the weather than the armour and corpse outside.

I lit another cigarette as I watched three Easy Company men burst through the door of the first building to my left. Flash and Jackson peered through the wide plate glass windows of the building to my right. I took a drag and watched them through the white smoke of my exhale. They were wasting their time; I knew that much.

'What do you think?' Sparks said as he stood beside me and lit his own cigarette.

'I reckon about the same as you,' I said as I turned my head forward.

We both looked down the main street. Before us were the tell-tale signs of everything we had seen before. Cyclone fence, barbed wire, train lines.

'We've been following the railways now for how long?' Sparks said as he took a step forward.

'Seems like an age,' I muttered before I turned to the rest of the men, beckoning them to fall in line. 'God knows I have aged.'

Sparks laughed. 'Yeah, you can say that again.'

For old times' sake, we followed the train lines, and something made me check my old watch. 6:18. The Lords hour, no doubt. No smile traced my face as I stuffed the watch back into my pocket. Somehow, I didn't find it funny anymore.

The railway tracks led us to another line of cyclone fence, a border within a border. Behind the fence a concrete and steel monstrosity rose up before us and seemed to devour the tracks as they vanished behind the enormous, closed steel doors. Where the tracks crossed through the fence, a checkpoint had been established. But rather than the guard house and a plank of timber to stop any would-be intruders, this check-point was constructed out of concrete, and housed an eighty-eight-millimetre cannon. Meanwhile, up on the concrete structure that bore the immensity of the steel doors, I could see four machine gun nests evenly spaced.

I walked through the checkpoint, the Thompson still low on my hip. The wind howled as it followed us through the concrete and it whistled around the eighty-eight. My men spread out behind me now, the boys from Easy Company holding their rifles semi-ready, unsure of what to expect. I flicked my cigarette to the ground as the shadow of the great structure fell over me. It seemed all at once that the world had gotten even colder. Like the last candle in the window had finally gone out. Thinking back, the coldness that I felt when that shadow fell over me, has never left my soul, even to this day.

As I neared the reinforced steel doors, I noticed that one of them was ajar. Only by a foot. It seemed so insignificant compared to the size of the doors themselves. Yet, the gap looked wide enough to go through.

I heard the crunch of gravel behind me and I turned to see Jackson, a look of deep concern on his face.

'You look old,' I said to him.

'I feel it,' he said. Then, as I went to turn away, he put a hand on my shoulder. 'Cody, what do you think we're going to find here?'

I frowned. 'Nothing good.'

'Then, do we need to go in there?'

I considered him, as we stood there on the brink. 'We're here to do our job.'

'Yeah, but Cody…'

I thought of all the times we had fallen short. All the times we had been too late. He didn't understand and goddamn him, he didn't have to understand. This was all about me and her, and he just needed to follow orders.

'Jackson, it's simple. We've been following these goddamned sons of bitches for too long now and I've just about had it with being too late. You were there in Bristol,' I said, lowering my voice, 'you saw them on that ship.'

Jackson opened his mouth.

'How can you look at me and try to get out of this now when you saw that?'

'Cody, that was almost eighteen months ago.'

'It doesn't matter,' I said as I took a step toward him. 'To be honest, it sounds like you think they're already dead.'

Jackson took a step back. 'They can't have survived, Cody. Tell me where you have seen any signs of life in this last year. Tell me.'

'There's been signs,' I said.

'Well?' Jackson exclaimed. 'Name one.'

I glared at him.

'We've been together from the beginning, Cody. We've been through all of this together and I'll follow you to the end, but I can't see anything good coming out of us going down there. And I don't know about you, but I've seen enough. Hell, I'd seen enough the first damned day of this war. I don't want to die, and I don't want to watch anyone else die.'

I spat at his feet. 'Then you should have stayed home.' I turned and slipped through the gap in the steel doors.

It took some time for my eyes to adjust to the low light inside the bunker. Although there seemed to be lights further down from the entry way, the cavernous doorway was extremely dark. Lights danced in front of my eyes and even a fading remnant of Jackson's face remained. I took a few steps, noticing my feet were falling on concrete now rather than gravel. I blinked a few more times as I heard men follow me through the gap, and I stopped when I saw it.

I think after all that time, I was surprised to see a train there. It wasn't anything special. The cars were old and the paint was mismatched and worn. All the doors stood open before the platform, the smell of piss and shit still thick in the air. I had to hold a handkerchief to my mouth as I peered into each of the open, vacant cars.

As before, it wasn't hard to follow where they had been taken. Small tokens, perhaps these were the signs of life that I was thinking of when I couldn't answer Jackson. Breadcrumbs to follow, but the further we walked, it seemed more apparent that no one would be following these breadcrumbs home.

From the tracks, we followed the trail down a long corridor that was ill lit. Lights flashed sporadically, as if the power of the facility was waning, but still, we pressed on. We had come this far. I looked down solemnly as we walked like cattle down this corridor, noticing each token as we passed it. A coat, dropped from someone's shoulders, a shoe slipping from someone's foot as they stumbled in the mass crowd. A man's hat, knocked from his head by a German soldier, never to be seen again.

Above us, the loudspeakers crackled and my heart sunk; surely there could be no further announcements. Surely the Third Reich was finished.

I looked up at the speakers and waited to hear the accustomed opening of Adolf Hitler's speech, the sounds of *Raise the Flag*, but it never came. Instead, it was the voice of an ordinary man.

'Sparks!' I barked. 'Translate for me.' I raised my Thompson in readiness as I continued down the corridor.

'It's all over,' Sparks said as the German man began to speak.

I stopped and looked at him.

'Of all the years we fought for the Fatherland, for our people and our leader. We were doing the right thing. Well, that's what we told ourselves anyway.'

I readjusted the Thompson's stock into my shoulder and continued.

'If I had my time again, I would have done everything – anything – I could for my people.'

The corridor opened into a large staging area. There were many warning signs, none that I ever had the time to ask Sparks to translate. Only one word meant something to me, and even with my lack of understanding of the German language, I was able to piece together what the word Königsjäger meant. King Hunter. My eyes lingered on the word as a bead of sweat ran down from my hair line to sting at my eyes.

'But I would have shot myself before I went there. There are things that I cannot unsee. And that I would never have done, nor ever wanted to know about. But cannot forget.'

I made the gesture for my men to spread out.

'We're finished here, Americans. No doubt you want to know, so I'll play it for you before I go.' I heard the German laugh, but it was sad. 'Maybe he was right, the last thing I heard Hitler say before he killed himself, his wife, and that damned dog. We may be destroyed, but if we are, we will drag a world with us. A world in flames.'

There was a scratching sound and a recording began to play mumbled voices. Sparks looked to me and said, 'It's a recorded speech from Himmler. I can't hear it well though'.

Then the sound cleared up as the man who was speaking said one word that needed no translation: 'Götterdämmerung.' Then as Himmler spoke and Sparks pushed forward to translate the speech, the speakers crackled as they echoed a pistol shot and the slump, as a body fell to the floor.

'You all accept happily, the obvious fact that there are no more Jews in your province,' Sparks said as the boys from Easy Company spread out around the perimeter.

'All Germans, with very few exceptions, realise perfectly well that we couldn't have lasted through the bombs and the stresses of the fifth and the sixth or even the possible seventh or eighth years of the war, if this destructive pestilence was still present within our body politic.'

The ground trembled beneath my feet.

'The brief sentence "the Jews must be exterminated", is easy to pronounce.' Again, the ground trembled and I saw small chunks of concrete dust and debris fall from the roof far above my head.

'But the demands on those that had to put it in practise were the hardest and the most difficult in the world. I ask that you only listen but never speak, of what I am speaking to you of, today.'

Again, the entire room shook this time and even the steel doors before me trembled on their hinges.

'We, you see, were faced with the question "What to do about the women and children?"'

'Jesus Christ,' Jackson said.

'Shut up,' I snapped at him as I leant in closer to Sparks. 'You should have stayed up above.'

Sparks continued, 'The hard decision had to be taken, to have this people disappear from the face of the earth'.

'Are you listening to this Cody?' Jackson said. He held his hands out to me.

I racked the charging handle on my Thompson, as the ground shook again.

'For the organisation that had to carry out this order, it was the most difficult one we were ever given. I consider it my duty, to speak to you, who are the highest dignitaries of the party, for once quite openly about this question, to tell you how it was. By the end of this year, the matter of the Jews will have been dealt with, in the countries under our occupation.'

'They're dead Cody!' he screamed. 'It's not too late for us.'

'Shut up!'

The steel doors trembled again against their hinges.

'You are now informed and you will keep the knowledge to yourselves. Perhaps later, we can consider if the German people should be told about this, but I think that it is better that "we together" carry for our people the responsibility.'

The ground shook again and I heard the slight sound of a hydraulic whine.

A hand fell on my shoulder. I turned and looked into Jackson's eyes. 'It's not too late. Get us out of here.'

'The responsibility for an achievement, not just an idea, and then take the secret with us to our graves.'

With a tremendous roar and the rendering of metal, the left-hand door crashed to the ground, and both Jackson and I turned wordlessly and stared at what came through.

3

The air was filled with the smell of hot oil and exhaust, and the howl of hydraulics and the cracking of concrete filled my ears. The monster moved through the gap it had created. An aura of steam and smoke seemed to surround it as one of its giant, armoured feet stepped through the doorway. The earth trembled as its immense weight came crashing to the ground, sending a spiral of cracks in the concrete superstructure out from its epicentre. The left-hand side of its upper bulk crashed into the remaining blast doors and the steel gave way under its power and its weight. Finally, with the sound of rending steel and tearing metal, it was through and we were left to face the entirety of its size in this new wonder weapon.

Up and up and up it towered, forty feet into the air. Forty feet of armoured steel and forged chassis that formed the basic shape of a man, but this was so much more. Squat in its stance so that it could hold its balance, the legs themselves were fifteen to twenty feet tall and at least four men wide. Its torso, which held the heavy diesels that powered the monster, was slender enough, giving the bulking monstrosity the appearance that it was one of the SS Leibstandarte of the old propaganda films of the mid-thirties. Men of iron, cold expressions and a commitment to the Führer that was unwavering and could never be tested.

Men with the will of steel. And essentially, this was what I was looking at. A forty-foot tall, mechanised SS man. A true testament to the name that it bore.

Hydraulics howled as its arms moved, and it stood before us in all its glory and size. I was vaguely aware that some men had broken at the sight of this monster and had started to run back up the Jewish trail toward the train, but I couldn't bring myself to scold them. I couldn't move my mouth to even utter an order. I was stunned by the sight of the armoured beast.

My mouth hung open as my eyes travelled from the thirty-millimetre pneumatic cannon that was bolted to its right forearm, to the balkenkreuz that was painted across its chest, to finally the long barrel of what looked to be a PAK 44, a one-hundred-and-twenty-eight-millimetre armament that was fixed to its back and extended up above its shoulder.

I noticed small lumps of metal all over its body and saw that they were the cylindrical grenade launchers that were fixed to turrets of Panzers. Hundreds of them. And finally, a sight that reminded me of the first freak weapon that I had encountered, rows upon rows of tubes that could only contain the Screaming Mimis, those damned Nebelwerfer rockets.

Why would they make something like this? Why would they hide this thing down here, down this trail, all this way? Why would this thing stand here at the end of the road?

All thoughts of this were swept from my mind as the mechanised monster roared for the first time. I don't know what sort of siren or horn made that sound, but my helmet was blown back off my head. I felt the flesh ripple on my face and even the air seemed to distort with the tremendous depths of its bellow as it clashed its two steel fists together in a war cry that brought specks of concrete down from the ceiling above us. Around me, more men broke away and ran for their lives as the Königsjäger's roar finally ended and its assault began.

As if instilled with a sense of purpose, the steel limbs of the monster all moved as one. As it took its first step forward, it squared its shoulders and cocked its arms. Then all hell broke loose amongst my ranks as thirty-millimetre, high-explosive shells ripped open amongst us. The sound of the pneumatic jackhammer was gut wrenching in this enclosed space, the smell of the fumes of the monster's engines made it difficult to breathe.

The sight of men from Easy Company getting turned to red mist before my eyes was horrific. One group of men was blown into the air by a ripple of shells that landed around them. Flesh was torn from their hides as they were thrown like children. I saw legs detach from their joints while boots that were still laced flew in a different direction from their owner. With each passing second, the blood of men filled the air and I knew we were all going to die down here. There was nowhere to hide in this open slaughter field of concrete. Throughout all this horror, the one thought that pressed through my mind was that Jackson was right.

It took another step and the ground shook, opening a crack in the concrete, allowing the blood of my men to flow down into the earth below us. Some of my men had started to fire on the beast. They may as well have had spit wads for the good they did. The beast swivelled its body and brought its course of fire across my men. Still, I stood there, gaping at what was happening until a shell exploded behind me and it was as though two hands that were on fire shoved me forward.

All the breath went out of me as I landed on my face. My Thompson skittered away on the concrete before me. I urged myself to breathe but my lungs choked on the exhaust of the monster. Again, I tried, as I threw one of my hands forward to drag myself towards my Thompson, an effort which now I don't understand, because it was useless to me at that point. But still, I dragged myself as I gasped for air. Finally, my lungs accepted the foul poison that surrounded me and stars danced before my eyes. I got to my knees and was about to follow four other men forward to where my Thompson was, when one of the great feet of the monster came down on them, ending their lives and destroying my weapon.

A crack ran outward from the impact and shot between my legs. I froze again for what was probably seconds but seemed like an age, as I slowly raised my head from the forming crack beneath me to the mass of the beast above me. I saw a jet of flame project outwards from its right arm and fall on my men. The screams were horrendous. Still, they fired on the beast. Still, they fought to survive. Those brave men. I knew I had to do something.

Two hands grasped my collar and dragged me to my feet and I saw Jackson. His face was whiter than I had ever seen it. Like me, he was frightened.

'It's killing us!' he screamed into my face. 'We need to do something!'

I didn't answer him, as he shook me and screamed the urgency of the matter into my face again. Maybe I was in shock, I don't know, but he drew his fist back as he screamed again and punched me as hard as he could. My head rocked on my shoulders and I was left to look beneath the legs of the monster, through the steel doors that it had burst from. That was our only option.

With a new sense of purpose, I snapped my head back to Jackson and my hands came up to grasp at his face. His initial thought was that I was angry at the blow he had given me and I saw him react and move to lash out again, but I stopped him.

'Listen!' I screamed. 'Listen to me!' He went to push me away, then saw that I was mentally present and stopped. His eyes were wide and waiting. 'We need to regroup. Get what men you can, go through those doors. Get past it!' I screamed as I pushed him away. 'It's our only hope!'

He gazed at me as I pushed him back, then over to the doors that stood vacant behind the monster. I thought that he might freeze, but another shell exploded behind him and the shockwave was enough to rattle him and send him on his way.

Jackson screamed as he ran off, waving his arms shouting for men to move forward as he did so. I thought that my time had come to do the same. I looked around as I bellowed and although the ground was thick with the bodies of men, there was still many up, alive, and fighting.

'Forward!' I screamed as I waved my arms. 'On me!' I howled as my legs finally began to move, and although the soot of the diesel filled my lungs, trying to choke me, I didn't cough and projected my voice above the rattle of pneumatic fire and the crushing weight of the Königsjäger's movements.

Men surged behind me, and I felt sense of pride in that moment of chaos. Like perhaps that I could stand beside Bill Carrera at the end of this and know that I deserved to do so. A man that people would die to follow, a true leader. But I think that's all rubbish, all desperate thoughts from a desperate man who was surging forward leading more and more men to their death.

Thirty-millimetre shells rippled around us as we surged forward and the Königsjäger brought its flamethrower around onto us, but we were too fast. In no time, we were under it and past it all together.

As I ran under the sizable mass of the beast, I turned and looked back and saw a hatch at the very base of its spine. An armoured door that no doubt led to its commander. That was the key to its defeat. Somehow, we had to get inside. Suddenly, small puffs of smoke rippled up the beast's arm and across its back, and my attention was drawn away from the hatch as I looked up at this new threat.

'Grenades!' a GI screamed as he threw himself to the ground. Metal canisters fell amongst us, smoke trailing after them as they fell. One by one they exploded as men dove for cover or were torn apart by the shards of steel and shrapnel that were hurtled through the air. I dove for cover and felt others do the same around me. The pop, pop, pop of grenades exploding in a sequence filled the air and a hot line of pain ran down my left thigh. I screamed as I rolled over and looked down to see a long shard of steel sticking out of my leg.

'I've got you, Top!' called another GI as he ran over to me and took a knee at my side. No sooner had he placed a hand on my chest to settle me, a thirty-millimetre round took his head off at the shoulders. His body collapsed on top of me as more grenades exploded around us and I felt his body ripple as shrapnel dug into him on all sides.

'God, save us,' I muttered as I used all my strength to push him off me. 'God, save us from this hell.'

I tore the piece of steel from my leg and screamed as I did so.

As the Königsjäger came about, caving in the concrete beneath itself as it did, I got to my feet and hobbled the rest of the way to the blast doors.

I was one of the first to cross the threshold, and as soon as the massive steel barrier was between myself and the Königsjäger, the din of battle seemed to diminish. Behind me, men were pouring through the opening the monster had made. Five at a time, yet still we kept running; there was nothing left for us to do but that.

The room we had entered seemed to be almost a thousand yards long and a hundred feet high. To my left was a docking station with scaffolding, fuel hoses and cranes, where no doubt the Königsjäger spent its time when not reaping American souls. Across on the opposite side was another dock, both of which were empty. Did that mean that somewhere there was another one of these monsters? None of that mattered now though; our situation was desperate enough as it was. There was no place left to run but forward, down this ramp that seemed to lead toward another metal object that sat at the far end of the room.

'On me!' I screamed as I sprinted forward, trying to gain as much ground on the Königsjäger as possible, before it breached the blast door and finished us off. 'Let's get to the end. Find some cover!' There must be cover. There must be something. *Please, God, there must be*, I finished in my mind as my eyes remained fixed on the thing at the end of the room.

Shaped almost like a bell, this metal shape with swastikas painted across it, loomed before us. Almost as large and imposing as the insane monster behind us. Large spindles of cables ran to either side to finally come to an end at control consoles that sat before massive cylinders, which contained God only knew what.

'Top,' a voice came from next to me. 'What the hell is it?'

I turned and saw Flash there. Where he had come from, I had no idea. My eyes returned to the Nazi bell, this enormous device that loomed in this forgotten facility, in this forgotten part of the war. Despite all the carnage that its protector reaped behind me, the question loomed: what the hell was it?

I opened my mouth to answer, but as I did, a horrible sound of wrenching metal came from behind us, and I turned to see the Königs-jäger tear the remaining blast door from its hinges, and let it fall to the ground in the slaughterhouse behind it. The sound the foot-thick door made when it crashed to the ground was earth ending and a wave of silt and dust rushed toward us, followed by the horrible roar of the Königs-jäger and the thrashing of its armoured fists coming together as it eyed its prey and sounded the knell that called us all to our end. But it wasn't the sound of the jackhammer that came next, it was even worse. As the Königsjäger braced itself in its stance, more hydraulics whined into life. I turned as I ran and saw the long barrel of the one-hundred-and-twen-ty-eight millimetre slowly angling down to bear on us.

There was no point screaming 'cover'; there was no cover to be had. Nor was there any other direction to run. The only weapon I had to wield was my sidearm, and all that was good for in this situation was to end my own life. I couldn't do that, not to my men.

The hydraulics whined and whined as the immense tonnage of the armament was brought to bear on us, and as I ran, I had a final thought run through my mind: *If God be us, then where the fuck is he?*

Königsjäger fired.

The report was deafening even at this distance. The muzzle brake shot great clouds of burning powder in a ring that made a halo of the Jager that wielded it. A line of red fire shot over our heads, well and truly off aim. I turned as if to follow it and saw the cylinders that lined the left side of the tunnel explode.

We didn't stop running. With fire consuming the world in front of us and the bellowing, steel monstrosity behind us, a wall of fire seemed like a soothing thought. Flame rippled through the air and rolled over and over itself in a fireball of such ferocity that it made me question what fuel had been ignited. As soon as that thought crossed my mind, the tanks on the right erupted in an explosion that made the first seem dull. A wall of air slammed me in the face and made me hesitate in my run. Someone collided into my back and our feet became tangled. We went down in a mess of flailing limbs.

As I crashed to the ground, I felt the soles of boots step on me, as the owners fled for their lives, desperate to escape the monster that was now reloading its main armament. I looked to the man that had fallen with me and saw that it was Jackson. His face was still white with fear but Christ, it was good to see him at that point. To know that he hadn't perished back in that chamber of death. That we were still together, ready to see this to the end.

I reached out to him as I watched men trample him, as they tried to escape. He reached back for my hand, and as we clasped our grips together, something happened before us that I cannot explain.

Through the smoke, and the haze of the explosions before us, purple light radiated outwards. Light so strong that it cut through the smoke in long, focused beams that shot out at odd angles. One beam illuminated the concrete wall to my left and in its focus point, I saw the reinforcement within the concrete walls. I saw the earth that clung to the other side, the stones and hidden rocks that lay buried for centuries now brought into the daylight by this invasive beacon.

Another beam shot straight at us, down the line, and with my free hand I covered my eyes while I clenched them shut with everything I had. Through my eyelids, I could see the veins coursing up my fingers and the bones of every finger in my hand. Beyond that, the skeletal structure of the men that stood before me.

Jackson screamed to my left and I wished that I could have joined him, but my speech was gone. Taken from me like the lives of everyone that had fallen to this point. As the light chased away the smoke and whisked away everything that was dark and impure within this room, we saw what was making it. It was the bell. It was spinning faster and faster as it rose up into the air. Sounds of lightning cracking and a hum filled the air. A hum that I didn't hear with my ears but felt in the middle of my head as it grew and grew and grew. The purple light was shooting not out from it, but from a sphere that had started to form beneath it. A pulsating sphere that was growing in size, its surface constantly tested by the surging power within it. Bulges appeared all over its rippling hide, as if the power inside was trying to reach out and claw at us, trying to drag us in.

Red lights were flashing in the tunnel and an alarm was ringing. A German voice came over a loudspeaker system that was still working somehow. 'Achtung! Achtung!' it cried as I redoubled my grip on Jackson's hand. 'Die Glocke…' But the rest was lost to me at that point, drowned out by the hum in my mind that had risen to such a volume that it could drown out even the bellow of the Königsjäger itself.

As I started to scream, the sphere exploded in a brilliant flash of purple light that I was sure would have blinded me. In a flash, I saw the skeletons of every man before me. I saw the metal of their rifled barrels through the timber of their stocks. And what was left was a circle. That is the only way I can describe it – it had dimension to it, but cast no shadow, and no light could touch it. Just a black hole before us. A black hole that began to suck.

Nobody ran anymore. There was no point. Men leaned back at first, fighting the magnetism that the black hole seemed to have on human flesh. Eventually, those that leaned back seemed to stumble as they fought for purchase on the concrete floor. The path forward to the bell looked like a trough. A chute to feed the hole. The soles of men's boots started to slide as the pulsing suction became stronger and stronger. I felt the pull at first in my shirt, it wanted to suck it straight over my shoulders. Then it was like a hook in my navel, starting to pull me forward while I lay there on my stomach. The roughness of the concrete did nothing to secure me to my spot.

The hum grew louder and louder as I was dragged closer. I looked over to Jackson as men started to fall, as their uncontrollable slides picked up speed. The fear in his eyes was replicated by the reflection of myself that I could see in his dilated pupils. He opened his mouth and said something to me, but I didn't hear a damned thing over the hum, that never-ending hum.

I watched in horror as men vanished once they hit the black hole. With each soul, a single flash of purple light radiated outwards. Barely even a second was all it lasted. Then men started to hit the hole five at a time and it became such a flurry that the world went purple and remained that way. Such a furious blinding light that I couldn't even see where I was anymore. I just knew that the end was here.

Just before the world went black, I lost my grip on Jackson's hand, as I felt an enormous pull from within, and I screamed in such horror for what I saw.

PART SIX

"Eine Welt In Flammen" – "A World in Flames"

Götterdämmerung

1

Weightlessness. That is the only word that seems fitting for the first sensation that came over me as I was first lifted from the concrete trough in that SS Bunker. Pulled at such velocity that even gravity itself lost its power over me, as I was sucked through the abyss. Words do not exist for what happened to me in this time, nor do they exist to explain the horrors of what I saw. Colours that transcended and twisted the memory of anything I had ever seen, whirled around me. A landscape that was not of this world, and structures that no man had made, at a distance made irrelevant by the size of the creatures that dwelt there.

I cannot say when I knew this was another world that I had been sucked into. Whether it was from the moment I saw the first man sucked into that black hole, or if it was the feeling of that hook under my navel. But I can recall the feeling I had, the one that encompassed me from the moment I opened my eyes and saw what lay on the other side. Fear. Pure and utter fear that shook me to my bones. The knowledge that we weren't alone, that the monster at the camp back in the Ruhr was not some Nazi construct and that these damned things, these horrible creatures, existed in a world of such hunger and despair that I wanted to die right then and there. As I've said before, I wish I had.

When my body hit the black hole, it felt as though I was thrown into a bath of frozen water. My head rocked back on my shoulders, and all the warmth in my body left me as if abandoning me to die. Time was irrelevant. I couldn't tell you if seconds, days, years, or even strange aeons passed in that moment, but it felt like nothing to me. Although my eyes were open, I don't know what it was that I saw. Perhaps, being at an age now where space travel has happened and looking back on this, perhaps I saw something somewhat relevant to what the men on the Apollo missions had seen when they had finally escaped the pull of the earth's atmosphere – but sped up fifteen-thousand times.

A dark smoke surrounded me, blocking out the light from my world and my home. The smoke was so thick and poisonous that I could feel my flesh dying at its frozen touch, like each cell gave up its existence, a dying brought on by some otherworldly chain reaction. I was completely and utterly alone. No one else that had entered was visible. We all made that journey by ourselves, like it was our turn for judgement with the Almighty.

Blistering lines of light shot past me as if they were comets tracing their way to their fiery end. Sounds of screams that could have either been men beyond the levels of hysterics, shrieking as if their own souls had been torn from their bodies and set ablaze before them. Or the horrible jets that the Germans had sent into the skies to try and stop the onslaught.

Then before me, starting as a pinprick in the darkness, was a clearing in the smoke. The rushing sensation became almost unbearable to the point that I opened my mouth to scream, not caring if the smog killed me, even hoping that it did. I pushed with my lungs and tried to scream but nothing could be heard over the warble of death and the rushing of the smoke, until the pinprick rose up with such speed and with such blinding light that my breath was sucked from my chest and I hung there suspended, gaping at what I saw.

The light rushed toward me, a circle of fire to replace the cold darkness that I had entered. When it hit me, it felt as though a man had stood before me on fire and had walked right through me. My eyes burnt in the heavy air; my hair clung to my face, already damp from the heat, whereas my extremities cried out for water. Pillars of fire shot up out of the cracked earth to the sky, where they met deep clouds of putrid smog that hid most of the chaos beyond. Only one part of the sky that I could see was not drowned in that horrible, life-ending muck and it was completely insane.

Two suns burnt beyond. One a massive red fireball that was somewhat relevant to our own, but twice the size, and it was overshadowed by the black colossus beyond that howled in the sky and shook my teeth in their moorings. I appeared in this world as if I was thrown off a cliff. As soon as its heat hit me, I began to fall. I saw the landscape: a wasted ruin of burnt earth and molten rock that bubbled from the heat. A great lake of fire sat out before me, and as I fell, I saw the head of a great being, a Leviathan of immense size. Its flesh glistened in the heat of its pool like the surface of rippling plate steel. A large crest began at the peak of its head and ran down its spine into the fire with the rest of its body. It opened its mouth and bellowed a sound that I could not completely comprehend. A sound that rippled the air even from this distance. Through it all, I saw its eyes. Those amber pits that I will never forget, almost like the one that I had seen in the Ruhr, but attached to this inconceivable beast.

As I fell, the lake of fire and the Leviathan that lived in it were obscured from sight by a large mountain. Rocks stuck out from the crest like the spines of another horned monster, and at angles that I couldn't comprehend. It was as if this world consisted of a dimension that our minds cannot understand and even so, as I fell and stared at this horrible landscape and the crest of this mountain, an eye opened in the side of the landscape. An eye that was larger than me. I saw its vertical pupil, a black slit on a horrible red and orange field, and it saw me. In its recognition, something further up the mountain shifted, and as I looked up and away from the eye, I saw the creature for what it was, revealed from its camouflage on its rocky outcrop as a large wing stretched out, and its mouth opened in a yawn as if I had awoken it from an ancient hibernation.

The stone dragon gnashed its jaws shut and settled its chin back on the ridge of the mountain as its wing flapped once and settled again against its stony hide. The eye blinked once, and I felt the light of it on my flesh, as if another fire was ablaze just before me. Then, its third eyelid rose up from the corner of its duct and the eye closed again, as if ignoring me. It was then that I saw its entire flesh was moving with other forms of life. They crawled on it like lice, an infestation of horrible creeping things that bit into its flesh and sucked the life from it as it slept. Horrible things that nested and bred all the while digging in and consuming this great beast, like a cancer.

As I fell away, I saw the other creatures that lived on the mountain, the smaller ones, almost anthropomorphic in the way they stood. With those horrible eyes, creatures that resembled the one that had taken Carrera's life. Slaves to the great ones, they dwelt below feeding on any scraps that the parasites let fall for them. They were moving, screaming as they ran. Some were larger than others, muscular beasts that leapt into the air and sent waves of dust and sediment sailing away when they landed. They bellowed and gnashed their jaws as they followed my descent.

As my body turned in its fall, I saw something that I couldn't believe within this landscape. Something man made. Rows of cyclone fence and razor wire, fields of crops, trucks with the balkenkreuz of the Wehrmacht emblazed for all to see. A barracks stood off behind the fields, where guard towers stood next to lonely silos. Into the distance, I saw a quarry, and a railway with cars filled with ore, but it wasn't iron. Even as I fell, I knew it was something else. Something alien.

I landed, crashed to the earth like a meteor. But I was unharmed. I cannot explain why – the distance I fell was immense but like I said, irrelevant in this world.

I looked up at the German camp before me and I couldn't believe what I saw. It was the sight from my dream, the tower that had been clawed by the great one, which stood above the railway tracks. Its great mouth open, and the gates clanging in the unnatural breeze. To either side, the weathered stone sat testament against the toxic climate. The glass windows were covered by steel bars, not to keep people in, but to keep those things out. The tower above lay dormant but even then, I could see the barrels of the machine guns that were pointed outward, not inward at the prisoners. I turned my back to follow the railway carts and I saw something else, something that could not have been man made. A large tower, almost gothic in its architecture. It stood upward, proud like one of the pillars of fire, but from its spire a light shone out. One that rose upwards and outwards. A purple light like the one from the Nazi bell, the one that radiated through me when we were sucked into this place.

As I stood there staring at the pillar of light, a purple orb swelled at the tip of the spire and shot up into the air along its current line of light. Once it reached its pinnacle the sky turned purple with an irradiated flash that made me blink, but even as I closed my eyes, I saw something appear way above me. It didn't make a sound as it fell, somewhat like me. But it was easy enough to follow its progress due to its size; it looked as though it would land in the quarry. I never got a chance to see the Königsjäger land, nor to know if it was damaged or still a threat, as between me and the tower a line of those creatures swelled down from the mountain. Their jaws gnashed and their cries were desperate as they ran towards me in a stampede of lust. I turned and ran for the camp.

I could hear their footfalls over mine as I raced for the safety of the German concentration camp. I wonder if I would have seen it that way, if I were to understand the immeasurable weight of the loss that the world of man had suffered from the sights of those gates. The words *Arbeit Macht Frei* in wrought iron, words that I still didn't understand. Despite it all, the safety and comfort I felt in this strange world, as I ran into the open jaws of that death camp and slammed the gate shut behind me, was the one thing that stopped my descent into insanity. There was a chain and a hasp littered on the ground and I barely had the time to fasten the gate shut before the vanguard of those creatures slammed into it with their full force.

The steel rattled and dust listed to the earth from the hinges of the great gates. The creatures howled as they reached inward and clawed at me while their eyes yearned for me desperately. Their horrible flesh rippled as they fought the steel, trying to get at me. They shook the gates and growled in protest as some of them bit the bars while others tried to climb, but there was nowhere for them to get through. One of them just stood there, its mouth open, panting as it stared at me. Those horrible amber eyes looked through you.

Something dug at the back of my mind and I remembered the creature at the Ruhr, how it controlled men, made them kill themselves. I felt my hand go to the hilt of my pistol; I felt the barrel slide out of the holster. I opened my mouth as I raised the pistol, felt my finger take up the tension and the pistol bucked in my hand.

The creature fell. One of its horrible eyes darkened forever. The rest of the creatures erupted in a flurry of anger and turned onto the fallen beast and started to tear it apart before me. I couldn't believe what I was seeing. They devoured the beast, fighting over the scraps. Clawing and gnashing at each other, leaving wounds and utter carnage in the chaos. I saw two creatures begin to fight over the arm, one of them falling victim to a slashing wound across its throat. The rest of the mob, sensing the life flee the wounded creature, began to tear it apart.

I left the commotion at the gate, completely horrified at what I had witnessed, and holstered my Colt on my hip. From everything I saw as I walked through that concentration camp, the Germans had set it up to be worked. The field of crops was a sight I had never seen. It was overgrowing with wheat, sorghum, and vegetables that were an immense size but had over ripened and were now black with rot. Tomato vines ran thick as my arm, the wheat stalks stood twice as tall as me – the grain so heavy they hung down almost flat against the stalks. I couldn't believe what I was seeing. As I walked, I kicked something hard, and I looked down to see a chunk of the ore that had been piled in the railway carts, tumble across the earth. I bent down and scooped it up. It was black, so deeply black I couldn't explain it, deeper than amethyst but with a red tinge and porous. I examined it, then placed it in my pocket and ventured to the barracks.

From everything I had seen, the Germans had mined and farmed this land. Had they been raping this land to fuel their fight in Europe? Their fight to conquer the world? If that was the case, where was everyone? I stepped into the barracks and as soon as I did, I drew my pistol. The smell was abhorrent. Something was living in this room, and it couldn't have been dead as if it was, surely those creatures would have eaten it. They seemed desperate enough to eat each other.

I walked through those barracks with the barrel of my Colt extended out before me, and I noticed the shake in my hand. A tremor that had been there for I don't know how long. It had been with me now for quite some time; would it ever stop?

I found the source of the smell, and I lowered the pistol when I saw the wasted shape. A woman, barely clinging to life. She was malnourished, and ill with something that had wasted her guts, the putrid waste that was coming out of her meant that she did not have long to live. I frowned as I looked down at her and she opened her eyes, looked at me and closed them again in her exhaustion.

I hesitated.

I took a step closer, and brushed her hair that was greyer than brown, away from her brow. Her flesh was dry from the time she had spent in this place. The moisture that had once filled her body was mostly gone. She opened her eyes again and looked at me once more as I placed a hand under her cheek and lifted her face so that I could consider her. And I saw it.

As wasted as she was, as ill as anyone could be, you couldn't remove beauty spots. Especially not three small ones that were clustered next to her left eye.

'I can't believe it's you,' I said as a tear rolled down my cheek.

She closed her eyes again and tried to pull away from me.

'No,' I said softly. 'Don't be afraid,' I whispered. 'Your father sent me.'

All those months ago, that old man in that shack. I suppose he had sent me, in the end. All these lives and all these failures had led me here.

'Kill me,' she said.

'No,' I whimpered. It couldn't all be for nothing, no. It couldn't be. 'No, no. Look, you don't understand.' I reached into my pocket and retrieved the photo that I had carried and loved for all this time and I showed her. 'See look, it's you. I've been looking for you for all this time. And now I've found you. It will be ok.'

I saw her eyes drift from mine and look down to the photo. I smiled as she did. 'See, it's you.' I followed her gaze and looked at a blank piece of photo paper that at some point could have had a face.

'No,' I whimpered again as I turned it over in my hands. 'It was you; I promise.'

'Kill me,' she whispered again and coughed hard, sending a splatter of blood across my shirt.

'Hey, hey, hey. No, come on. You can't die, Bonnie.'

She opened her eyes and looked at me. 'My... name?' she croaked. 'How?' Her breaths were so shallow that I could barely hear her, but I understood.

'Your father sent me,' I whispered and kissed her forehead. 'I'm here to take you home.'

'Home,' she whispered.

'I missed you at Bristol I tried to save you, but we....'

She looked at me, seeing me really for the first time. There was recognition there. I knew from that look that she saw me there in the Jeep, bloodied and half dead as the ship pulled away. She knew that I tried, and she knew that it was me here now and that it was her photo that I carried. She knew it all, and...

I cried as I placed her down on the pillow. The tears from my cheeks dampening her dry, now dead flesh. I ran my fingers across her lips and traced the features of her face that I knew so well, but had never touched. I kissed the beauty spots to the side of her eye, grateful for their existence, as how would I have ever recognised her if not for them? I ran my fingers through her hair and kissed her forehead again and then her lips. I was too late. Again. I was too late.

I heard the rattle of a Browning Automatic Rifle in the distance and I looked away from her. My vision blurred from the tears streaming freely down my face. I retrieved my Colt again as I sniffed and placed the muzzle against my temple. If those fuckers at the gate wanted me to kill myself so bad, then fine. What did it matter anyway? I was a complete failure. Every damned time I thought there was hope, I was wrong. Every time Perry spoke about the hope in the Lord, he was full of shit, because this was all that hope had ever given me. False dreams of happiness in this world of starvation and horror and the death of men.

A Thompson and what sounded like a platoon of M1s joined the volleys from the Browning.

There was no hope. There was no freedom.

I could hear the words now, the screams and the horror of those that fought.

There was only this as the end. And if every man and woman in Europe had come here to fall, then I would be the last to join them.

2

The muzzle of the Colt felt cool against my temple. I found it funny how something so dead, something that could take a life, could be so cold. I thought this as I looked out of the dormitory window at the surreal landscape that laid beyond the Germans' fortifications. So cold, when this entire world was on fire. It didn't make sense.

Over the sounds of their gunfire, I heard the screams of men. I closed my eyes as I felt my finger take up some pressure on the Colt's trigger. Seconds could be related to pounds. Each ounce of weight I took up with my finger, sucked the seconds away from my life. Time of death, 6:18. But then a thought crossed my mind, as I sat there next to the woman who had consumed my life from the moment I received a glance from her eyes. If she could hold that power over me, then what did Jackson have? What about Flash? Those were men that had fought beside me. Jackson had kept me alive since Northern Ireland and here I was throwing everything they had sacrificed to the ground. What a coward I was.

As my finger released the pressure off the trigger, I felt the time that remained in my life suck back to me. My heart uttered a tremolo in my chest, but I didn't know if it was in relief or anticipation for what was to come.

As I stood, I holstered the Colt and turned to her one last time. Death had brought a calm to her that no photograph could capture. No stress or worry could touch her now. No concern for hunger, pain, or remorse could crease her brow.

I ran my hand through the hair that had once been a luscious brown, now as dead and as grey as the hide of that Leviathan that lived in the fiery lake. The eyes that struggled to remain open in their pain, now wide, accepting the horrors that had come and gone. Accepting the death with open arms, so to speak. I frowned as I looked down on her… maybe in the next life.

'Maybe,' I whispered in her ear before I kissed it. I turned my back and left her there. Alone.

The sound of the fighting was fiercer as I moved through the crops. One thing that amazed me was that I could even hear bullets thumping into flesh. It was a deep sound, almost like the bass of a drum the wallop would come back over the sounds of the gunfire. I heard screams again and I started to run. I wasn't surprised to see that the gate was free from those things; no doubt they were attracted by the sounds of the fighting and once they had devoured their own, they had left in search of their next meal. All that remained were the half-eaten corpses of those that had fallen. The bones of their ribcages stood out from the mess that was left. Limbs that were torn from sockets lay spread amongst the ground, the blood that had soaked into the earth darkening it even further.

The chains rattled against the iron as I unlocked the gates. I looked up and around to make sure that nothing had been aroused by the sounds I had made. The chain rattled to the ground and I drew the gates open, without suffering any further attention from those creatures.

I walked out under the words of death that some unknown number of souls had seen before their demise, *Arbeit Macht Frei* or "Work Makes You Free", and a sense of unease washed over me. I felt so exposed as a breeze whisked up the red earth to sting my eyes. I held up my hand to shield them as I advanced, and headed toward the gunfire.

The sound was coming from the direction of the tower and hence I started down that long road, which was bordered by the mountain on one side and the quarry on the other. As I progressed, it seemed like even this world itself was against me. I cannot imagine that Earth has any place like where I was or harboured any creatures such as these. It could not be.

Nonetheless, the wind hurtled itself at me as I leant into it and shielded my eyes. Sand that felt like shards of glass created a blistering barrage of artillery for me to progress through. I couldn't keep going through this, I couldn't see. No doubt the creatures that inhabited this unworldly place would be more adapt and I would be easy prey out in the open.

I held my hands close to my face and turned toward the mountain. It was difficult to say, but it looked as though there was an opening. A cave or a tunnel of some description. I made a line for it, hoping to get out of this horrible sand storm. As I approached, the sounds of the gunfire became louder and louder. I broke into a run, which was more of an amble, as I was blown off balance by the wind. Finally, I entered the darkness and the blessed stillness of air. And it was deafening.

The boom of rifle cracks that sounded like cannons in the confined space reached out to me as I progressed through the tunnel. The horrible red light from the twin suns diminished quickly the further I moved, yet I only had to listen to find the men that were still alive. I had only progressed around a hundred yards when I found the first body.

The GI was slumped against the tunnel's wall. A pump action shotgun lay against his chest, resting after its work had been complete. The gore from the blast had spread the man's head up the wall his back rested against; his thumb was still looped through the trigger guard.

A shiver ran up my spine as I thought back to the Ruhr and the monster that controlled that GI through its eyes. Then the one at the gate that had tried to control me. It was a horrible feeling. Worse yet was the feeling of resistance I felt when I tried to pull the shotgun away from the dead soldier. Not only was his thumb looped through the trigger guard but his right hand still held the pump. His fingers had locked around the grip, seizing with rigor mortis. His arm slowly lifted. I removed the man's thumb and pulled, watching as his arm stretched and fell back, stiffening as his grip finally gave way.

As I held the shotgun in my hands, a hideous roar that made the tunnel ripple with its force echoed toward me. I turned to face it as the sound trailed off and was replaced by the sound of padding feet. The horrible feeling in my stomach washed away as it was replaced by fear and hate. I worked the pump on the shotgun and readied myself for what was to come.

It happened quicker than I thought it would. My vision only stretched about twenty feet before me. The pace the creature came at me closed those twenty feet in about two seconds.

I shot it within seven feet of me, hitting it in the mid-section. The force of the shotgun lifted it and threw it backward, where it landed and lay still. I worked the pump again and took a step towards it, but my eyes snapped upwards as another two came out of the darkness at the same time. I remember seeing the glow of those eyes and the drool running down their chests as they panted for the taste of my flesh. One of them leapt at me, arms outstretched in its hunger.

The shotgun roared again in the tunnel, sending my hearing into the dark ages as the creature fell lifeless to my side. I had enough time to work the pump on the shotgun again but not enough time to aim it. I drove the butt of the weapon outward and into the mid-section of the creature that had closed the gap to nothing now and felt it drive into flesh that was hard as iron. It had no effect.

The creature hit me like a brick wall. I was thrown back down the tunnel by the force of the blow and almost lost my grip on the shotgun. If I had, that would've been the end. I have no doubt about that. But as I landed and the creature closed the gap again and threw itself forward to land on top of me, I fired.

Its lifeless weight fell on top of me. I cursed as I struggled to free myself as more of them came toward me. *This must be it*, I thought, as another three came toward me. The shotgun would be lucky to have another two shells in it. I wouldn't even have enough time to get those two shots off. Nonetheless, abandoning my struggle to remove the creature's corpse, I worked the pump. I aimed it at the closest monster that had now leapt into the air and pulled the trigger.

Clack.

'Oh shit' was all I had time to mutter before it hit me and I was on the ground with its hot breath in my face and its drool running down my neck and pooling on my chest. It snorted as it sniffed me, then lifted its head and opened its mouth horribly wide, wider than any human gape could ever possibly open. Its lower jaw split open at its chin and it swung its head and slammed its jaws shut onto the flesh below.

In its desire for flesh, it didn't notice that it had sunk its teeth into the dead creature that lay between us. It tore strips of flesh away, swallowing them without chewing, and returned for more. The other creatures joined in, tearing and fighting amongst each other while I lay there as still as could be while they tore the dead thing apart. Only once did I suffer any damage, when one of the creatures grabbed a hold of my arm instead of the others as it tore a hunk of lifeless meat free from its dead comrade. One of its claws punctured my skin – nothing dramatic, just a slight wound.

A metallic sound came from down the tunnel. Metal sliding against metal. The sound of a rifle being charged. All three of the creatures froze. I felt one of them turn its head slowly to gaze down the tunnel where the sound had come from. Seconds passed like hours, then finally as if they had somehow communicated it between themselves, all three of them surged toward the sound at once. Their sudden movement was met by the deafening fire of a Browning Automatic Rifle. The heavy calibre shells ripped through the creatures as if they were paper mâché. The steady stream of fire was unrelenting, and although I was eager to see the creatures get torn apart by good old American firepower, I had to press myself flat to the tunnel floor to ensure I didn't find myself in the way of the blistering fire.

Two of them died quickly. The third was wounded and had lost the use of its legs. It lay there in agony trying to move, when the GI emerged from the darkness. It was one of the Easy Company boys. Blood was smeared all over him, his overcoat torn in a jagged tear down his front where one of the monsters had gotten to him. He advanced on the wounded creature, determined to finish it. The GI was within five yards when the creature snapped its head up and stared at him with those horrible amber eyes.

From where I sat, I didn't see what the GI saw, I only saw his face and what came over it the moment the creature stepped into his soul and took control of his body.

The Browning fell to the ground, too large to be used to kill one's self. All sense of being left the man at that moment, wiped from his face like chalk from a board. There was nothing left in those eyes, no sadness or horror or anything else, just the blank darkness as if the lights had been turned off.

The man stood straight, pulled a Colt from his side, and shot himself where he stood.

The creature hissed as the man fell and started to move towards him, but it was weak. As if using the energy to force that man to kill himself weakened it somehow. It stretched its arms out slowly and began to pull itself forward toward the dead man.

That was when another GI emerged. He ran, paused slightly as he positioned his M1 over the head of the creature, and fired before he moved on. I held up my hand and grasped at him as he passed. The GI went to shake me off. He spared a glance down as he tried to move past the mess of the half-devoured creature that covered me. I could only imagine what he saw as he looked down at me in the darkness, but if there truly is a God up there, he gave Jackson the ability to see that it was me, peering up at him.

'Holy shit,' he muttered as he leant down to grab me by the hand. 'Cody. I–'

'Just get me up, man.' I groaned as I took him by the hand.

More GIs came out of the darkness. Flash and Sparks were amongst the five or so that emerged.

'I-I can't believe you guys are together,' I stammered as I finally gained my feet.

'We won't be if we don't keep moving,' Sparks said shakily. I noticed he didn't hold a weapon. He had both of his arms clasped around a leather satchel. He was shivering.

'Yeah, come on. You don't want to see what was back there,' Flash said as he started back down toward the tunnel mouth.

'Hang on,' I said as I moved back down the tunnel and retrieved the BAR as well as the man's bandolier. I reloaded it as we moved out.

'What's the plan?' I asked.

'Live.' Sparks shuddered.

'I don't know,' Flash muttered. 'But we can't stay in here, the tunnels are infested and that... that... I don't know what the fuck that thing was back there, but it's a hell of a lot worse than the others.'

'We can go to the camp,' I said. 'I was safe in there before, but we won't be able to stay forever.'

'We won't be safe in there,' Flash said.

'I–' I didn't get a chance to finish as the earth began to shake under our boots.

'Oh, fuck it's coming.' Sparks began to cry.

'Run!' Flash screamed.

We all did, as fast we could. Back to the mouth of the tunnel. The entire earth was trembling and we feared that the tunnel would collapse on top of us. Sparks as well as some of the other GIs screamed the entire way. A scream that was not that of a man. It was insane. Absolutely insane with fear.

We breached the tunnel mouth and ran into the open. We were relieved to have escaped the tunnel but our relief was short lived. The six of us were surrounded. At least thirty of those tall creatures stood around us at a distance. Some stood above the tunnel mouth, others thirty feet to either side, while the edge of the road was cut off from us by a thin line of them.

Some of the men raised their rifles, but none of them fired. We just moved to the centre of the road.

'Close in, keep your wits boys,' Flash said as we created a circle with Sparks in the centre.

The creatures didn't advance on us, they just stood there, drool running down their chests as they watched and waited. Their amber eyes glowed but none of us sensed any intrusion. They wanted us alive; they wanted us to see.

'What are they doing?' one of the Easy Company boys asked.

'Just hold your fire, they want us for something. Be ready,' Jackson said.

The earth continued to shake, trembling under our feet with such force even the iron sights of the Browning were impossible to focus on. What happened next is difficult to put into words. Words weren't meant to describe such things.

The sound that each of those creatures made was horrible. They mewled as if pining for something. And that something was not far away now. The mountain, the entire mountain, began to pulse. Like it was a living, breathing thing. Part of its centre moved, shifting like it was always meant to. When I say that mountain moved, I don't mean many rocks moved and it gave that impression. I mean that they moved and shifted their shape as if they were molten. As if they were scared out of their molecular construction so that even rock became malleable.

The mountain hitched as if sucking a breath, a major heave of life and then it fell in on itself, as fire reached up to the skies surrounded by a pillar of billowing smoke and ash and death. The suns were buffeted from the skies, hidden by the smoke that had flown forth on the batting wings of death that carried it from the centre of the earth.

Whatever it was that had hidden beneath the scrim that was the mountain, came forward now. Too large to fit through, yet still it came. Up and up and up it stretched. Flesh that was grey like an elephant's hide and cracked like the fiery earth. Two horns stretched out from its head. Horns that were cracked and ridged like those of a buffalo, rotten with age. Its flat face ended in a mouth that sat below a nose that was skull-like. Rows and rows of teeth lay exposed with no lips or flesh to cover them and as it opened its mouth, the smell that came out of it was death.

It roared. A scream from another world, so loud that it shook the earth beneath us, rattled the bones in my spine and set flight to any sense of sanity that remained to us.

Words were not meant to describe such things.

3

Rocks as large as houses broke their foundations and tumbled down the mountain to land on the road where they shattered. Not like stone; they shattered like glass on the road, spreading out like pebbles to be lost amongst the dirt, forever forgotten. The world was in darkness, no light could ever win through that smoke, that fog. That veil of death that had come forth with it.

The monster from my dreams, the one that had been behind everything. Finally, the answer to the question was answered. 'If God be for us, then who be against us?' This is what it was. This was the Anti, the great power in the dark that lurked there, waiting, now come forth in all its power – and it was horrifying. Words could never describe everything I felt, everything I saw, and what happened in those seconds without taking an aeon to write. The only thing I can say now, is that the underlying feeling was not fear, nor horror, but that we were alone. If this was the Anti, then where was God? Where was he to stand against Satan, as he stood so clearly before us now?

Its roar trailed off in a shudder, a shudder that spoke something to us and all at once I knew it all. My hands went to my head as I closed my eyes as I felt it in there, raping every part of my mind as it called out, looking for what it desired. And the word that it used, was Juden.

I heard it so clearly in my mind, spoken through a mouth that was not physical and was never intended to speak the language of man. But Jews were not what it wanted. That much was clear.

'*Juden*,' it said again, with a tongue that was raspy and not of this world, and as it spoke that word, I felt what it wanted. I felt what it was all about. Everything from the letters to the empty camps. And it was hunger. Undying, unrelenting hunger that would never end, and never be satisfied no matter how many tonnes of flesh that it devoured. The word echoed in my mind. '*Juden, Juden, Judenfrei....*' It was the word the Germans used when they referred to the people that they fed to the creatures. It was the word that they used when they rounded them up. The word became more than a belief system when the creatures used it. Then, it became life itself. For them, Juden meant food.

We saw this place for what it was now: a quarry, a farm, a death camp. This was the reason why there was no one left. All those towns, all those cities. Generations of people, cultures, gone. But not for political reasons, not for genocide's sake, or even religious beliefs. It came down to the fact that they needed meat.

I began to scream. Perry died where he stood. I have no way to know if he had killed himself or if he just perished in his horror. But he fell at my feet without a sound, his hair turned pure white. Others were screaming, lost in the madness. Some of them turned to run, but the creatures that surrounded us had moved in; it was as if we were the final sacrifice.

Sparks held that leather bounder close to his chest as he screamed in horror, over and over. He expelled every ounce of breath in his lungs only to draw in a fresh breath and expel it again until finally his voice tore, leaving his scream a ragged gurgle of fear. Flash held his hands to his face. Blood began to run rivers down between his fingers and over his wrists as he clawed his eyes out to finally put an end to that horrible vision. The screams were hysterical, no sanity was left in this.

Jackson was the worst. He held me. Close. I felt the wetness of the front of his pants against my thigh as he clutched me to him. The desperation in his touch was matched only the pleading in his voice.

'Dad, I don't want to go anymore,' he whimpered into my ear. 'Just let me stay home. I promise I'll be good; you won't even know I'm here.'

These words I heard over the screams, over my own screams. I think because it wanted me to hear them. It wanted me to see and to know the complete and utter breakdown of the mental capacity of my entire team before it took us. I screamed and screamed as the creature turned its eyes on us and the world went silent.

As the amber glare came over us, it was as if we were all caught in a beam of heat. The world seemed to shimmer, and instantly we all stopped. The screams died in my throat. Jackson let go of me and stepped away. Flash pulled his bloody hands away from his face and stared up at the creature in awe, looking with eyes that could no longer see. The leather binder in Sparks' hands fell to the earth; it no longer mattered to him. All of them looked up in adoration at this beast, while it stood there above us, its mouth gaping and drool running down its gullet. Enough liquid to fill a dam. All were fixated but me.

I could see everything. I could feel that something was digging in the back of my mind, but it was far away. Like they were digging in the wrong spot. It was the men from Easy Company that went first. The creatures that surrounded us moved in, close enough to bore their eyes into the sockets of those that remained. They let their full concentration work on them without concern. The Easy Company men, too low a rank to carry a sidearm, pulled their bayonets from their scabbards. They were silent as they did, uttering not a word as they plunged the tips of their own weapons into the hollows of their throats. They didn't even blink as they did it. Blood rushed forth over their hands and I swear that one of them even smiled up at the great beast before his life finally left him and he crashed to the earth.

Flash and Sparks stepped forward next. They walked toward the great beast. I wanted to call to them. Trust me, I did. But perhaps the digging in my brain was not to control me, perhaps all it wanted was for me to see all of this, before it turned its focus onto me. That's all I can think, because I watched everything that this malevolent, insane deity did to my men. And I'll never forget.

Flash knew to step over the dead as he walked open armed. He knew to lift his leg when he had no eyes to see with. That's how I knew he wasn't in control of himself, if nothing else was evidence to the fact. They walked right up to the creatures that had stood before the Easy Company men and the creatures hissed as they approached. Their lower jaws gnashed together in a pincer movement, drool running rivers down their fronts as they frothed for the feast that was to come.

My two friends pulled their pistols, held them to their temples and fired. The acts happened at the same time. Synchronised to the second, from the moment they reached for their sidearms to hammer falls of the Colts. To the second.

My heart stopped as I watched this, and I wanted to scream. But there was a disconnect between my mind and mouth, my hands, and my feet. I wanted to cry, but even my tears seemed to belong to some-one else. As I couldn't lash out, I used the only thing I could. My mind. My thoughts projected outwards my hate for everything, focused into the point of a needle, and I pushed it outwards with everything I had at the great being before me.

'*You're weak,*' my thoughts said. '*Relying on these gaping idiots before me, to do all your work for you,*' I roared with my mind.

Jackson started to walk forward. I wanted to grab him. I wanted to reach out and pull him back, but all I had left to me were my thoughts, and they weren't strong enough.

'*You've taken her from me.*' I spat as I projected the image of Bonnie lying wasted in the bed outward. '*But you'll never take what she meant to me.*' I overlayed the image that I carried for all these years over the top. Proud of my memory, I held her before me. Perfect to the finest detail and above all the three beauty spots. Two above and one below. I sent her image outward. '*You'll never understand how strong something like that can be. Because you're weak.'*

Jackson stopped. He turned and stared at me. His mouth was slack and opened slightly. A single tear ran down his cheek, carving a clear path through the dust and soot that caked his face.

'I don't care what you do to me. But you'll never take my spirit. None of ours. We're too strong for you.'

Jackson advanced on me. I wanted to close my eyes. I wanted to turn and hide from what he was going to do. But nothing belonged to me anymore apart from my thoughts. And even those didn't really feel like they were mine anymore.

'You couldn't take his faith,' I projected, as I thought of Perry, lying there white haired on the ground. *'If God be for us, then you stand against us,'* I thought. *'God be for us.'*

Jackson stood before me now. His mouth moved and the words he spoke were not his own, nor was the voice human that came from his mouth.

'No God...' It spoke, and behind those words I heard the true language that it spoke. Ancient and decaying. Only the creatures that stood before me now could understand it, and they all cocked their heads and mewled as the words filled the air. *'Only I...'*

Jackson, now standing with his nose barely an inch away from mine, put the muzzle of his pistol under his chin and fired it. His blood spattered against my face and I felt the heat of the explosion against my throat. And then he was gone. Gone from my sight, gone from the world, life fleeing from him, like his sanity had only moments before.

And now, I was alone. Completely and utterly alone…

4

Now that it was only me that stood before this great being, the other creatures closed in. I tried to fight. I tried to move any part of my body, even to strain my muscles, but nothing would work. It was like there was wire between my brain and the rest of my body, and someone had cut it. Yet there were things that I was allowed to feel. Like the feel of Jackson's blood spattered across my face. That was real to me. The feeling that the end was near and that I would face it alone and afraid. That, I was allowed to have. But nothing else remained to me apart from my sight and my thoughts.

'*You bastard!*' I cried in my mind. I looked to every one of those creatures that edged closer to me now and I couldn't allow any ounce of fear to show in my eyes as they advanced on me, their mouths open in a gape of hunger and fixation. Their amber eyes searched within me for the levers to make my body move. I could feel them in there. But they wouldn't have me. That much I knew. '*Come on, you fuckers!*' I screamed mentally at them. '*Come closer, and stand before me, as I die.*'

One of them stopped, while the others came closer. There was something in the eyes of the one that stopped. Maybe it knew that I was different, but how much thought processes beyond the basic desires of feeding these things have, I will never know. Nonetheless, it remained at the rear while five others advanced.

'Come on then, if my God is dead and you're all that's left, then let's finish this. Let it be done.'

They closed in, their eyes close now. Their feelers reaching out, caressing the levers that controlled my body, and involuntarily, I felt myself move and stop. I focused my eyes on the creature in the middle. I bore down on the cat-like irises that glowed before me, as I felt the drool from its mouth drop on the toe of my boot.

I actually felt it and I blinked.

My hand continued to move. Up above me, the great being edged closer, eager for it to be over. Wanting nothing more than to finally feast and to come forth. My hand closed on the hilt of my Colt and I felt the metal slide against the hard leather. More drool landed on my other boot and I felt their breath against my cheek.

'A thousand shall fall at thy side, ten thousand at thy right hand. But it shall not come nigh thee,' I projected as I felt the pistol come upwards and my finger crept around the trigger.

'Only with thine eyes shalt thou behold and see the reward of the wicked.' The muzzle of the Colt pressed into flesh and my finger began to squeeze the trigger.

The creature before me spoke. It spoke in a tongue that I could understand but the words were printed across my brain in English, as if they were planted within my mind. *'Finish your prayer and die so that we may feast on your flesh, like the millions that came before you.'*

'He shall call upon me, and I will answer him.' I squeezed the trigger and the Colt bucked in my hand.

The amber eyes of the creature that stood right before me, went dark instantly. As if the power that had illuminated them had instantly been cut. Its head rocked backwards and its legs went out from underneath it. The other creatures didn't react. They were so fixated on me and feasting that they never even knew what had happened, they were just waiting for me to fall.

The Colt bucked again, and another one went down, black blood trailing in the air as its body collapsed. The great deity above us roared but nothing could stop my progress now.

The Colt bucked again and again, two more collapsed and finally I didn't even hide the pistol for the final one. I held it out before me and looked the creature full in the face, turning my head to do so.

'God be for us.' The Colt fired again and I saw the lights of its eyes vanish as it too fell backwards, its arms flinging up in the air in its death throes.

There was only one shot left in the pistol, and something told me that it was for me. Something that came from deep down. If now was the time, then so be it. I had come all this way to be here. I had done so many things that I could not be proud of, and the only thing I wanted in all of this had been taken away from me. As had Flash, Sparks, Carrera, Little, Skinner, Perry… all of them and worst of all, Jackson. My brother.

If there was nothing left, and I was alone, then I'd let my body fall. Perhaps I'd end it as they were ripping my guts out with their claws. Perhaps one of them would finally find the right levers to work my mind and they would force my hand in the act, but somehow, I didn't think so.

Of all the things I did in that moment, I did the one thing that I doubted the bastards would have ever expected. I laughed.

I don't even understand why I did or how I managed it at that point. Perhaps I imagined the creature that had remained to the rear with a look of surprise across its face. A look so impossibly human, that it made the whole race seem like a joke. I laughed hysterically, long, deep, and booming. The sound echoed in the desolate climate, so insulting in its waves that the great beast itself turned on me. It continued to glare down at me, but the shimmering effect that its eyes had on me was gone. Nothing held me to the spot anymore. Its power over me washed away, now all it could do was kill me with its strength.

It threw its head back and bellowed as it flexed its arms and clawed at its own chest, tearing strips of flesh away from itself in a fit of rage that seemed to drive it mad in fury. Its scream ripped through the air, sending the earth into a rumbling tirade of dissent.

The creatures that surrounded me all bore the look of fear across their face. Some of them ran. Others looked around, as if trying to understand why the ground was shaking. A few fled into the tunnel's mouth that we had just escaped from, only to be crushed under the earth as the tunnel collapsed as the great being moved toward me.

I laughed even harder at the sight of this. Even the sight as the primal great one descended on me, was not enough to make me stop. Only the words and the vision that came with it, the message that it planted within my brain as it raped my mind for the final time as it reached toward me, it had the power to do that.

'I will kill you all!' it shrieked in its own tongue but the message was clear to me, and the vision that it projected now was the most horrifying thing that I had ever seen. It wasn't because it contained death and fire and destruction of a world, and that the vision had millions of these creatures crawling across the globe. It horrified me and stole my laughter from my breath, because the world that I saw was my own. I saw the Brandenburg gates, broken down. A lone Tiger tank sat dormant, the bodies of Wehrmacht men littered the ground around it, but "bodies" was not the right term. Skeletons that were picked clean; not one ounce of flesh remained to those bones. They gleamed white as the world of fire around them consumed everything.

I saw the Arc de Triomphe. Although standing, it did so above the wrecks of American armoured vehicles, even the tail of a B17 Flying Fortress could be seen amongst the fires that consumed everything below. The stone dragon flew into view and perched upon the Arc and howled a horrible sound through the air.

The fall of Europe would come, and not by the hand of the Germans. Germany would be the first to tumble in a series of countries and continents, all of which I saw images of. Some of them I didn't even know, but of these I did. I saw Buckingham Palace, the Sydney Harbour Bridge, I saw the statue of Christ the Redeemer, in Brazil.

All these things in a world of flames that only Hitler could predict. All these things that led to the end, which was the burning ruins of the United States of America, the final image that I was presented.

I saw the Statue of Liberty, broken and in the sea. Only the crest of her crown and the torch that she held were visible now in the depths of the waters that bubbled ferociously as if it was boiling. From the depths rose the steel-plate Leviathan that I had seen in the lake of fire. Its third eyelid rose up to protect its horrible eyes and it screamed in triumph while the city burnt behind it. Burnt to the ground while millions of the tall creatures scoured the earth. My earth. Scouring the ruins for any human that remained so that their flesh could likewise be consumed. The United States, although the last to fall, it was shown to me that it would happen. The fall of man would be upon us, and this was only the beginning.

My laughter was gone, and fear took hold. But it wasn't fear for myself. I was already resigned to the fact that I was dead. Remember, I knew the bullet in that pistol was meant for me. The fear that gripped me now, was not for my own soul but for everyone that remained. The Germans, the French, if there were any. The Brittons and my fellow countrymen. As the palm of the great beast descended on me, I began to scream, but the sound of my voice was nothing over the rumble of the earth and the single phrase that it repeated as it came to collect me.

'I will kill you all.'

5

I took another breath and continued to scream, feeling as though the last scrap of sanity that I clung to was gone forever. The sky was black from the smoke and soot, risen from the eternal embers that burnt from where this great beast had torn itself out of the earth. Yet, as its mighty palm descended on me, a shadow was cast over the road. It appeared that all the light that remained in this horrible, horrible land fled from its grasp, leaving me and the few creatures that remained to quake in fear in the darkness that existed beneath it.

Lines were carved into the flesh of its palms, crevasses so deep they made the hide of the beast look as if it was ancient stone with the fissure that only time itself could carve. Slowly it came down on me, and it became harder to even focus on the descending death, as the ground trembled with more ferocity the closer it seemed to come. I closed my eyes as my scream finally left my lips and waited for all the weight of hell to come crashing down on me.

But a sound filled my ears. A sound that I had not heard for some eighteen months. One that in many places seemed to be alien, but one I recognised as completely and utterly human in this surreal world. As if in a sign from the heavens, I felt the heat that followed. I opened my eyes and saw the aftermath of the detonation from the high-explosive rockets that had rushed in to explode against the goliath's mid-section. The shockwave of the explosives was enough to drive me to my knees.

Suddenly, the hand, the coming doom, was no longer descending. It was falling away from me. The shadow vanished across the land and what skerrick of light that existed came flooding back.

Amazed, I looked up and saw the great beast stumbling backward. Put off balance by the blow, it roared a tremendous shriek of surprise. The other creatures that remained on the road all turned to face something that was behind me. Their mouths opened in snarls of reproach as they looked up.

Up, I thought. *Why were they looking up?* A sound cut through everything, the rumble of the earth, the roar of the titan, and the beating of my heart that was growing louder and louder with every second. A horn of war. One that I had only heard twice in my life. And I turned, and joined the creatures looking up at the Königsjäger, again at its full height. As the smoke that listed out of the chest-mounted Nebelwerfer tubes dissipated, it emitted its cry of war to this alien world, and then charged.

The scene was chaos. As the Königsjäger advanced, the road surface shattered under its weight. Cracks in the earth shot outward in all directions as the crust splintered and erupted in all directions. The creatures that remained on the road surged toward it and the thirty-millimetre pneumatic jackhammer on its right arm, began to bark once more. The sound had never sounded so good.

I needed to move. I knew this, and as all the feeling came flooding back to my body, I noticed that the ground under my right knee was considerably softer than the cracked earth under my left. Beneath me was the leather binder that Sparks had carried. I could see the imperial eagle clutching the swastika burnt into its hide. It must have been important, so I took it with me as I rose and tucked it down the back of my pants.

As I once had, perhaps only an hour ago, I summoned all the courage that I had left, and ran beneath the steel legs. Bodies were everywhere, those of my men, my friends, laid behind me, while pieces of the creatures that were blown apart by the shell fire fell around me. The world turned bright as the flame from its left arm shot outward and the road behind me was doused with the same fire that these things lived in, and they hated it. They burnt and howled screams of agony that needed no translation, while their amber eyes had no effect on the steel titan that advanced on them. Again, the Königsjäger sounded its horn of war as hydraulics brought its shoulder cannon upward into its reload position.

Around me, the creatures were surging, seeming to appear from nowhere. Some were on fire. Others had lost limbs, torn away by the savagery of the thirty-millimetre cannon. Limping, I watched one still eager to fight the Nazi war machine get crushed under one of the mighty feet of the metal titan.

I narrowly avoided being burnt alive, and so far, the cannon fire had only surrounded me. If I remained there for much longer, I wouldn't be so lucky.

As I again ventured under the legs of the machine, I heard something and looked up. The rear door of the machine was open. Clinging onto the jamb of the door, was a man. His piercing blue eyes stood out even at this distance. He was looking down at me and beckoning with his hand.

'Komme, Amerikan!' he screamed down at me as he waved again.

I looked around and saw streams of the creatures surging towards us now from almost every direction. Returning my gaze toward the Nazi in the machine, he tossed a rope down to me. I holstered my Colt, which seemed useless to me now, grabbed the rope and started to climb.

If you've ever climbed a rope, you'd know that it's hard enough. Climbing one that was attached to a lumbering five-hundred-tonne monster, while a thousand creatures were trying to kill it around you, was almost impossible. When I was halfway to the door, I saw puffs of white smoke emit from the cannister holders that lined the Königsjäger's body, what seemed like hundreds of them. The sound, although dull, so many combined meant that it was loud enough for me to hear over the din of battle.

'Schnell!" the German called as he hurriedly waved me up the rope. 'Granate!'

I didn't need a translation. I had seen the grenades tear American souls from their bodies in the facility. I knew what would happen here. As the grenades landed all around the machine, only to be swallowed by the mass of bodies that was surging around its feet, I looked back up and saw a clawed hand reach down and grab the German by the hair.

As the grenades exploded and flesh, blood, and strips of hide were thrown into the air in all directions, the German screamed. He was torn out of the doorway by a creature that had perched itself high on the machine's back. The claws of the creature's hand dug deep into the German's scalp and I could see the rivers of blood flowing over its fingertips and coursing down the Nazi's face. I climbed faster. Nazi or not, there weren't many of us left now.

Faster and faster, I climbed, while the metal titan fought on. The German screamed again as the creature held him in front of it. Its jaw was open and its drool dripped on me as I climbed. The German screamed an unintelligible phrase as the creature sunk its teeth into the man's throat. He pulled his Luger from his hip and fired the weapon five times at the creature's temple. Both German and creature fell to their deaths as the war around us waged on.

I hoisted myself into the back of the machine and retrieved the rope so that I could shut the hatch.

'Come on, come on,' I muttered as I pulled the rope, feeling it snag on one of the titan's legs as it ascended. Finally, the last of it slipped through the opening in and I started to close the door. Another creature's hand grasped the bulkhead. I stomped on its clawed hand but still it rose and soon its face was visible as it tried to climb up through the doorway.

Grasping the hatch with both hands, I slammed it shut as hard as I could. The creature's head was caught in the jamb and there was a sickening feeling as heavy steel crushed its skull. Its amber eyes locked onto me as the door came crashing down on it, and for the briefest moment, I felt its claws in my mind. Then as the door crushed the life out of it, it was as if a light was turned off inside. The claws in my mind paused and shot out as if in nerve pain, then I felt them slowly slip away as the creature itself fell away from the hatch and I was finally able to fasten it closed. I was lucky to have killed the creature so easily, remembering the way the creature back in the Ruhr tore through us. If it had managed to get into the hallway with me, I feel my story would have ended there.

In agony, I got to my feet and almost fainted, supporting myself against the closed hatch. The pulsing red light illuminated my path to the end. The world was filled with the boom of the titan's feet impacting the earth, the hydraulics that whined as the metal moved and the rattle of the pneumatic cannon on its right arm.

Suddenly an artificial German voice spoke over a loud speaker system. 'Achtung. Achtung,' the computer announced. 'Panzerabwerkanone fuering um drei, zwei, einz.'

This was a countdown, I thought, as I looked up as if the voice was an artificial deity.

'Aus–' The entire structure shook with force as a monstrous explosion echoed above me. The sound inside the machine was tremendous, and I fell to my knees holding my hands to my head with the concussion of the force.

I knew in my head that the shoulder-mounted cannon had just fired. The thought rocked through my head that the concussion was worse for the Germans than it was for me, standing on the outside. I advanced again, shakily, and through the strobing red light, I found a ladder and climbed it.

6

At the top was the control room, where just one German sat. A man that spoke quickly to himself, he stood in the middle of the room; each of his legs were lashed into what looked to be oversized pushbike pedals that had linkages attached to them. Large levers stood up either side of him like ski poles that he worked like the gear shift of a manual truck. He constantly adjusted the grip of his right hand to turn a wheel that was attached to sprocket and chain.

'Klaus!' he exclaimed and was partway through another phrase when he turned and saw me. He paused, and I felt the entire machine pause with him. He looked down at my shoulder, saw the blood running down my front, and returned his gaze to the forward position where he looked through the dark armoured glass.

'Klaus?' he questioned and shook his head.

'Yeah,' I said, imagining that the name Klaus belonged to the man that had saved me. I too shook my head, thinking it was a poor expression to explain the end of a man's life, but in this instance, it would need to do.

'Scheisser!' The German exclaimed beneath his breath and I didn't know whether the profanity was directed at the death of his friend or for what we were seeing through the armoured glass before us. I stood at his shoulder and watched the horrible, horrible scene unfold. Masses of creatures were swarming the earth around us. But worse yet, much worse, was the sight of the great beast rising again. Its eyes glowed through the dust, smoke, and fire that surrounded it. It seemed that all that the rockets had managed was to knock the beast off its feet.

A rumble emitted from the great beast as it rose, a rumble that grew into a roar as it lumbered forward. I watched in exhausted horror as the earth shook even within this great metal casket, with each footfall as it approached. The German began to yell what I can only imagine were curses to the great beast. The bravery of the man I cannot overstate.

As he roared words that were meaningless to me, he hammered his fist down on a button and the Königsjäger uttered its war horn again and began to advance on the great beast. As the German used the controls, I watched and saw what each seemed to yield. I saw how the wheel he turned directed the angle of fire from the thirty-millimetre canon, which he directed to fire on the great beast.

Black clouds erupted up the beast, starting from its legs and working their way up its midsection. Each black cloud impacted momentarily after the report and shudder from the cannon. Closer and closer the great beast came. Still the German screamed as he worked the controls and pushed the metal titan toward its greatest foe. Closer and closer still, the black impact clouds worked higher and higher and eventually began to impact on the beast's face. It roared as it turned its head. The German shrieked in victory and drove the Königsjäger forward.

The impact as the great beast and the metal titan came together was earth shattering. The German brought up a massive steel fist and drove it into the head of the great being. It echoed a roar as its head rocked back sickeningly. I watched as the Königsjäger's metal hand clasped the monster by the jaw and it shrieked as the thirty-millimetre fired rapidly directly into the creature's face.

The German leant forward as he continued to pummel the goliath, chanting something that made no sense to me. Over and over, as he worked the machine to end the great one's life.

He pressed a button and the German artificial voice echoed 'Panzergranate laden' before the entire structure vibrated. The German began to laugh.

Suddenly, with a screech of steel and a horrible roar, the structure shifted and I almost lost my balance.

'Achtung, Achtung,' the German artificial voice declared, but the rest of the words I had no understanding of. Whatever this stood for, it drew the German's attention to the left. I followed his gaze and through the dark, armoured glass I saw the edge of something. The right hand continued its fight against the great being, but the left was unresponsive. The German shifted the controls and the steel titan came around, and I saw it. The left arm was on the ground, completely detached and swarming with those disgusting parasites, which I now saw were larger than even the seven-foot-tall creatures.

'Scheisser!' the German screamed as he turned his attention back to the great being that he had still clasped in the Königsjäger's right fist. With quick movements from the German, the thirty-millimetre stopped firing and the remaining arm drove the beast away. As it stumbled back, the German swung the machine to the left in search of what had attacked us on our flank. Slowly our vision panned and I thought it was a mistake; whatever it was that had attacked us, I didn't feel safe turning our back to the goliath that was far from dead.

I tried to convey this to the German, but the language barrier was too great and all he did was wave his now free left hand to me and utter words that I didn't understand. Still, we panned. I scoured the landscape and couldn't see a trace of anything that could have hit us that hard. Nor did the landscape suggest that anything that large had touched it. In hindsight, I should have known what that meant, but I was near fainting again from the pain in my shoulder. Looking back now, I suppose it doesn't matter if that was an excuse or what, because it happened anyway.

The stone dragon descended on us again. Somehow, I feel that the creature knew where to attack, as its blow went right to the source of where we were. As quick as the German's reflexes were, no hydraulics could move that fast. The stone dragon descended out of nowhere, shrieking as it extended its talons.

The dark, armoured glass shattered under the blow as one of the talons penetrated inward. The Königsjäger seemed to slump. Suddenly, the right arm swung wildly and although we couldn't see it, there was a crash of steel and the dragon fell to the ground. The German uttered a groan as the right arm came into view once more. We watched, no longer protected by any form of glass or steel, as the thirty-millimetre opened fire on the dragon.

The beast howled and writhed as FLAK fire ripped up its back. Then the structure shook again and I heard steel scream and the German voice called its warning one more time. But the German didn't react.

The structure was shifted, almost thrown around. How the giant SS mech didn't fall, I still cannot explain. It stumbled backward. As it did, I saw that my concerns in turning our back to the goliath had been justified. Chunks of steel were in its hands, torn from the rear compartments of the machine, and I could hope that the main armament still remained.

'Kill it!' I screamed, but there was no answer from the German.

I turned to him and started. 'Come on! What are you…' I stopped when I saw a large shard of the armoured glass sticking out of his chest. He now slumped over it, blood running down his legs and pooling over the controls of the machine. I swore as I moved to him. Now alone once more, in a machine I didn't know how to use to even defend myself. There was nothing I could do but try.

I heard the great being utter its horrible roar behind me as I worked to free the German. I let his body crash to the ground as I took his place at the helm. I positioned myself to where the German had stood and I looked up at what faced me.

On the left, the stone dragon was getting back to its feet. It didn't look at its metal foe – instead its eyes were locked on me. Such hatred flowed through its eyes that it made me sick. It knew it was fighting a small man; the illusion fooled no one. Between it and the great being, the Leviathan from the sea was coming for me. It slithered along the ground as if it were a snake, while the great spikes that lined its back slowly stood up on end. The earth that its body touched was turned to fire from the heat of its hide. Its eyes glowed even from that distance. Then as the great being stood there, smoke shot from its nose in two hot jets, as if it was breathing fire. Its horns low, it tilted its head ready to charge.

To my right stood the tower that I had seen when I first got here. The long line of purple light continued up into the sky. But something was moving before it. Halfway between myself and the tower, the ground opened, revealing another great monster and the last that I saw. Another snake-like creature that was every colour of the earth and more. There were colours that we have no words for, and the way the earth moved and parted for this creature made no sense. It couldn't have happened. The earth didn't tumble over itself, pushed from its moorings to escape the beast's movements. No, it simply just ceased to exist, as if the hole that this creature created was always there and that the earth was just another scrim, finally revealed to be false.

This great snake of many colours opened its mouth and screamed. But it wasn't a roar; it was a literal human scream but from the mouths of millions. I don't know how I knew this, but like the great being, the way its words echoed in my own language within my mind, I knew that those screams belonged to everyone, every human being that had died here. There were men, women, children. Jews, Christians. The old and infirm. Wehrmacht men, SS officers. Jackson, Sparks. All of them were contained in that one shriek of horror and finally it ended in a low growl that I feel was what the sound was below its horrible representation of the human cries.

The great being advanced first. The other three came slower, but they would all hit me at the same time. I knew this was the end. It spoke in its own language, but the translation echoed in my head, with each step it took. It spoke more and more and the shrill shiver ran up my spine.

'*All your thoughts of gods are wrong. It is us who waits for you. There is no salvation, no loving or peace that awaits you. Only us and the world of fire that you see here.*'

I looked down to the levers as the words ran through my head. There was one there that I hadn't seen the German use and I knew at once what it was for. I flipped it and all at once hydraulics whined as above me the long barrel of the one-hundred-and-twenty-eight-millimetre cannon began to lower.

'*Your weapons will do nothing to save you,*' the voice said in the centre of my head.

A unit lowered next to me at the same rate as the cannon. It contained a telescopic sight and two adjustment wheels that were astonishingly like what I remembered in the Sherman tank all those years ago. I held my eye to the telescopic sight and adjusted the crosshairs to the best of my ability. In the end the target was large and the canon was powerful. 'Who said I wanted to be saved,' I muttered as I slammed the trigger of the cannon.

'Achtung, Achtung.'

'*When will you people learn?*' The great beast echoed as the monsters closed the gap.

'Panzerabwehrkanone fuering.'

'*You were meant to be our food.*'

'Um drei.'

'*Give up and become the offering that you were meant to be.*'

'Zwei.'

I laughed as I pressed the horn and the Königsjäger uttered its war cry for the last time. The sound was horrible and triumphant and a sound I will never forget until the day I die.

'Einz.'

'If you want your meal, you'll have to work for it. You ugly son of a bitch!'

'Aus—'

The cannon fired. The sound was deafening and the concussion from the monstrous brake rippled the flesh on my face and stopped my heart momentarily. The monsters roared together as they closed the gap; none of them were affected by the cannon fire. But none of them were the target.

In the distance, just before they all hit me, I saw the detonation. It hit exactly where I had aimed. I laughed as the world shimmered with the purple shade of the twilight of the gods.

7

The great being stopped just before me as it turned to look at the tower. As it did it blocked the destruction from my sight. Another flash of purple came, so bright that I saw through the great one. I saw its skeleton; I saw every piece of its eternal structure. I saw that of the Leviathan and the snake of many colours too. But words cannot describe these things that I saw. They were never meant to. I laughed, hysterically now. Exactly what had happened in the bunker was happening now. There was no Nazi bell this time though; I had destroyed the portal on this end and trapped them here, doomed them to starvation. But I had forgotten what had happened when I was brought here, when the bell was set to surge by the chain reaction.

I laughed as even from this distance I felt its pull. I stepped out of the control section and moved to the threshold of where the armoured glass once stood. There the pull was stronger.

'*What have you done?*' the great being cried.

'I have ended it,' I said as the pull finally became strong enough to carry me and I let it lift me and pull me towards it.

I laughed as I flew, onwards and away from it all. Laughing hysterically as if finally, I had gone mad. Until my momentum stopped.

A hand closed over me. A hand as large as a city block is what it felt like. The way it moved, it was so fast I cannot explain, but suddenly I was there before its eyes. Its great amber eyes.

It said to me mentally, *'This is only the beginning'.*

As it spoke, I saw the stone dragon attempt to take off and fly away. But it was flying backwards. It disappeared over my shoulder, and in a bright flash of purple light I never saw it again.

'I will see your kind again,' the great one said. *'And it will be you.'*

I saw the Leviathan slip past. Over and over, it tumbled as it roared, helplessly caught in the pull of the purple light. Another bright flash and it was gone forever.

'You, so brave, that will bring about the fall, as it should be.' With that, it let go of me and I whisked away. The air rushed past my head, at such a speed that I cannot explain.

I saw two noteworthy things before I entered the purple light again. Two things that I will write here as testament to what I saw. The great one turned and walked away. Against the pull of the light. It walked away, past the wreck of the Königsjäger. As I turned and the crumbled remains of the tower came into view, I saw the snake of many colours caught in the pull. It screamed as it tumbled but it wasn't the scream of humans this time. It was the war cry of the Königsjäger. The last thing that it had heard. Then it hit the light and the world became purple once more as it vanished.

I was helpless now but to let the pull of the purple light take me. I had no thoughts in my exhaustion, only a hope that this was all behind me. Nothing but a nightmare that I would try to forget. I couldn't have been more wrong. As I have said before, words cannot describe the things that I saw, nor could they describe the feeling that I was left with as I hung there suspended above the chaos and death.

'Goodbye, Jackson,' I said, although it was plain he would never hear me. I closed my eyes and let the purple wash come over me. And I prayed for the first time, that I could die and never think of this place again.

EPILOGUE

1

So, there it is, the long-winded story of how I came to be here. How I fought across Europe. How I missed the actual D-Day but took part in one of the largest invasions in history. Just not your history. Sometimes I wonder if it's even my history at all. I know this has left so many questions. If I were to put myself in your shoes I could start with a few.

Was I shocked when I got here? Did I look for anyone that I knew? Do I have any evidence to back any of this up? Well, my educated friend, the answer to most of this is 'yes'. And I will do the best I can to summarise this for you, although I am becoming weary of writing and my time is near. The main thing to consider is that I was a man who had spent the last two years of my life fighting my way across Europe. I was dressed as a soldier; I carried a pistol that had one round left in it. Half dead, blood all over me, and I woke up in a post-war Europe. Think about that before you read on, and consider the shock that some of those poor people had when they saw me. I can only thank the Lord above that I didn't "arrive" in the middle of a populated area.

2

I woke up disillusioned, exhausted, and near death in the middle of a forest, half buried in leaves. I have no idea how long I had been there. But it couldn't have been for that long. I have reason to know this as what I brought back was not damaged by moisture nor exposure to the elements. One of the first things I did when I woke up, was to sit up. Something made that almost impossible. On top of the fact that I had no energy, I was near starved, and had lost somewhere between half to a full quart of blood, there was something jammed down the back of my pants. In the state I was in, I couldn't even think what that could be.

What I discovered was the binder that Sparks had clung so dearly to. I remember sitting there in my state of exhaustion, looking at the swastika and the imperial eagle burnt into the leather. Being alongside the last Germans in that fight for humanity, had made me feel different towards them, but the swastika and what that stood for will never be right. Not in my eyes, not ever.

I tucked the binder back down the rear of my pants and set out through the forest. I had no bearings. Although the weather was warm, I could not see the sun for the dense canopy. I could not tell you how long I walked, as I was in and out of consciousness. Eventually, I came to a ditch. A ditch that had a creek running through the lowest point.

I stumbled down through it and limped up the other side to see a great field. A field that had cows grazing in it. It was bordered by a stone wall that led up to a road, with a small cottage that sat opposite an intersection. I hope this is feeling somewhat familiar to you, because it was to me. The big difference is that the field was full of cows and not twelve-foot poles with wire strung across them. The type of wire and poles that would turn a WACO glider and the men inside into mincemeat.

I don't know why I decided to go back to that cottage. Maybe it was because I was delirious? Because if I had been in my right frame of mind, I would have remembered that it was no longer there. But there it stood – despite seeing the wreckage and feeling the flames when one of those Screaming Mimis, the Nebelwerfer rockets, had thrown the lorry into it.

In the state I was in, I didn't think anything of it, until I saw her. I was still in the tree line at that stage, so she didn't see me. For that, I am thankful.

I watched Bonnie run from the front door of the cottage, into the arms of a young man. He picked her up, twirled her around and kissed her.

That's all I remember. I fainted then. When I woke up the second time I was in another cottage. In a bed, naked. I had been washed. As it turned out, the cottage belonged to Bonnie's neighbour, who owned the field and the cattle and had seen me and had followed me to make sure he hadn't gone mad, seeing an American soldier, five years after the end of the war.

That had not only been a wake-up call for me, but had been difficult to explain. How had I, an American, and an armed American for that matter, appeared in his field five years after the war? Not to mention with Nazi artefacts? Well, you know, kids and their fancy-dress parties. Too much alcohol and too much imagination. The documents, I passed off as fraudulent documents I had found and used as a prop, and the wound I suffered from a dog attack, which I no doubt received while walking through people's fields drunk at night.

This seemed to satisfy the curious neighbour, to some extent. In the end, I feel he was happy to see the back end of me, even if it cost him a set of clothes.

I had received some answers from that. Most of the answers I needed. It was the 1950s; exactly when, I don't know. But there had been a shift in time. The war that I remembered, wasn't exactly what had happened. At least not here. Bonnie was alive. I know now that the United Kingdom suffered through the Battle of Britain, but still, her house stood where it had been. No crater marks, no Rommel's asparagus. Too many things had changed. I had to be careful moving forward. I had to come up with a story, or be labelled a madman. I, for better or worse, chose the story and clung to it for dear life.

3

I managed to make it back to the United States with some help from the US embassy. Hell, I had dog tags, I had a pistol and scars from the war. Although, apparently there was no record of a John Cody, nor any record of our unit. I put it down to scrambled brains after the war – hell, I couldn't even tell them what I had done for the last four years. In the end, the story earned me a trip home. If you could call it that.

What I found was some other family living in my house. No one knew me, not even my neighbours. Apparently that family had lived in that home for the last forty years. Who was I to argue?

I suppose I did what any lost soldier would do when they reached times of trouble. I turned to my superior officer for guidance. It took me five months to find Bill Carrera and another month to approach him. The day I did, he was working in his garden, in his nice, tidy New England home, as he tended to do most Saturday afternoons. I walked along his white picket fence, which would lead me directly to him. He looked up at me from the weeds he was pulling and gave me a smile.

'Hey there,' he called as I approached. 'Fine day for it.'

I didn't know how to answer him. Bill Carrera, the man who had ended his own life to save us, was pulling weeds on a fine New England afternoon.

'You ok, son?'

'Yeah, sorry sir.'

'Sir?' he laughed as he stood up. 'Son, no one has called me that since I left the military. Did you serve?'

He obviously didn't recognise me. 'Yeah. Yeah, I sure did. Europe.'

'Yeah, so did I. Bravo Company. 2nd armoured.'

'Easy Company, Five Oh Third,' I replied, thinking of the men I served with at the end. It must have sounded right because he didn't question me.

He nodded and extended his hand. 'Bill Carrera.'

I returned the gesture and shook his hand. I looked him in the eye as I said my name.

'Pleased to meet you, Cody,' he said, then paused, as though there was a glimmer of recognition.

'Say, did you serve with a Jeff Gordon?' I asked, trying to move past it.

Carrera's eyes lit up. 'Flash?' he laughed. 'Yeah, I served with that peckerwood. One of the bravest damned sons of bitches I had ever met.'

I laughed. 'Yeah, and one of the biggest mouths too.'

'Hey, you are not wrong.' He pointed at me and squinted. 'Did I see you with Flash at one time or something?'

'No, I don't think so, sir. I just remember having a beer with Flash while on leave once and I remember him saying Carrera. So, I just put two and two together, you know. I can't believe I could just remember that like this. Say, you don't know where he settled down do you? I would like to look him up.'

Bill looked at me, not really convinced, but there was a scream and suddenly a child was at his hip, tugging at his shirt.

'Daddy, daddy,' the boy called.

'Woah there, sport,' Bill said as he bent down to collect his child. 'Cody, I'd like you to meet my boy, Daniel.' I greeted the child. 'Cody here was a soldier like your pa. What do you say son?'

'Thank you for your service,' Daniel said timidly.

'Oh, no problem,' I said as I looked over his shoulder and saw a beautiful young woman standing there with another squalling child on her hip. 'Looks like the missus has her hands full with that one,' I said as I recalled the letter that she had written him. Instantly a foul taste filled my mouth.

'Bill,' the wife called on cue and her husband's eyes wandered over to her.

'Yup,' he agreed solemnly. 'She sure does. Hey look son, do you want a beer?'

'No. I best be going.'

'Really, it's no problem.'

'No, sorry, I really must be somewhere,' I said and took a step back. 'But pleasure to meet you,' I said and extended my hand again.

'Pleasure was all mine,' Carrera said and winked. 'If you're over this end of town again, make sure you call in. And try Clear Lake Iowa – I get a postcard from Flash every now and then. That was where the last one came from, anyhow.'

It took everything I had not to cry at that point. Even then, I only lasted twenty steps before the tears started running down my face.

I took his advice and followed my nose to Clear Lake. On the fourth day of looking, I found my old friend Flash and on one occasion, I shared a beer with him at the Lakeside Landing. Like with Carrera, he did not recognise me, not at first. But the conversation with Flash was the last time I tried to contact anyone.

On that occasion, I had found Flash at this watering hole, having a quiet beer by himself as he read a novel. I got my own drink and sat down a few tables away. I had wondered how to start any of these conversations and I supposed that all I really had for obvious common grounds was our war service, so I started there.

'Say there, you wouldn't have served in France by any chance?'

Flash looked up at me and considered me for a while before he answered. 'Yes sir, I was one of Omar Bradley's boys.'

'Armoured?'

'Two in a row. Do I know you, soldier?'

'Ahh.' I wiped a hand over my face. 'I think we might have shared a beer while on rec leave in Paris one time.'

'Is that right?'

'Yeah, I think so. Say you didn't serve with a guy called–'

'Carrera?'

I swallowed hard. 'Yeah, how did you…'

'How did I know you were going to say that?' He laughed and took a pull from his beer. 'Could be intuition. Or it could be that Bill Carrera phoned me up not five days ago and said that I might have someone call in on me.'

'Is that right?'

'That's right,' Flash said as he looked me full in the face. 'Said he had some guy walk past and they got into conversation and I came up. He said that this guy used my full name. Said that we had a beer together on rec leave and that he recalled me dropping Carrera's name. Sound about right?'

'Yeah, well, it sure does.' I swallowed again.

'Yeah. He also said that something about this guy seemed familiar but he couldn't quite put his finger on it. Like there was something he was forgetting, something important, and that every time he stopped to think about it, he got a real bad feeling.'

I didn't answer him. I just stared at him.

'Now, here you are, getting to talk to me, and I know how he feels. I know you. But I don't know where or why. I have a feeling I know what your name is but I don't want to say it.'

'It's–'

'And I don't want you to say it either.' We sat and stared at each other for a little while at that point. 'I'd like you to say what you came here to say and leave me alone.'

I took a pull from my beer and set it down on the table. I stood up and extended my hand. Flash looked at it. 'You don't remember, but you did something for me at one point. I just want to say thank you.'

'I'm not shaking your hand,' he said coldly and unblinking.

I held it out for a little while longer, then let it fall to my side. 'I'm sorry to have bothered you,' I said before I turned and left.

4

The next thirty years I would like to say I spent trying to move away from that life. But in the end, all I did was to compare my time and what I knew, to this period and what I had access to. I moved to Europe, I learnt German, and out of boredom, French. I studied the rise and the fall of the Third Reich and learnt a lot about the shortcomings of the German war machine and how it fell apart. All of this I wanted to do, to learn why they did what they did.

I read the documents, those files that were included in Sparks' binder. What they entail is the documented recordings of the quantity of tonnage removed per month and year of grain, and a material that I have been unable to name until now. This number is offset against the number of people that were transported to this world. I leave the documents with you, that you may read them and understand the magnitude of the crimes that were committed and the number of lives that this world and these resources consumed.

What this comes down to, and what all this leads towards, is that Germany was lacking resources. They were dependant on the resources of other nations to fuel its war machine. In your timeline, once they lost those streams of incoming resources, the wheels started falling off the proverbial wagon. In my timeline, they didn't need the international resources. What they needed were sacrifices. At first, no doubt, it seemed like a gift from the gods. A land so bountiful and resourceful they even named it Großdeutchland, meaning Greater Germany. Then, the war was going well for them. They were winning as they had ample resources. They had achieved their goals and now the time had come to walk away. But the order was given to stay.

More men were required to keep the creatures at bay, more sacrifices required to satisfy the hunger that seemed to be ever growing. When the people started running out, the Germans found themselves in a predicament. They had become dependent on not only the food, but the mineral red mercury which they were mining. Remember the quarry I mentioned? IG Farben was hydrogenating the red mercury to use for fuel. The Ruhr Stahlwerker were using the red mercury in their treatment of highly specialised armoured steel.

When I recall the pounding that the Panzer MKVIII Maus had sustained in the Ruhr, this would make sense. The steel that was available in your period would not have lasted against the barrage that the Tiger had given it.

Even Rheinmetall and Krupp had become dependent on this red mercury for armaments – how else could something like the Königsjäger have ever existed? Even today, nothing of the sort has come to be in this timeline, almost forty years after its fall in mine.

So here the Germans found themselves no longer in need of resources such as food in times of peace, but in a requirement for red mercury to sustain the peace. A material that they could not source from any other location. Hence to continue, they needed souls. Once the souls of one conquered land ran out, they invaded the next. Sudetenland, Poland, France, England. For them, it was easy, they just broadened their classifications of what it meant to be a Jew. But I will let you decide for yourself in these words that are attached.

But listen to me. This is NOT the reason why I write this. I have known you now for the better part of fifteen years, so why would I wait until now to bring all of this up?

I suppose it all lies in what I left you with. My last paragraphs or so from the last chapter of my life. I didn't come back alone. There are three of them here. And I have looked, high and low. And I can't find a trace of them. The closest thing I found for a multi-coloured snake was the Australian Aboriginal Dreamtime based around the Rainbow Serpent. But how could that be? Those stories are from thousands of years ago. But as there is no expert on travelling through dimensions along the line of purple light, who's to say when they could have arrived, or where? I arrived four years after my departure on the other side of Europe. I was lucky to arrive on land. But for them, it wouldn't matter.

So, I suppose I am partway through discussing with you the evidence I have to back up my story. I feel this is the only question now that has somewhat been left unanswered. Even the documents I know you will try to discredit, and that is up to you now. Where I am going, I suppose I won't really care. But if anything, please at least read the summaries of three separate newspaper articles that follow.

Found from the Portland Press Herald, dated November 27th 1986. On November 25th of that same year, Bill Carrera turned seventy. His family held a party. Those who attended were his wife, his two sons, both of their wives, and a total of six grandchildren. When the time came to bring out the cake and blow out the candles, Bill sat there smiling as they sang happy birthday. Part way through the song, something heavy fell from Bill's hands and rolled across the floor under the table. Ever dutiful, one of the grandkids bent down and retrieved for his grandpa a MKII Grenade. It exploded in his grandchild's hand, killing everyone at the table instantly, except for two.

One of those poor survivors was one of the grandchildren, who clung to life for another three days and then died of their injuries. The other one of those two was the wife of Carrera's youngest son, the one I had seen squalling at his mother's hip all those years ago. She said that Bill was adamant that her husband was not his son, accusing his own wife of adultery even in front of the grandchildren. In their defence, they probably thought that Bill was having a turn and did what most children did with their elderly parents – smiled and nodded. At other times he had mentioned something that they didn't understand.

"You guys remember the eyes, right? How they make you just want to do it? Make you want to blow your brains out." They gave him some tablets and put it out of their mind; he obviously wasn't himself that day.

Around the same time, I came across the second article, which was from the Clear Lake Mirror Reporter, where it was reported that on the 25th of November, Flash Gordon, a Clear Lake resident, had invited all of his old war buddies to celebrate their lives post war and brag about how many kids each of them had raised.

Invites were sent out to all surviving veterans of that platoon. Sadly, Carrera was unable to attend as he had prior family engagements. Nonetheless, those that did attend played poker, talked about the good old days in the 2nd Armoured, drank beer and coffee, and had a bar-beque. One man said that it was coming close to the end of the night when Flash asked if they remembered landing in England. When the others agreed and spoke about what they remembered, Flash got angry. He claimed that wasn't true, that when they landed there was machine gun fire, Screaming Mimis and Rommel's asparagus, and that so many died.

He had apparently even pointed at this one man and told him that he had died. Obviously, as Stewart Leach was now telling this story, that was not the case, but Flash had really gone off the rails. Then some men started leaving and it got worse.

Flash stood up and drew his service pistol and started shooting the men that should have been dead. He screamed that they were ghosts. They were all ghosts. When the others tried to overpower him, he shot himself. The names of the men that he killed were Joe Skinner, Mark Laffey, Timothy Clark, Matt Walker, and Jacob O'Reilly. Reading those names and remembering the young men that had died in Ireland made such a hole in my heart.

The final article is from Bristol, and was released on the same date. I suppose you can gather where this is going. Mother of five, Bonnie Wright, invited all her children and grandchildren together two nights ago. After she fed them and watched, making sure that all of them had eaten enough, she said that she was glad that they had come, because no child of hers was going to die in that camp.

How do I know this? One of the grandchildren didn't like the taste and was topping up her brother's bowl when Nanna wasn't watching. The entire table was suddenly stricken ill. Wild vomiting overcame them all, including Bonnie, who couldn't live in a world without her children.

I would like to say that this one had nothing to do with me, but sadly this is not the case. The final words of that article detailed that a neighbour commented that Bonnie hadn't been exactly right for the last thirty some years after she and her husband had helped him drag a drunk American back to his cottage for rest. She said that there was something about the man that had disquieted her. According to the neighbour, Mrs Wright had suffered from sporadic nightmares ever since.

Still not enough? That's fine, there is very little that I can offer you now. If my word and these small tokens that I leave to you are not enough, then I suppose only this chunk of red mercury will do. Take it to any geologist. They won't be able to identify it, trust me, I have tried. But I would rather you didn't – the less questions that are asked about any of this, the better.

So, why then did I tell you? I tell you out of fear, my friend. I know this is real and I know these horrible things can happen again. What I want from you is to make sure they don't. If you hear anything about these creatures, you must kill them. Find a way, if anyone can, Rheinmarsh. It's you. Whatever you do, leave the red mercury alone. It's useless unless you can kill every damned one of those things. If the Nazis, the most successful killers in history, couldn't do it, then no one can. Let it be.

Before I go, I suppose you may be wondering if I had looked up Carrera and Flash, then surely I would have looked up Jackson. Well of course I had. But it took some time before I found him. Funnily enough it was June 6th 1964 when I finally came across my old friend. Perhaps the date can give you some indication of where it was that I found him. Standing on the shores of Normandy in France, listening to the waves crash on the sand, I was taken back to Northern Ireland. How the men stormed the beaches. Normandy, Millisle. Different countries where the same soldiers died. How the men crashed to the sand, just as the waves did now. Every time I think of it, it almost brings me to tears.

I walked amongst the veterans that had taken the pilgrimage for the twentieth anniversary. I looked closely into their eyes. Saw the emotion, the remorse, and the fear of being back here once more. And my heart bled for them, as I knew how they felt.

I eventually found Jackson, and we talked plainly. I told him everything that had happened to me since I ventured into this timeline. I told him about Bonnie, I even cried when I did. Even to this day, I think that this was the first time I had cried in front of him. But I'm sure he understood. I promised to go back and visit him from time to time, but I never have. I'm not sure why. Not sure if I could bring myself to do it – just seeing his name there on that cross would give me more heartache than I could handle. But I suppose I will, before the end. I even memorised his plot location.

For now, my friend, I have one bullet that has had my name on it for over thirty years and it's calling me. The watch that I leave you will have the time of my death. Just like so many. I will not become an offering, and I will not bow down to them. If only my actions could have averted the fall, I should have used that last cannon shell to remove the great one's head and not to have prolonged my own life. That was a coward's way out. I won't make that mistake again…